DUE PROCESS

Recent Titles by Ted Allbeury from Severn House

BERLIN EXCHANGE

COLD TACTICS

THE NETWORKS

NEVER LOOK BACK

RULES OF THE GAME

SPECIAL FORCES

DUE PROCESS

Ted Allbeury

severn House

This title first published in Great Britain 2003 by
SEVERN HOUSE PUBLISHERS LTD of
9–15 High Street, Sutton, Surrey SM1 1DF.
Originally published in 1983 in Great Britain
under the title *Pay Any Price*.
This title first published in the USA 2003 by
SEVERN HOUSE PUBLISHERS INC of
595 Madison Avenue, New York, N.Y. 10022.

British Library Cataloguing in Publication Data

Allbeury, Ted, 1917-
    Due process
    1. Mafia - Fiction
    2. Espionage - Fiction
    3. Suspense fiction
    I. Title
    823.9'14 [F]

    ISBN 0-7278-5971-4

Printed and bound in Great Britain by
MPG Books Ltd., Bodmin, Cornwall.

With love to Laurie Beaty, Headmaster, and the staff of St Mark's C. of E. Primary School, Tunbridge Wells, for caring for and teaching my two girls, Lisa and Sally, in the years that matter most.

Let every nation know, whether it wishes us well or ill, that we shall pay any price, bear any burden, meet any hardship, support any friend, oppose any foe, in order to assure the survival and the success of liberty.

JOHN F. KENNEDY
Inaugural Address
20 January 1961

1

Although Cambridge, Massachusetts, is only separated from Boston by the arbitrary meanderings of the Charles River, most people feel it has succeeded in preserving its separate ethos from the depredations of its large neighbour. Buildings, streets, houses, are on a more human scale. You can walk even the main Cambridge streets at a leisurely pace. It has the air of a nineteeth-century village inhabited by civilized and cultured people. With Harvard University at its centre to emphasize the point.

In one of the older houses the Symonses were holding a small party to celebrate the graduation of their son Anthony.

Arthur Symons was perhaps the most respected brain surgeon in Massachusetts. He was certainly the most financially successful. Amongst his medical contemporaries there was some argument from time to time as to how much his success was due to the rich girl he had married, and how much to his own undoubted charm. Charm is not a characteristic rated highly by surgeons. Unless they happen to have it. It is not too common an attribute among either the rich or the medical profession. But even Arthur Symons's more acid critics would not deny that his charm was both real and natural.

Their son had an inferior version of his father's charm, and he also lacked his father's patrician good looks. The son's best features were his dark brown eyes and their heavy lashes; the rest of his face was a little too smooth, a little too rounded. But the pretty girls hung on his words, and there was no doubt that he had a gift for words, and a soft molasses-brown voice that gave teenage girls a tendency to close their eyes when he spoke. In his case the charm was calculated and spurious. But useful nonetheless. And Tony Symons had one talent that was not shared with his father. He played the piano with a skill that made him constantly in demand at student parties and the like. Whatever style you fancied, Fats Waller, Teddy Wilson, Errol Garner or Ellington, Tony Symons could play it.

Just after midnight he slipped out of the white door that led to the small garden. He and the girl walked hand in hand across the lawn, keeping to the shadows and away from the floodlit shrubs and borders. Half an hour later they were in his apartment near City Hall Plaza. And ten minutes later they were both naked on his bed. It was only the second time they had enjoyed each other's bodies but it was also only the second time he had dated her. The girl had been madly in love with him for months but the young man had eschewed all pleasures for the last four months until his final exams were over. He uttered no word, even during their love-making, which could possibly be interpreted as indicating that he loved her or was even 'in-love' with her.

When it was over he lay beside her, feeding chocolates into her soft, sensuous mouth. She smiled up at his face and her hand reached down to excite him again, then frowned slightly as he moved his body out of reach.

She said softly, 'Don't you want to do it again?'

He nodded. 'Later, maybe.'

She looked at the brown eyes. 'Did you like it?'

'It was beautiful, honey. How about you?'

'It was fantastic, Tony. I'd like to do it all the time with you.'

'I think I've got to do my post-graduate at UCLA and that's not going to give us much time together.'

She leaned up on her elbows. 'But why? Why go to UCLA?'

'Garfield wouldn't recommend me for post-grad at Harvard.'

'Why not?'

'God knows. I don't think he likes me. Or maybe he doesn't like my old man.' He smiled. 'Anyway I think he's got his eye on you. He's a horny bastard. I think he's jealous of me.'

'You mean he wants to sleep with me?'

'Yeah. He's not the only one. I guess he knows he hasn't got a chance, so he takes it out on me.'

'You mean if I let him do it to me he'd let you stay?'

'You bet he would, provided he knew that I'd put the good word in for him.'

'Shall I let him?'

'Of course not. He's just an old goat.'

Her hand touched his face. 'Let me, Tony. I'd do anything for you.'

She saw the dark sweep of his lashes on his cheek. Every girl on the campus envied him those lashes. When he looked back at her he said softly. 'Are you sure?'

'Of course I am.'

'Shall I tell him?'

'Yes.'

'When shall I say you'll see him?'

'Anytime. Tomorrow. Let me get it over with.'

And Judy Powers was the first person he sold out to serve his ambition. Even the weasel-words 'Are you sure?' had been coldly calculated. They clinched the fact that she had already agreed to do it, cutting off any retreat, and at the same time made the responsibility entirely hers. During the last year of Symons's post-graduate studies he published two papers that led to a little correspondence with practising psychiatrists, and two or three meetings with research psychologists. The first paper was titled *The*

11

Physiology of Emotion, and the second was a much longer paper – *The Hypnotic Block*.

It was that second paper that led to enquiries being made into Symons's academic and private background, and two months later he was approached and recruited by the CIA. The package of temptation that had been put together to attract him had been based on a shrewd evaluation of the obvious pattern in his academic background. Symons was demonstrably ambitious, having sacrificed his practical day-to-day experience with patients to the demands of his published papers. In addition it had been carefully noted that his ambition was to a large extent power-motivated. Symons had a need, some thought a compulsion, for power over people, and as a charismatic man he found no difficulty in finding suitable subjects.

Most charismatic figures inevitably use their power over an extensive audience. Like Stalin, Jack Kennedy or Winston Churchill in the manipulation of whole nations, or like certain film stars and entertainers in the manipulation of national and international audiences. Some charismatic figures are content to be the sun in quite small constellations. Schweitzer in Lambarene. Whether your interest or satisfaction is to do good or evil, it is more recognizable when the canvas is small. If your urge is towards power over individuals then the CIA provides an ideal camouflage and a constant flow of human material.

The operations room was busy. Marines sat watching the radar screens and directing the US Marine jet fighters and US Navy Constellations back to base. Atsugi base, a few miles south-west of Tokyo, was responsible for controlling a vast area of air-space, using radar to direct aircraft to their targets, and radio for communications with pilots in the air.

All the Marines on the base were hand-picked, their backgrounds checked out by the CIA. Marine Oswald was highly thought of, and that evening he accepted an extra hour's duty to cover a colleague's absence. And for the first time, Marine Oswald and his fellow operators heard a radio call from a pilot requesting weather details for an altitude of ninety thousand feet, an altitude far higher than that used by any plane they had ever heard of. Similar requests for weather information at this extraordinary altitude were to come over the air in code during the next few weeks, but it was almost a month before they learned that the planes were U-2s. The so-called spy planes that were flying deep into Soviet and Chinese air-space to bring back revealing photographs of army, navy and air-force bases, seaports and factories.

When his relief came Marine Oswald showered, changed, and took the base bus into Tokyo. He didn't join the return bus which took his fellows back to the base just before midnight. He had a free morning the following day when an operator was allowed to lie in before his afternoon shift.

The 'Queen Bee' was Tokyo's most expensive and exclusive nightclub. Mainly patronized by Japanese businessmen, diplomats and US officers, its hostesses were reckoned to be the prettiest in Japan. Marine Oswald, in civilian clothes, was a regular visitor to the nightclub and his girl-friend was one of the prettiest of the girls, and apart from dancing with her most of the evening he generally spent the night with her. And spending the night with one of the pretty hostesses cost roughly what a US marine earned in a month, including overseas and specialist allowances. He was the envy of most of his colleagues and disliked by the others.

When orders came through that the unit was being transferred to the Philippines there was disappointment all round. It was at that point that Marine Oswald's excellent service record ended. He shot himself in the arm before the unit left, to try and avoid the posting. It was only a minor wound but it earned him a fine and twenty days' hard labour. Not long afterwards Marine Oswald applied for, and was granted, release on the grounds that he had to look after his sick mother. Nobody had checked but his mother was, in fact, in excellent health.

2

The girl sang with her lips close to the microphone, her hands lovingly caressing its chromium stand. Her voice was thin and little-girlish, its range too narrow for the song she was singing. But in a Texas army camp if you're young and pretty and you sing 'Tie a Yellow Ribbon Round the Old Oak Tree' you're going to get applause enough to satisfy your show-biz ego. And if you're a stunning blonde in a pale blue bikini you're going to bring the house down. As the applause crashed around the hall she smiled and bowed, the deep, pseudo-humble bow that singers give to kid the audience that they are sole arbiters of the singer's fate. Then, against the roar of the applause, she sang the opening lines of 'The Yellow Rose of Texas' and the soldiers fell silent again. And when she had finished they clapped and shouted and stamped enough for half a dozen curtain calls before the spotlight was cut off to allow her to escape.

Debbie Rawlins was born in Bradford, Yorkshire. She had escaped to London when she was fifteen, and with her pretty face, her long legs and well-developed breasts she had earned her living performing in half a dozen Soho strip clubs night after night. Freed from a father who abused her sexually, and a mother who hated her with a fury and energy that were frightening, her life in the sleazy clubs suited her well. The middle-aged Maltese who owned three of the clubs was besotted by her young body. And sleeping with him gave her all the protection she needed from the animals who ran that square mile of vice in London's West End. Cheerful and happy-go-lucky, she was friendly with them all. But nothing more than friendly. Maybe she sometimes allowed an influential hand to wander inside her sweater, or even under her skirt when it was diplomatically sensible, but that counted as no more than mere amiability in those circles.

She had gone one weekend with the Maltese to Brighton and there she had won a talent competition in a pub, singing 'Long Ago and Far Away', and an agent in the audience had contacted her a few days later and offered her a six-month contract singing in the Lancashire clubs. The Maltese had immediately asked her to marry him; but even at eighteen she had wisdom and ambition enough to sign the contract.

The contract had been extended to a year and she was in constant demand. The pretty face, the beautiful body and the little-girl voice were just what they wanted. But the American contract had been her real step up the show-biz ladder. Both Guild and Equity rules had been relaxed because she was entertaining only American troops including active service zones. Several shows at overseas bases and scores of shows at army camps in the United States had made her a real professional. Sure of herself and capable of negotiating her own contracts. Well aware of the limitation of her talents but equally aware of how to use what she had to the full. She was billed as a singer and she no longer stripped, but her act started in a pale blue chiffon evening gown and ended in the pale blue bikini. She didn't consider herself promiscuous, but she took it for granted that good bookings sometimes had to begin on a leather couch, and from time to time she slept with men just because she fancied them. But there were no emotional entanglements. Not on her side anyway.

In the officers' mess after the show that night, dressed now in the blue gown, she was persuaded to sing one last

16

song before she retired for the night. She pleaded that she couldn't sing unaccompanied and a young officer was pushed from the crowd and forced to the piano. An old but in-tune Bechstein grand. She asked them what she should sing and they shouted out half a dozen different titles. She turned to the pianist and he grinned and winked as he played a slow introduction, and she smiled as she recognized the tune. As he came to the chorus she sang softly, '. . . *and when two lovers woo, they still say I love you, on that you can rely . . . no matter what the future brings . . . as time goes by . . .*' There was complete silence as she sang, and for a few moments after she had finished, and then the applause was real. Not soldiers' applause for a pair of long legs and a bit of nostalgia, but genuine show-biz applause that made her blush and turn to look at the pianist. Ten minutes later, after one last drink, a US Marine colonel escorted her to her quarters, and half an hour later he was in bed with her. And he drove her himself to the air-strip the next morning.

It was two months later when she met the pianist again. He was a captain now and he took her out to dinner after the show at Fort Huachuca. It was one o'clock in the morning when he drove her back to the camp. He had stuck in her mind for two reasons. He wasn't in any way handsome, but she found him attractive. Most men spent the meal-time gazing down her cleavage as they, arrogantly or diffidently, according to their natures, sold their virtues and importance; but the piano-playing captain asked her about herself and listened attentively as she gave him a strictly censored version of her life and career. He was sufficiently sympathetic for her to expand the details far beyond her usual bowdlerized scenario. The other thing that impressed her was that he didn't proposition her, and even sitting in his car in the moonlight outside her hut he didn't make a pass at her. Just a peck on the cheek as he left her on her porch and then walked back to his car.

She was twenty-six then, and she guessed that he was just

turned thirty; but he had an almost fatherly attitude to her. Caring and concerned, and undemanding. She thought about him often.

Mrs McVickar had the look on her face that her husband recognized all too well. As a busy consular official at the US Embassy in Moscow he often had to absent himself from cocktail parties and even their own private dinners. And his frequently delayed arrival at even normal meals was a constant source of friction. But being a professional diplomat he reacted patiently because he recognized the inconvenience and frustration that he caused.

As he pulled out the chair for his wife he said, 'Well, I thought I'd seen it all but that little scene was absolutely . . .' he paused '. . . I can't think of the right word . . . bizarre's probably the only word to describe it.'

'The strawberries are the last we shall get in Moscow this year, John. And the tomatoes too.'

'Thanks for the warning. I'll have the chicken if you'd prefer the turkey.'

'There's plenty for both of us so don't go all diplomatic and sacrificial.'

'Were there any phone calls for me?'

'Two. The details are on the pad.'

'Who were they?'

'I don't remember.'

John McVickar took the hint and got on with his salad.

'I can never understand why cold chicken tastes so much nicer than hot chicken.'

'Tell me about the bizarre scene,' she said, ignoring his comment.

'This lunatic comes bouncing into my office like the Demon King. Throwing his passport on my desk. Practically foaming at the mouth. He wants to renounce his American citizenship. He wants to announce officially that he has defected to the Russians and intends telling them all the

18

secrets he knows.'

'What's the secret? How to make Coca-Cola?'

'No. He's an ex-Marine from a high-security base in Japan. He's only a kid. Says he's going to tell them all he knows about our codes, our methods, the lot.'

'What does a Marine know anyway? I thought they spent all their time stamping their boots on parade grounds and trying to bed the local girls.'

'I'm afraid not, honey. He knows a lot that could be useful to our friends up the road.'

'A funny attitude for an ex-Marine to take.'

'Yes. And even odder in one way.'

'What way?'

'When he said his little piece it was almost as if he had been tutored by someone . . . seemed to be using words he had learned but didn't really understand.'

'What do you think the Russians will do with him?'

'They'll certainly suck out all that he can tell them, but I doubt if they'll make a song and dance about him. They'll probably be suspicious.'

'Why?'

'Well, like you said, it's abnormal behaviour for an ex-Marine. When they want servicemen to spill the beans the KGB do it deliberately. Sex, money, whatever works. Volunteers, they don't trust.'

It was a good sized sitting-room in what was one of the older buildings in Minsk, and apartments had been bigger in those days. But despite its size it was crowded that day, the last day of April. Both children and adults were enjoying themselves, and the dining table was piled high with *zakuski*, caviar, salami, fish in aspic, and bowls of fresh fruit.

Vanya Berlov rose unsteadily to his feet. 'Valya, what is wrong with your cooking today? Things are always so tasty at your table but today they are bitter.'

19

The other guests smiled and shouted '*Gorko, gorko*', and looked meaningfully at the young groom and his bride. The old Russian custom was that all food and wine tasted bitter until they were sweetened by the newly married couple's first kiss in public.

The young girl blushed but eventually submitted to her groom kissing her full on the lips. From time to time someone would shout '*Gorko*' and the couple would kiss again.

It was after midnight when the celebrations ended and the young couple, Alik and Marina, walked the few blocks to their new home, the young man's small apartment. It was on the fourth floor and she was a well-built girl, but her new husband gallantly lifted her up and carried her up the stairs.

While her husband was preparing for bed Marina looked at the marriage stamp in her passport and idly picked up her husband's passport to look at his stamp. And with a shock she saw that his year of birth was 1939. That meant he was only twenty-one, and he had told her that he was twenty-four. She wondered how much of the rest of what he had told her was true. At least he hadn't lied about his name. It was there in the passport: Lee Harvey Oswald.

The two brothers sat side by side, directly opposite the hard-faced man and his legal advisers on the other side of the long table. They were both handsome men, the brothers; stylishly, but not ostentatiously dressed, their eyes intent on their adversary's face. Jimmy Hoffa, boss of the Teamsters Union, despised and hated the two young men who relentlessly pressed their questions for the Senate committee investigating corruption in the unions.

Hoffa's bull-neck was thrust forward aggressively as he spoke.

'The fact is this is a strike-breaking, union-busting Bill. In my opinion.'

Hoffa leaned back in his chair, a defiant, self-satisfied smile on his face. The elder of the two brothers leaned forward towards the microphone in front of him, the TV and film lights emphasizing the white cuff of his shirt as his hand jabbed up and down to emphasize what he was saying.

'Mr Hoffa, the fact is that this is not a strike-breaking, union-busting Bill. You're the best argument I know for it. Your testimony here this afternoon . . . your complete indifference this afternoon to the fact that numerous people who hold responsible positions in your union come before this committee and take the Fifth Amendment . . . because an honest answer might tend to incriminate them.'

Hoffa sat there, his eyes angry, closing his thin mouth to hold back his violent temper as his lawyer whispered in his ear to keep quiet.

Ten minutes later that session of the hearing was over, and as Hoffa walked with his hoodlums towards the big doors he said loudly, 'That SOB. I'll break his back that little sonofabitch.'

And the next day the first question to Hoffa from the committee's chief counsel, Robert Kennedy, was typical of the implacable determination of the two Kennedys to expose the Teamsters Union.

Kennedy gestured towards Hoffa's entourage. 'While leaving the hearing after these people had testified regarding this matter, did you say, 'That SOB – I'll break his back?'

'Who?'

'You.'

'Say it to who?'

'To anyone. Did you make that statement after these people testified before this committee?'

'I never talked to either one of them after testifying.'

Kennedy pressed on. 'I'm not talking about "to them". Did you make that statement here in the hearing room after the testimony was finished?'

21

'Not concerning him as far as I know of.'

'Well, who did you make it about?'

'I don't know . . . I may have been discussing someone in a figure of speech.'

'Well . . . whose back were you going to break, Mr Hoffa?'

'Figure of speech. I don't know what I was talking about, and I don't know what you're talking about.'

To most of the onlookers it seemed a small incident, but in front of his henchmen it was yet another humiliation at the hands of the Kennedys. And in that moment he was determined to smash them both. He would fire the first shot that night.

The man sitting opposite John F. Kennedy in the hotel room had been in the US Navy with the Senator. They hadn't liked one another then, and neither of them had had any reason to change their opinions since. But the man was now wealthy, important, and an influential local figure in the Democratic Party. He was dressed formally in a dark blue business suit, white shirt and subdued tie. He looked amiably towards the Senator as they sipped their drinks.

'I'm not asking you to go easy on them, JF. Just to . . .' He made a see-saw gesture with his well-manicured hand. '. . . how shall I say it. Keep a balance. A perspective.'

The Senator smiled as he put his glass down on the table beside him.

'You could have fooled me, Ray. I'd have said you were doing a pitch, asking for the committee to lay off your pal Hoffa.'

'No way, old friend. The law has to take its course and all that jazz. But people are beginning to see it as a personal dogfight. The Kennedy brothers versus the Teamsters.'

Kennedy smiled. 'And people would be right. It is.'

'But why, for God's sake? We need their support. The party needs their votes.'

'How many votes has Hoffa got?' Kennedy raised his eyebrows.

'Who knows. But we all know we need them.'

'James Hoffa has one vote, and as far as my campaign is concerned he can shove it.'

The other man opened his mouth to speak but the Senator held up his hand to silence him.

'The Senate subcommittee has been set up to investigate union corruption, and that's exactly what it's doing.' He wagged a monitory finger. 'And that's what it's going to go on doing. They don't command their members' votes. Their members may be too scared to do anything but apparently accept what they're told to do. But in the ballot booth they do what they choose.

'You know as well as I do that the mob are running the Teamsters, not Hoffa. And they're running the other big unions too. You've got union funds, huge amounts, being transferred into private bank accounts, gangsters acting as union officials. Murder. Torture, for anyone who complains or resists. What more do you want?'

'But none of this can be proved, JF. None of it.'

Kennedy smiled. 'Don't rely on that, Ray. And tell your friends not to rely on it. We've got a lot of people working on it. Good people. Incorruptible.'

'But why make it all so personal?'

'It's very personal for their victims.'

'I don't understand.'

The Senator winced and moved his back to make it more upright in the armchair.

'Well, for instance, there was the union organizer from LA who went to San Diego to organize juke-box operators. He was told he would be killed if he didn't stay out of San Diego. He went back again the next month. He was clubbed unconscious, and when he came to he was soaked in blood and had terrible stomach pains. He tried to drive himself back to Los Angeles but the pains were so bad he

23

stopped at a hospital. He had an emergency operation and the surgeon removed a cucumber from his backside. A large cucumber. Sounds jokey if it isn't you. When he got home he got an anonymous call saying that next time it would be a watermelon.'

'You mentioned murder, Senator.'

'I'll give you just one. There was a little guy named Rubinstein. Lived in Chicago and was a runner for Al Capone. In 1939 Rubinstein was involved in the murder of a local union boss in Chicago; Rubinstein was the local union secretary. It was that murder that let the Mafia into the Teamsters.'

'You know, Jack, if you go on too far you could bring down very powerful figures in the party. You must know who I mean.'

'One of my senior investigators told me the details, Ray. I've given the appropriate instructions.'

'I'm glad to hear that. Very glad.'

'Yes. I told my man to go back and build up the best case they can against those men.' He paused for a moment. 'We have a rigid rule around the subcommittee, Ray. If they're crooks, we don't wound 'em, we kill 'em.'

The man looked uncomfortable. Leaning forward as if he were going to speak, he hesitated and drew back. The Senator watched him, half-knowing what the man was going to say on behalf of the hoodlums who owned him.

'Say your piece, Ray. It makes no difference to me. But you'll be able to tell them that you delivered the message.'

'Who told you about the message, Jack?'

'Nobody. But I know how those bastards work. Give me the good news and then we can call it a day.'

'They've declared war on you, Jack. You and Bobby. If you stand for President they'll be against you all the way. They mean trouble. Real trouble.'

Kennedy nodded. 'Is that it?'

'Yes.'

24

'Let yourself out, Ray. Turn right for the elevator.'

The band was playing a Latin-American version of 'America, America' and the two men standing in the wings were watching the chorus line on the stage. The girls were all hand-picked for their good looks, their long legs and full bosoms. Their scanty costumes of silver sequins only emphasized what they were supposed to hide. The Tropicana Club in Havana was reckoned to be the biggest nightclub in the world.

The bald-headed, tubby man said, 'Who's the chick second from this end, Santos?'

'God knows. It'll be Rosa, Maria or Anita. They're all called that. Why? Do you want her?'

'She's a real doll, pal. A real doll.'

'Do you want her, Jack, or don't you? Just say for Christ's sake.'

'I guess the answer's yes.'

Santos Trafficante walked across to the stage-manager and spoke to him before coming back to his guest.

'She doesn't finish until one o'clock. Her name's Maria. She'll come to your room at the hotel about two.'

'You're a lucky man, Santos, with all these pretty girls.'

Trafficante said irritably, 'What they've got's no different to what the broads in Miami or New York have got, my friend. My job here's money not screwing.' He paused, 'You got any idea how much I'm sending back to the States every month?'

'I heard it was nearly fifty grand a month.'

'Double it and you'll be in the ball-park.'

'Is Castro gonna make any difference?'

Trafficante smiled a grim smile. 'He's been in Havana a couple of weeks now and I ain't seen hide nor hair of him. OK, maybe he'll stick us for more than Batista did, but they all want something. Whatever it is we'll give it to 'em. I'd better get back to the office, Jack.'

25

'I'll come with you, pal.'

There was a man sitting at Trafficante's big desk. A young man in torn and stained battle camouflage. His hand was resting on a Kalashnikov lying on the desk top. As Trafficante stood in the open doorway the soldier looked at a photograph lying on the desk in front of him. He smiled at the American.

'Is time to go, Señor Trafficante.'

'It's time for you to get out of my goddamn chair, little boy.' He reached for the phone and went to dial a number before he realized there was no dialling tone. He slowly replaced the receiver and looked at the soldier.

'What's going on, soldier boy?'

'You're under arrest, Mr Trafficante.'

'Who says so?'

'Fidel says so. Who's your friend?' The soldier nodded towards the bald man.

'I've no idea. He's not a friend. He's just a customer who I brought back for a drink.'

'What's your name, señor?'

'Jack Rubinstein. I'm an American citizen.'

'OK. Where are you staying?'

'At the Hilton.'

'OK. You go back to Hilton. We see if you OK.'

The bald man backed out of the door looking for some indication of what he should do from Trafficante. But Trafficante was busy taking a thick roll of dollars from his inside pocket as Rubinstein closed the door and headed for the exit doors. It was eleven-thirty and the stage was strangely silent and empty. A few stragglers were still queueing to get out of the club. A dozen scruffy-looking soldiers were wandering around aimlessly, trying to look as if they knew what they were doing.

Outside there was an armoured car and half a dozen battered jeeps, with weary-looking soldiers standing around, smoking cigarettes, their free hands touching the guns in

26

their canvas holsters as if to check that they were still there. They shook their fists at him as he walked by.

The next time that Debbie met the piano-playing army captain was in Honolulu. She had given four performances that day and as she walked off the stage in the evening she knew there was something wrong. Her throat felt as if it were on fire, and there was a bitter taste on her tongue. She found swallowing painful. Her escort insisted on sending for the medical officer. And when the doctor came to her quarters she couldn't believe it. She hadn't even realized that her piano-playing captain was an army doctor.

He checked her throat and then switched off the torch putting his hand gently on hers.

'Did it come on suddenly?'

'My throat felt a bit sore yesterday. Like I might be starting a cold. The real pain only started when I was playing my last number tonight.'

'And the bitter taste?'

'I didn't notice that until I was walking off-stage.'

'Well, my sweet Debbie, you've got an abscess at the back of your throat. A fair-sized one. And it's burst. The bitter taste is the pus. I'm going to give you some antibiotics. A shot in your arm right now, and tablets for ten days. You've got to stay in bed for at least two days, then we'll see how you're doing. If the pus doesn't come out I might have to help it on its way. But I'm hoping the penicillin will be enough.'

'But I've got engagements I've got to keep.'

'Forget them, honey. You couldn't sing anyway, and if you don't stay in bed you'll have a temperature like a furnace and your throat won't heal at all.'

He bent down, opening his black case, checking through the phials until he found what he wanted. He turned to look at her.

'Go and get into your night-things and into bed. The

27

injection will make you sleepy.'

When she was out of the room he filled the syringe from the phial. The label on the phial said 'MKULTRA' in capitals, handwritten in black ink. He knew that it was too good an opportunity to miss. They could work out how to use her later.

As he swabbed her arm and pressed up the pale blue vein he said, 'It'll only be a slight prick.' And as he was saying it he slid the needle smoothly into her arm and pressed the plunger as he smiled at her.

'Are you feeling sleepy yet?'

Her eyes were closed and she nodded her head. When he could see from her breathing that she was almost asleep he said softly, 'Can you hear me, Debbie?'

She sighed and her lips said 'yes' without speaking.

'I'm going to count to ten, Debbie, and you're going to go deep asleep. One, two . . . nice and relaxed . . . three, four . . . deeper and deeper . . . five, six . . . seven, eight . . . soft and warm . . . nine . . . ten. Now you're asleep. Can you still hear me?'

She nodded.

'When you wake up you won't remember anything. Just that you were asleep. Is Debbie Shaw your real name?'

'No.'

'Tell me your real name.'

'Debbie Rawlins.'

'Is Debbie short for Deborah?'

'Yes.'

'Have you ever been into drugs? Heroin or cocaine or LSD?'

'No.

'What about grass, marijuana?'

'No.'

'Have you had drugs for illnesses?'

'No.'

'Do you trust me, Debbie?'

28

'Yes.'

'Will you do anything I tell you?'

'Yes.'

'Will you let me have sex with you?'

'Yes.'

'Now?'

'Yes.'

'What's your favourite girl's name?'

'Nancy.'

'When I talk to you like this your name is Nancy. Do you understand?'

'Yes. Nancy.'

'Nancy Rawlins.'

'Yes. Nancy Rawlins.'

'You'll never use that name unless I tell you to. And you never talk about what we're saying to each other now.'

'OK.'

'If I ever say Nancy Rawlins to you, you'll go to sleep like this and do everything I say.'

'Yes.'

'And you never go to any other doctor but me. If you want me for anything, wherever you are you phone Washington 547-9077 and ask for Joe Spellman. If I'm not there you leave your telephone number and I'll get straight back to you. If I can't see you I'll tell you who to see. Understand?'

'Yes.'

'Tell me the number and the name.'

'Washington 547-9077. Joe Spellman.'

'Good girl. Now I'm going to wake you up and you won't remember any of this. Wake up when I've counted from ten to one. Here we go . . . ten, nine, eight . . . you're beginning to wake . . . seven, six . . . lighter and lighter . . . five, four . . . you're waking up and you feel fine . . . three, two . . . open your eyes . . . one. Now you're awake.' He paused as her eyes fluttered open. He smiled. 'How do you feel, kid?'

She smiled. 'Fine. What about the injection?'

'You've had it, sweetie.' He stood up. 'I'll see you tomorrow. A nurse is coming over to look after you. So sleep tight.'

'I'm glad you're the doctor. That was really a lucky break for me.'

'See you tomorrow and sleep well.'

3

As the warning lights went on Boyd fastened his seat-belt. He wasn't looking forward to his assignment in Washington. Liaison officer between the CIA and SIS was worse than any field operation. If you got on well with the CIA then London began to be suspicious that you were taking the easy way out. Keeping in with the Americans. If the CIA hinted that they weren't happy with you London went through the motions of urging you to try harder. Probably going along with Langley's criticisms but urging patience and forbearance. Both sides' assessment of your usefulness was based on whether they thought you were helping them get away with more than they should. There were no winners in the Langley job. Just a question of losers, bad losers, or ineffectives. Somebody had once said that if CIA/SIS liaison in Washington ended up with his guts hated by both organizations it was the nearest you could get to knowing that the job had been well done. There was only one consolation. Unless you really made a genuine hash of things there was automatic promotion when you returned to London.

Twenty minutes later he gathered up his hold-all from under the seat and joined the queue for the exit. At the bottom of the steps a man in a blue suit touched his arm. 'Boyd?'

'Yes.'

'My name's Schultz. Otto Schultz. Langley. I've told them to clear your bags straight through. I thought we

31

could have a meal here at the airport and then I'll take you home.'

'Thanks. Isn't it a bit late to keep you working?'

Schultz smiled and reached for Boyd's hold-all. 'Not this particular night. Maybe you'd forgotten. It's election day here and we'll all be staying up for the results on the tube.'

'Of course. When I got my travel orders I noticed that I'd be arriving on the day but it had slipped my mind.'

Schultz smiled. 'Let's go and eat first. It's not a bad restaurant.'

They chatted mild 'shop' until the coffee was served, when Schultz said, 'There's nothing in our background stuff on you about a wife. Is there one?'

Boyd shook his head. 'No. I'm afraid not. Not even a steady girl-friend.' He grinned. 'But to save them the trouble of finding out, I'm not queer either.'

Schultz made no pretence of not being interested in Boyd's statement but he smiled and said, 'We'll have to see if we can't fix you up over here.' He waved to the waitress and signalled that he wanted his bill. 'Meantime let's go back to my place. We're putting you up in the spare room for tonight and we'll talk about something permanent tomorrow.'

Boyd was introduced to Patsy, Schultz's wife, and four friends who had come round for election-night drinks.

By 10.30 local time it looked as if Kennedy was a landslide winner and Patsy turned to Boyd. 'You must be tired, Jimmy. Don't stand on ceremony. Just go off to bed as soon as you feel like it.'

Boyd looked at Schultz. 'Are you going to stay on, Otto?'

'Yes. It matters to Langley who wins. And Kennedy's only picked up what he could expect so far. The ball-game's not over by a long way yet.'

By midnight it looked as if Schultz was wrong. Kennedy's margin by then was over two million and the first returns from Los Angeles County looked as if California was falling

32

to the Democrats. But by 3 A.M. it was certain that Nixon was going to take more states than Kennedy.

They were having breakfast when Schultz came back from the telephone. Their guests had left and Patsy was in bed. As Schultz slumped down at the table, reaching for the black coffee he said, 'That was a call from the office. They just heard that the Secret Service team has moved into the Kennedy compound at Hyannisport. That means they already know that he's won.'

'Does it matter to Langley who wins?'

'You bet it does. It matters a lot.'

'Who were they hoping for?'

Schultz shrugged. 'Not the one we got.'

'Why not?'

The American leaned back in his chair until it creaked. 'The Republicans are professionals. They want law and order maintained so that big business can get on with the job. Kennedy has got his support from the students, the blacks and the Southern States that Lyndon Johnson brought him. We're never going to know where we are with Kennedy. He wants to look good and that isn't what makes a good president so far as Langley's concerned.'

'Does that influence your personal vote?'

Schultz laughed drily. 'No way. I voted for Kennedy. When all the votes are in you'll find that it was damn nearly fifty-fifty between him and Nixon. How about we get some sleep and I'll take you in to the office late this afternoon.'

'I can carry on if you want?'

'Do you mean that?'

'Sure I do.'

Schultz nodded approvingly. 'Fine. Let's go. I'll introduce you to a few people you'll be working with apart from me.'

The snow started falling on the streets of Washington about mid-day and by the time the office- and shop-workers were heading home the streets were covered, and all through the evening the snow fell relentlessly, building up until, by mid-evening, the District lay frozen and gripped under a carpet of ice and snow.

Soldiers were using flamethrowers to melt the ice around the inauguration stand and, as the snow still fell, open fires were lit along the Mall in an attempt to keep it clear for vehicles.

President-elect Kennedy and his wife were attending a concert in Constitutional Hall and they were not back in their Georgetown home until 3.30 A.M. Ten minutes later the snow abated but the icy-cold wind from the Potomac and the Tidal Basin was whipping-up frozen snow that stung the faces of the troops who had just come on duty. It was the early hours of Friday the 20th of January. Inauguration Day.

By noon that day there were still ten degrees of frost, but the crowds had assembled despite the punishing cold. At 12.30 John F. Kennedy appeared on the stand and the crowd cheered their man and the thought that they could soon be back in the warm. But Cardinal Cushing was not the man to forego the opportunity of such an important convocation. As he spoke the sun came out to camouflage the cold. At 12.51 Chief Justice Warren administered the oath.

The President stood there, hatless and coatless, the harsh wind whipping at his hair, leaning forward, a posture that was to become familiar, to emphasize his words, and as he spoke into the microphones the Boston accent seemed suddenly to represent and symbolize the vigour of a new style of administration.

'Let the word go forth from this time and place, to friend and foe alike, that the torch has been passed to a new generation of Americans . . . unwilling to witness or permit the slow undoing of those human rights to which this nation has always been committed, and to which we are

34

committed today at home and abroad . . . Let every nation know, whether it wishes us well or ill, that we shall pay any price, bear any burden, meet any hardship, support any friend, oppose any foe, in order to assure the survival and the success of liberty . . .'

34,221,463 of his fellow Americans had voted for their new-generation President. And those who watched knew that they had got what they wanted . . . a knight in shining armour who spoke political poetry not prose. Better even than Lincoln.

In 1960 there were only thirty-five convictions in US courts for offences connected with organized crime, but after John F. Kennedy became President of the United States and his brother Robert became Attorney-General there were hundreds of such convictions. Apart from the growing staff of lawyers and field investigators there was a special group known as the 'Get Hoffa squad'. No attempt was made to hide the fact that the Kennedy brothers had declared war on organized crime, and in the slow war of attrition there were signs not only that they were winning but that the syndicates knew it. The Mafia leaders and the men they controlled were not intelligent men. Their thinking was always crude and obvious. Violence, murder, money and sex were their only weapons, and their experience had proved that these primitive weapons always worked.

Senators, Congressmen, judges, lawyers, police-chiefs and tycoons were men. Their motivations were much the same as those of the Mafia bosses. Power, status, money and good living. Rich men lusted after yet more money or power, and simpler men who sat on judges' benches rationalized their pay-offs as little more than reasonable enhancements of their inadequate pensions. And for all manner of men there was the awareness that their Mafia contacts could fix anything, anywhere. You had only to ask and it was delivered.

It was always Christmas with the Mafia, and you didn't have to know how it was fixed, whether it was tickets for the big fight or a pretty young blonde for the weekend. They arrived on time and they were always the best. And those were just the crumbs. The votes or the money were the protein at the feast. And you didn't have to do much to earn it. A word in an influential ear, a vote against unfriendly legislation, a liberal attitude on the bench to an 'accidental' homicide, a word to a city gambling board when an application for another casino was meeting opposition. You could easily convince yourself, if you wanted to, that the Mafia was only the working boys' version of the Ivy League.

There was a feeling too, amongst the racketeers, that the Kennedys themselves were a kind of Mafia. They looked after their own; and who had more patronage to dispense than the President of the United States? But one thing they recognized for sure. The Kennedys weren't looking for money. They'd already got more than they needed.

There were many meetings in luxury hotel suites and lush casino offices about how to deal with the Kennedys, where all the traditional weapons of suborning the influential were discussed. Only money was excluded from the considerations. The Kennedys were rich but this generation of Kennedys wasn't greedy. And they didn't need anything fixed. The President of the United States, whoever he was, commanded all the fixing that the mob had to pay millions of dollars for. But there must be something. Every man had his price. It was just a question of working out what it was.

Sam Giancana was the Mafia *capo* in Philadelphia and when he appeared before the McLellan Committee he did them the honour of removing his dark glasses. There was nothing wrong with his eyesight and his glasses no longer gave him any protection against being recognized. His big nose, the wide, thin-lipped mouth, and the restless eyes were

36

instantly recognized by all who had reason to fear or hate him. As he sat with his lawyer he was concerned that the cameras should show him as being completely at ease. There was no reason why they shouldn't, because he was completely at ease. He tried to make that clear by probing with his tongue at his yellowed teeth, his mouth half open as he listened to the committee's counsel reading another long statement of evidence before putting yet another question.

Giancana's shifty eyes wandered along the line of committee members and settled on their senior counsel as he turned over to the last page. There was no doubt he was a good-looking fellow, with a round face that reminded Giancana of those plump *puzzi* on the church ceiling back in Palermo. But he wasn't as good-looking as his brother, the President. The older man had what the media called *charisma*. Giancana reckoned that he too had *charisma* even if he wasn't as handsome as Jack Kennedy.

Then his lawyer's elbow brought him back from his day-dreaming. 'He asked you a question, Sam.'

Giancana said loudly and with sincerity, 'I respectfully decline to answer under the Fifth Amendment on the grounds that an answer might tend to incriminate me.'

Bobby Kennedy glanced briefly at the cameras then back to Giancana.

'Mr Giancana. Do you realize that you have pleaded the Fifth Amendment in response to thirty-one questions from this committee?'

Giancana shrugged, smiling amiably. 'If you say so, counsellor.'

Kennedy wasn't smiling. 'Would you tell us, if you have any opposition from anybody, that you dispose of them by having them stuffed in a trunk? Is that what you do, Mr Giancana?'

When Giancana sat silent Kennedy picked up the next statement and started to read it aloud. And in that moment

37

Sam Giancana had what he thought was an inspiration.

In the morning, before the Las Vegas sun was scorching the dusty city, the cavalcade went out to the Sahara Country Club, and the President drove the first ball off at the first tee and handed the driver to Frank Sinatra. It was a pro-amateur match in aid of charity and the driver was to be auctioned later in the clubhouse.

In the early evening the President spent almost an hour at the University of Nevada and then went on to Paradise Road and the Convention Center to start the basketball game. Two hours later he was back at the University campus, but this time in a tuxedo and black tie for the concert in the Judy Bayley Theater. It was an Aaron Copland and Samuel Barber programme, but the pro-moters had been aware of the fact that John F. Kennedy could be restive at orchestral concerts and they had included a lush piece of Korngold to go with the *Adagio for Strings* before the interval. But despite this, anxious eyes noticed that the President was paying rather more attention to the pretty, dark-haired girl sitting two seats along from him than to the all-American music.

In the interval one of his aides made the usual diplomatic excuses about the war injury to his back, and the President was driven to the airport where Airforce One was waiting for him. A different but equally diplomatic aide made out a press pass for the pretty, dark-haired girl who now sat with the secretaries and radio operators in the main cabin. She had been granted a half-hour interview with the President in his private quarters on the plane. She made no notes because she wasn't a journalist, but in her handbag was a torn page from a diary, with the President's direct-line telephone number.

For several months Boyd helped smooth out the routine snags that occurred between the two stylistically different

38

intelligence organizations as they placed their differing emphases on one aspect or another of joint operations. And translated the objectives of one to the other when their intentions appeared to be in conflict. But it wasn't until mid-April of the following year that a serious problem arose. Schultz called Boyd at his apartment and they met in the Washington Hilton for a drink.

'We need your help, Jimmy. You'll have guessed what it's about.'

'The newspaper headlines. Cuba.'

'Yep. It's a total disaster. I saw the situation reports coming in during the night. Everything that could go wrong went wrong in spades.'

'I doubt if we can do much in that area.'

'That isn't where we need the help. The President's going berserk. Blaming it all on the CIA.'

'Wasn't it a CIA operation?'

'Sure it was. Eisenhower gave the go-ahead and Kennedy had to pick it up when he took over. But he made it into a half-assed operation. Took away air-cover and resources. He knows that he's got to carry the can in public but behind the scenes he's gonna chop off heads. And most of them will be CIA heads. And the Kennedys aren't just sticking to the Cuban mess. They're gonna settle a lot of old scores with that as the excuse.'

'What do you want me to do?'

'Tell your people that a good word for us in the White House right now will get London a lot of cooperation in the future. It's raining blood in Langley and it's gonna get worse in the next few days. Every country in the world is going to enjoy hauling us over the coals in the United Nations. OK, we can take it, but if somebody doesn't stop what's going on in the CIA at the moment the damage is going to take ten, maybe fifteen years to repair.'

'What exactly do you want?'

'A phone call to the White House from somebody right

39

at the top in Westminster. No need to pull any punches, but just pointing out that life has to go on, and damage to the CIA is damage to the whole of the free world.'

'That's hardly likely to make them stop putting Langley through the mincer.'

'I know that. All we ask is that the White House stop in their tracks for just five minutes and think about what they'll do when they've carved up Langley.'

'I'll see what I can do. But it won't be the PM, he's far too shrewd for that. Maybe Selwyn Lloyd or Lord Home could be persuaded. It would be as individuals, not officially.'

'That's OK. Just so that somebody makes them stop and think.'

'I'll go to the embassy now and use their radio.'

'Can you let me know the reaction when you get any?'

'Yes, of course.'

A senior British Minister with an American wife found reason to visit the Washington embassy and had ten minutes with Bobby Kennedy after a theatre party, and the ambassador himself said a few words to the President while delivering the British government's top-secret report on the Soviet Union's launching of its first manned space-rocket. Neither approach made any perceptible difference but Langley noted the attempts and were grateful.

4

'Sweetie' Dawson was 22. Just over six foot tall with wavy blond hair and freckles across his nose and cheeks. Athlete, ball-game player to a high standard, he had chosen the army rather than the scholarship to UCLA. He wasn't intelligent but he was sensible in a slow easy-going sort of way and the army could give him almost the same athletic facilities as the university without the pretence of attending classes that would bore and confuse him. As a second lieutenant he was drawing 690 dollars a month plus some benefits like special training, free time for representing the army at sporting events and no great disciplinary pressures.

He met Debbie after her performance at an army camp just outside San Diego. He thought she was the most beautiful girl he had ever seen and had been surprised when she accepted his invitation to the beach-hut he hired at La Jolla. When she seemed to take it for granted that she would spend the night with him he was overwhelmed. He had several regular girl-friends who slept with him from time to time when his training programme allowed such therapy. His sex-drive was normal but not excessive despite his opportunities, but his first night with Debbie he looked back on with embarrassment. He was sure that she must rate him as some kind of maniac.

He was sitting on the steps of the shack the next morning looking out across the ocean, trying to think what excuses he could offer when she woke. The fact that she was a foreigner made it even more difficult. 'Sweetie' Dawson was a nice young man from a small town in Kansas and he wanted to do the right thing. And he had fallen for Debbie right from the start.

He turned to look as he heard her footsteps. She was wearing his towelling bath-robe and she was smiling as she settled down beside him on the steps. He waited for her to speak so that he could decide what to say.

'God I'm hungry, Sweetie. Where can we get a real good breakfast?'

Smiling with relief he said, 'We'll go into town to Joe's Place.'

She looked at him, her eyes screwed up. 'You look kind of uneasy. Are you overstepping your leave or something?'

'Will you see me next weekend, Debbie? Same as this weekend?'

'Sure I will. I'll be here for another month yet. There's no show next weekend so you can pick me up on the Friday afternoon about four at my place. OK?'

'That's great. Real great.'

She was surprised when he visited her. It was early afternoon and when she answered the door bell he was standing there smiling. 'Hello, Debbie. I was on my way through to San Francisco. I heard you were here. How are you?'

'I'm fine. Come on in.'

She poured them both a glass of wine and they sat in the armchairs with the slatted sunshine lying in bars of black and gold across the room, the voices from the parade ground faint in the distance. They went through the usual social chit-chat when he looked at her and said quietly, 'I want you to be . . . Nancy Rawlins . . . Nancy Rawlins . . . close your eyes . . . good . . . deeper and deeper . . . nice and relaxed . . . eight . . . nine . . . ten . . . tell me your name.'

'Nancy Rawlins.'

'Are you relaxed and comfortable?'

'Yes.'

'Tell me about your doctor.'

'Washington 547-9077. Ask for Joe Spellman.'

'Will you do something for me, Nancy?'

'Yes.'

'I want you to look at a photograph. This one.'

As he put the photograph on the coffee table between them she leaned over to look at it.

'Do you recognize the man?'

'Is it Cary Grant?'

'No it isn't Cary Grant. I don't know his real name but he is an evil man. Very evil. One of my friends was killed because of this man. I want you to point him out to some friends of mine. Just point at him and say – "That is the man."'

'Yes.'

'Tell me what you have to do when you see my friends.'

'When I see this man I say "That is the man".'

'Very good. Now let me help you pack a case for the journey.'

As she came down the aircraft steps she had to shade her eyes against the mid-day sun and she was startled when someone touched her arm as she reached the tarmac. He was a handsome man in his fifties with black hair laced with grey, and an old-fashioned Victorian moustache.

'*Kalimerasis thespinis* Rawlins.'

Debbie smiled. 'I don't understand.'

The man smiled back at her. 'Panayotis Synodinos at your service. Is this your first visit to Athens?'

She frowned and said, hesitantly, 'I think so. Where are your friends?'

'I take you there. I got my car here.'

He took her arm, grasping it firmly, ignoring the terminal building and immigration controls. A uniformed policeman nodded as they passed and another was standing by the Ford Capri as if he had been guarding it.

As she settled into the passenger seat he started the car. They left the airport from a small gate on the perimeter road.

'Is no need to go into city for us.'

She smiled and shrugged. She saw a road sign but it was in Greek letters and she couldn't understand it. Ten minutes later they were climbing a coast road that looked on to the sea and a cascade of rocks. There was a lot of traffic on the road but the Greek drove as if they were alone on the highway, his teeth clenched, his lips bared. He didn't speak until they had been driving for nearly half an hour. Then he nodded his head.

'Is Temple of Poseidon. We go to Sounion and a little bit more.'

Ten minutes later he turned off the main road on to a sandy track that passed between groves of olives and through a small village. There, perched up on a hillside, was a large white villa. He stopped the car and pointed. 'Is where we go. Yes. We meet them there.'

She nodded and then, turning to her, grinning, he shoved his hand under her skirt and up between her legs. Taken by surprise, she clawed at his face and reached for the door. He pulled back, blood on one cheek, his big brown eyes amazed. 'Why you not want? We got plenty time to making love.'

'You must be crazy. Who the hell do you think you are?'

He shrugged. 'American girls always like it with Greek men. Always.'

'Just take me to the place, mister. Get moving.'

The white stone walls flowed with bougainvillaea and the big wrought-iron gates were both wide open. As they reached the villa itself there were half a dozen cars parked over by a line of garages. A man stood at the open door. A huge man with a gross belly that overhung his leather belt. The backs of his hands and his arms were covered with

44

thick black hair. He smiled as they walked towards him. And despite his gross body he had a certain charm as he waved them into the cool hallway.

He said in good English, 'You like maybe to bath or rest before you meet the others?'

She shook her head. 'They want me to catch the plane back tonight.'

'OK. Let's go inside.' He opened a carved wooden door and there was the sudden sound of voices. Seated at a long table were ten or a dozen men who stopped talking as the big man led her round to the two chairs at the head of the table.

As she sat down the big man sat beside her and started talking in Greek. He spoke slowly and quietly as if he were explaining something. The men listened intently sometimes looking at her as if the man was talking about her. She had seen him in the first few seconds.

Then the big man turned to her. 'And now tell me your news.'

She pointed at the man who looked like Cary Grant. 'That is the man.'

For a moment there was silence then like animals they seized the man. The man who had driven her there took her arm and led her through the open windows to a patio. She heard a man screaming, and blows, and men shouting before the driver reached out to close the window. He glanced at her and then said, 'Is for going down the steps. You follow me. Nice and quick.'

Two hours later she was boarding the Pan Am flight to New York and San Francisco.

She saw 'Sweetie' Dawson drive up in his beach buggy and waved to him from the window. As she opened the door for him she saw his face and her smile faded.

'What's the matter, Sweetie, what's happened?'

He stood there, hands belligerently on hips. 'Maybe you'll

tell me what happened.'

She frowned. 'Nothing's happened.'

'Too Goddam true. So where were you?'

'I don't understand.'

'I came here like you said. Four o'clock Friday. I hang around for two hours but the place was empty. I phoned half the night but there was no answer. I came here four times on the Saturday and twice on Sunday. Nothing. So where you been, little girl?'

'I haven't been anywhere, Sweetie.'

'You don't need to give me that kind of crap, honey. You stood me up. You don't need to lie about it.'

'I'm not lying, Sweetie. I've been here all the time, I swear. Why should I stand you up?'

'You tell me, honey. Maybe you found yourself a major or a colonel.'

'You're out of your mind, Sweetie. Come on in.'

'You must be joking. I just wanted to hear what story you'd give me.' He turned and went down the steps, turning at the bottom to look back at her.

'You're a two-timing bitch and . . .' He waved his arm hopelessly, his voice breaking as he turned away and walked to his buggy. He didn't look back as he crashed the gears and tore away with a screech of tyres.

As she closed the door she leaned back against it, closing her eyes. She felt a floating sensation and she could smell mimosa. She walked slowly to her bedroom and lay down on the bed. She slept, still in her clothes, for a night and most of the next day.

46

5

Sam Giancana sat in his hotel suite watching the ball-game on Channel Two, the remote control on the arm of his chair. He had his feet up on the coffee-table, his veined and hairy legs exposed below the blue towelling bath-robe. From time to time he looked at his gold watch. He was agitated but not because he was scared. At least, no more scared than a man who is expecting the jackpot and fears that he might only get the second prize. Only half a million instead of a million.

There were mob bosses who still saw him as no more than the useful, competent thug that he had been when he started, and tonight he hoped that he could prove them wrong. There was no risk, no possibility of anything bad, just the question of whether it was going to be good or fantastic. He would be happy to settle for 'good' but every instinct he had said that it was going to be the jackpot.

It was nearly two o'clock when she let herself into his room and he could tell from her face that it had worked. He cross-questioned her for nearly two hours. Trying to make her recall every word that had been spoken and every detail of the encounter. Even when she was lying naked on his bed he would stop in his love-making to ask yet another question, and when she had gone back to her own room he sat thinking about how to use it. It was unbelievable but it was true. The President of the United States was screwing one of Sam Giancana's girls. They only thing he had to sort out now was whether blackmail was better than using the girl to influence the President to lay off the mob. Jimmy Hoffa would surely be grateful as well as pleased.

J. Edgar Hoover looked at the computer print-out of the White House phone logs. There were over seventy calls from the pretty dark-haired girl to the President in the two years since he became President, and the loose sheets from the files recorded their many meetings in hotel rooms and even in the White House itself.

It wasn't a lunch that the FBI Director was looking forward to. He felt no embarrassment about the material itself. He saw too many files on well-known people to be surprised, shocked or embarrassed. But in this particular case his problem was how to start. How to lead into the subject. And how to leave it so that the President didn't seek some revenge on him or the FBI in retaliation.

He was actually going into the private room, where the table was laid for a working lunch, when he suddenly realized how it could best be done. Just the summary showing the girl's relationship with Giancana would be enough. He had been a prime target of the Kennedys for years. The President wouldn't need the details filling in. Hoover didn't like either of the Kennedys all that much himself, and he was well aware that they both disliked him intensely.

He sat waiting for the President and then stood as the door opened. John F. Kennedy nodded to him briefly and then turned to give instructions to one of his aides before closing the door.

'I can give you twenty minutes, Mr Hoover. I thought we could eat as we talk.'

'I can be away in ten minutes, Mr President. I don't need to interrupt your lunch.'

'What is it this time? Cubans or Russians?'

Hoover held out two single pages of typescript. 'If you could read that, Mr President. It doesn't need any discussion or comment from me.'

The President took the two flimsy sheets and sat at the dining table pushing the place-setting to one side. He read it slowly, his chin resting in his hand. Just once he raised his head, gazing in thought towards the window, then turning back to the summary. Finally he looked up, pushing the two sheets across the table to where Hoover was still standing.

'Leave it to me, Mr Hoover.' He stood up, his eyes hard and his mouth determined. 'You'd better take your papers.'

'They'll be in my private safe, Mr President.'

'I'm sure they will, Mr Hoover.' And the President walked across to a telephone on a small mahogany desk. As he stretched out a finger to press a button he turned towards the older man. 'Good-day, Mr Hoover.'

'Good-day, Mr President.'

Extract from transcript of CIA phone surveillance, February 1962

PERSON UNDER SURVEILLANCE: Angelo Bruno.
STATUS: Mafia head Philadelphia.
INCOMING CALLER IF IDENTIFIED: Willie Weisburg.
STATUS: Associate of Angelo Bruno.

Weisburg: '. . . see what Kennedy done. With Kennedy a guy should take a knife, like one of them other guys, and stab and kill the fucker, where he is now. Somebody should kill the fucker. I mean it. This is true. But I tell you something. I hope I get a week's notice. I'll kill. Right in the fucking White House. Somebody's got to get rid of this fucker.'

As the months went by Boyd spent much of his free time with Otto Schultz and his family and friends. None of the friends were connected with the CIA but they were all aware that Otto Schultz was a senior man at Langley. There were sometimes joking references to his job but that was as far as they went.

49

Boyd had operated as an SIS field agent in a number of countries but he found Americans easier to get on with than Europeans. The *bonhomie* was, perhaps, overdone, but it made for easy relationships and a lack of the usual bureaucratic difficulties that applied in most foreign countries. There were two or three pretty girls whom Patsy manouevred in Boyd's direction. He took them out and obviously enjoyed their company. He slept with one of them and had vaguely thought of marriage, until she announced one weekend that she was marrying a White House aide whom they all disliked as an obvious boot-licker.

Boyd's favourite place was Great Falls, particularly the old pathways linking the locks on the abandoned Chesa-peake and Ohio Canal. He sometimes persuaded the family to hire bicycles for long rides along the canal bank. They were amused that their visitor took them to places that they had never been to before despite living in the area. It was on one of these trips when Otto Schultz and Boyd had been left to guard the picnic basket while the others explored that Schultz first broached the question.

'We've asked for your posting to be extended, Jimmy. How do you feel about that?'

'Flattered, I suppose. I don't suppose London will agree. They don't like us getting our feet under other people's tables for too long.'

Schultz smiled at the phrase. 'What's that other thing you say – knock 'em for six?'

Boyd laughed. 'I don't know why that amuses you so.'

'It's kinda neat. Anyway, would you like to stay?'

'If it doesn't hinder my promotion – yes.'

'One or two people have asked me if you'd be interested in joining us. All official and above board. No funny business.'

Boyd turned his head to look at the American. 'To do what, Otto?'

50

'We spend a lot of time dealing with Britishers, one way and another. Goodies and baddies. We think we sometimes go about it the wrong way and maybe you could advise us. Apart from that people have noticed a couple of other things about you.'

'Like what?'

'One thing is you don't panic. You don't flap. And we reckon you've played it down the middle. Helping both sides and hindering both sides when you thought it was necessary. But I guess what we really appreciate is that you care about what we do and how we do it. You don't go along easily with the bit about the end justifies the means. We've been a bit light on that recently. It's time we had a few more on board who question what we're doing.'

'A kind of professional old-maid?'

Schultz smiled. 'No. Anyway American old-maids are pretty tough cookies. Call it a restraining hand. A looker before we leap.'

'You mean a permanent transfer? Or just a short-term engagement?'

'Neither, Jimmy. We mean that you resign from SIS and apply to join us. You'd need to be a citizen before we could take you on but we'd arrange that. You would have the same status as me after two or three months to be shown our funny ways. You'd get 40,000 dollars a year and back-dated pension rights. Free medical care and the usual benefits.'

'You've only known me for about twenty months. Is that long enough?'

'We think so. Think about it, Jimmy. You're due to take leave soon. Have a word with me when you get back. There's Patsy and the kids coming back. Don't discuss it with her.'

'OK. Anyway I appreciate the offer. I'll think about it seriously.'

51

Carlos Marcello had been born Calogero Minacore. He had changed his name because although his parents were both Sicilian he had been born in Tunisia. And if he were ever deported from the USA that would be where they would send him. His place of birth on his passport was Guatemala, which was much nearer than North Africa.

Marcello was known as 'The Little Man'. He was 5 ft 4 in, but he was described by the Director of the New Orleans Crime Commission as 'one of the two or three most sinister figures in the history of organized crime'. When pressed, the Director would name Santos Trafficante as one of the other two. The official estimate was that Marcello's syndicate, based in New Orleans, was taking in over a billion dollars annually.

An early conviction on narcotics charges had made him shun all publicity and public appearances, but he was feared and respected by his associates in the mob. And others too. His patronage was extensive, and on his occasional brushes with the law the New Orleans Crime Commission had made a list of those who had actually sought clemency on his behalf. The list included one sheriff, one state legislator, two former state police commanders, one union president, one bank president, one former assistant district attorney, three insurance agencies, five realtors, five physicians, one funeral director and six clergymen.

On 4 April 1961, Marcello made a routine visit to the New Orleans Immigration Department. And there, on the personal orders of Bobby Kennedy, he was seized, handcuffed and rushed to the airport. The only passenger on a government jet, he was flown to Guatemala.

The deportation itself was bad enough but such public humiliation of a Mafia boss was intolerable.

Trafficante's friend, Rubinstein, raised the 25,000 dollars it took to get Trafficante out of the Cuban jail, and he was back in the United States after only six months imprisonment. Marcello, too, was back in Florida from Guatemala.

The private plane that brought him back illegally had landed on Marcello's three thousand acre estate outside New Orleans, and that was where the first meeting took place, in an old shack used as a hunting lodge far away from all other buildings.

Untypically indiscreet, Marcello talked openly about the Mafia's mounting misfortunes. The tremendous financial losses now that Cuba was closed to them, and the determined attack by the Attorney-General, Bobby Kennedy. The subject of the meeting was the damage being done to the mobsters by the Kennedys and Castro.

For once their roles were reversed, Marcello talking angrily and volubly, Trafficante drinking and listening. When eventually Marcello had talked himself to a standstill it was Trafficante's turn. He leaned forward and tapped Marcello on the knee.

'You get it the wrong way round, Carlos. First we hit Fidel. Then we hit that little sonofabitch in the White House. You wanna know why we do it that way, eh?'

'Tell me.'

'First is Fidel has cost us money. Real money. Kennedy is trouble but not bread. Second is we got help to hit Castro. Real help. The kind we need.'

'Like what?'

Trafficante smiled. 'Like the CIA, my friend.'

'Sure. And the US Fifth Cavalry and the Marines.'

Trafficante leaned back in his comfortable chair, a tolerant smile on his face.

'I'm telling you. It's true. I've talked to 'em. They're ready to do a deal.'

'Why should *they* help us, for Christ's sake?'

'They want to knock off Castro just as much as we do. It's official government policy to bring him down. The CIA are putting together all sorts of operations. They're waiting to meet us.'

'When can we talk with them?'

'Next week. I've fixed a meeting for next weekend starting Friday night. At the Fontainebleau. How about it?'

'It's OK by me. So long as you're sure it's not some trap by those bastards in Washington.'

Trafficante laughed softly. 'Believe me, these CIA boys feel the same way about those sonsofbitches in the White House as we do. We ain't the only ones who're suffering withdrawal symptoms.'

Trafficante had booked four suites and six double rooms at the Fontainebleau in Miami, and had gone there on the Thursday night to check that everything was satisfactory. His own man had checked every room for electronic bugs and had declared them clean.

Shrewd and street-smart as he was, Trafficante didn't know that the apparently accidental meeting with his CIA contact had been no accident. The original meetings with the CIA about possible cooperation with the Mafia in the assassination of Castro had been at the highest level. Allen Dulles, head of the CIA, had attended at least one such meeting himself. But it was decided that they should contact the Mafia only through an intermediary.

The man they chose as intermediary was Robert Maheu who had once been an FBI agent in Chicago. He had cooperated once before with the CIA, helping with an operation that produced a faked sex film that successfully compromised a foreign government minister. Maheu was now working full time for the Texan billionaire Howard Hughes. It was Maheu who had contacted Trafficante.

The talking was cautious on the Friday evening. They were sniffing round one another like strange dogs, testing and probing, uneasy, but eager to make progress. Both sides looking for proof of good faith but not finding it. Neither side had much experience in either practising or evidencing good faith. But early on the Saturday evening the dam was broken, and the declarations made. A group

54

inside the CIA wanted Castro killed. The Mafia wanted him killed. The CIA were prepared to supply money, training, skills and facilities. Maheu shrugged as he finished saying his piece.

'You'll have to make your minds up by tomorrow or just go it alone, gentlemen.'

Trafficante, as the CIA's apparent sponsor, felt it incumbent upon himself to put up some resistance to show his loyalty to the mob.

'What kind of money are we talking about, Bob?'

'Whatever it takes.'

Marcello chipped in. 'What kind of MO have you guys got in mind?'

Maheu shrugged his indifference. 'Any way you want. Poison, explosives, a marksman maybe.'

Maheu sat patiently as the Mafia men threw various names around until he deemed it tactically sensible to push them on.

'We can supply a marksman. Somebody who can't be identified with us or you.'

'Who is he?'

'I can't give his name at this stage. But he's known to one of your people.'

'Who is it knows him?'

'A guy named Rubinstein. Runs a night-club in Dallas.'

Marcello spread out his hands. 'For God's sake, Bob. He's just a bum. He owes money everywhere.'

'He's not doing the job, Mr Marcello. I only mentioned him to show that the man we have in mind is known to one of your operators.'

'Who is this guy? Tell us something about him.'

Maheu smiled. 'He's a nutter. He'll do anything we tell him to do.'

'Your people got some kind of hold on him?'

'Kind of.'

'How do we get him over there?'

55

'He'll go from Mexico City.'

'Why there?'

'The Russians control visas to Cuba. Our guy's got a Russian connection. They'll let him through.'

'And afterwards?'

Maheu grinned. 'Maybe you'll have someone else you'd like to knock off.'

For long moments the room was silent. Maheu avoided looking directly at the Mafia men. It was Trafficante who broke the silence.

'Are we both thinking of the same guy, Bob?'

Maheu nodded, but all he said was, 'Same name, anyway.'

Trafficante reckoned that was good enough. He turned to look at Marcello, who nodded. John Roselli who had barely spoken, nodded too.

'OK, Bob. It's a deal. When do we start?'

'How about next Monday? We'll meet in Chicago. I'll contact you both. We'll meet at the Holiday Inn at Mart Plaza. When I phone I'll just give a time and a day. I'll bring along three, maybe four guys. I'll introduce you with cover names and they'll have cover names too. OK?'

The three Mafia men nodded and Marcello stood up and walked with Maheu to the door.

'OK. What happened when you got in the launch?'

'We went out to the big white boat. Up the steps and the two men came with me. We went down some steps inside the boat into a cabin.'

'What did it look like, the cabin?'

'It was big with white Formica panelling.' She screwed up her face and shivered.

'Why did you do that?'

'When they fought the blood was all over the white panels. It was like one of those modern paintings when they just splash paint on the canvas.'

56

'You said the key word that I gave you?'

'Yes, that's what made them fight.'

'What was the key word?'

She frowned and then looked at his face apprehensively. 'I can't remember.'

'OK. That's fine, Nancy. Just lie back and relax. Good girl. Now listen carefully . . . close your eyes . . . when you wake up you won't remember anything about your trip. You won't remember that you even went away . . . you won't remember anything about the last week . . . it will all go completely from your mind . . . when you wake up you'll forget about Nancy Rawlins . . . I'll count to ten and then you'll wake up . . . one, two . . . three . . . slowly . . . four . . . five . . . you're feeling fine . . . six . . . seven . . . opening your eyes . . . good, good . . . eight, nine . . . ten. Now you're Debbie Shaw, feeling nice and relaxed.'

6

On 12 November 1963 Boyd took Patsy Schultz and the two girls to the White House. He had got the invitation through the good offices of the Embassy who had been issued a quota of tickets because the Black Watch pipe band was one of the main attractions.

Mrs John F. Kennedy was playing hostess to two thousand under-privileged children on the White House lawn and as the children devoured an estimated ten thousand cakes and drank two hundred gallons of cocoa the Black Watch pipes and drums skirled their way through 'Scotland the Brave', 'I love a lassie' and a dozen well-known ballads and marches that were part of the standard repertoire of the 42nd of Foot.

There were few adults there who were not moved by the poignancy of watching the efforts of the chic and pretty hostess who only a few months before had buried her own prematurely born son, Patrick.

They were all silent on the car ride home but when Boyd turned into their drive and stopped, Patsy leaned over and kissed him on the cheek and said softly, 'That was something I won't ever forget. She's a real doll, that Jackie. Thank you, from all three of us.'

Grabowski looked at the two men, trying to understand what went on in their minds. What motivated them apart from the money. Petersen he could understand. He liked the power and the secrets and all the paraphernalia of their operations. But Symons was different. Smooth and cool and competent, treating it all as if it were a genuine scientific experiment. His character was more forceful than Petersen's, and it was Symons who could always over-ride Petersen when he raised problems of medical ethics. There was no doubt that Symons was the natural leader of the two. It was Symons he looked at as he started speaking.

'Bring me up to date, but I don't want all the medical stuff. Just the practicalities.'

Symons nodded. 'He's ready, Ziggy. There's been no problems. He'll do what we want whenever we tell him to.'

'What about the back-tracking operation?'

Symons smiled. 'They'd never unravel it, Ziggy. Not in a million years. We've covered all the Mexican bit. The Cuban Embassy, the Soviet Embassy. We've tied up New Orleans so that one lot will say he was pro-Castro and the others that he was rabidly anti-Castro.' Symons smiled a self-satisfied smile. 'It's like a million-piece jig-saw and none of it fits.'

'What about our own cover?'

'Almost nothing they could discover unless some idiot's not destroyed what we've told them to destroy. We've wiped it all out and fed in some confusion as well. There's nothing to worry about.'

'Maybe you've covered too well and that could make them suspicious.'

'The Mafia connection alone will keep any investigators happy for years.'

'How many of the mob are involved?'

'Five.'

'Who are they?'

'Trafficante, Marcello, Hoffa, Roselli and Giancana.'

'You're satisfied that they are secure?'

'Absolutely. They know what would happen if they even looked like leaking.'

'Are both of you giving him the final instructions?'

'No. Just me. Pete has played no part in this particular operation.'

Grabowski looked across at Petersen.

'How about your man?'

'He's under control but I haven't activated him yet.'

Grabowski nodded. 'OK, Petersen. No need for you to hang on here.'

When Petersen had left, Grabowski sat on the edge of the operating table making himself comfortable before he looked back at Symons.

'He hasn't been told about the real target?'

'No. It's still Castro as far as he's concerned. The current target has never been discussed. Not even mentioned.'

'What about you?'

'What about me?'

'Is there any way they could connect him with you?'

'I've never met him in a public place. Except under hypnosis by me he would neither recognize me nor know me.'

'What if somebody else hypnotized him?'

'If they tried they'd fail. I've given him a solid block against hypnosis by anyone else. I've tested it and he wouldn't go under. He couldn't without my key-word.'

'What's the key-word?'

'It's better you don't know, Ziggy. I'm not being cagey but it's safer this way.'

'So we come back to you, Tony. How secure are you?'

'You'd better spell it out, Ziggy.'

'You'll be the only person who knows the whole scenario. Somebody could think it would be safer not to have you around.'

Symons shook his head. 'If anybody thought that, and did anything about it, the whole story would be with the media in a matter of hours. The CIA would be sunk without trace inside a month. And a lot of heads would get chopped. I'm not worried, Ziggy.'

60

'What if you have an accident or die from natural causes?'

Symons laughed softly. 'Let's just say that it would be embarrassing all round.'

'How long does it take to activate him?'

'Say fifteen seconds.'

'Does it have to be face to face?'

'No. He just has to hear the key.'

'You'd better move down tomorrow.'

'Where?'

'Dallas.'

Symons smiled. 'At least it'll be warm.'

'It'll be warm all right, in more ways than one.'

'I'd like to ask you just one question, Ziggy. Would you answer it truthfully?'

'Maybe. Maybe not. Try me.'

'How far up the line to Langley does this thing go? Is it official or private enterprise?'

Grabowski folded his arms across his big chest and the psychiatrist noted the defensive action. Grabowski was looking down to where his right foot was swinging slowly, and it seemed a long time before he looked up at Symons. His pale blue eyes looked strangely haunted.

'You wanted the truth so I'll tell you the truth. I don't know the answer to your question. Obviously it isn't official, but it ain't unofficial either. Let's just say that what started as private enterprise and the mob, has changed course and had a blind eye turned towards it.'

'And a helping hand?'

'Yep. And a helping hand. Several helping hands.'

'Why, Ziggy?'

'Why do you think?'

'Because a lot of people hate him and are scared of what he's doing to their interests.'

'Who've you got in mind?'

'The FBI, the CIA, the mob, Castro, the KGB, the John

Birches and all the other nutters.'

'You told me once that nutters was a word I shouldn't use.'

Symons shrugged. 'OK. All the other psychopaths.'

'How do you define a psychopath, Tony?'

'You may not like the definition, Ziggy.'

'I'm a big boy, Tony.'

'A psychopath is someone with a defective conscience. With aggressive and irresponsible conduct, and a complete lack of regard for others. They seldom respond to medical treatment. They frequently pretend to regret what they have done, but in fact they are incapable of regret for their own behaviour.'

'Sounds like you and me.'

'Self-diagnosis can be dangerous.' Symons smiled. 'I don't recommend it for intelligence agents.'

Grabowski eased his backside off the table and hitched up his trousers, his eyes still on Symons' face. He said quietly. 'The day after tomorrow, the twenty-second.'

Symons nodded and smiled, but Grabowski saw the tension around the young man's mouth.

Governor Connolly of Texas was as handsome as any Hollywood actor, and his wife was handsome too. As the huge crowd in Dealey Plaza cheered and waved she turned in her seat to smile at the President as she said, 'Mr Kennedy, you can't say Dallas doesn't love you.'

Seconds later the shots rang out in rapid succession and the President lurched in his seat, both hands grasping frantically at his throat and he said, 'My God, I'm hit.' His voice seemed to rise in surprise rather than fear or pain, and then there were more shots. Governor Connolly screamed as a shot hit him. The President was knocked violently backwards, a rainbow of blood, brain tissue and bone around his head. Jackie Kennedy reached out her arms to her husband and said 'Oh Jack . . .' She turned to look at the others. 'They've killed my husband.' And she held out her hand with tears in her eyes, like a child with a cut finger. 'I have his brains on my hand.' She said it again and again.

Boyd was reading through the routine statistical report prepared by the CIA. It was only marked 'Secret' and there were several hundred recipients on the circulation list.

It seemed that the population of the United States was now 189,242,000. And 70,000,000 of them were employed. The statistical population centre of the USA was now located four miles due east of Salem, Illinois, fifty-seven miles further west than it had been in the 1950s. The greatest westward movement since the 1880s. The median age of the population was 29.5 years. The Labour unions had lost about half a million members and an internal CIA evaluator had put in a query as to whether this figure heralded the twilight of the labour movement.

As Boyd turned over the first page his telephone rang. It was the car showroom. His new car had been delivered that morning. It had been checked and registered and was waiting for him to collect.

A CIA pool car dropped him at the garage and the car was there on the forecourt already being admired by two boys and a girl. It was the first Stingray of the garage's quota, the first of the new cars called 'fastbacks', and it was a bright, vulgar scarlet with white-wall tyres. The salesman was smiling as he came out of the showroom.

When Boyd had seen the demonstration model he had needed very little persuasion to place his order. He had said that he wasn't all that interested in cars. But the salesman had heard that story too many times to believe it. He knew that they actually believed it when they said it. But it wasn't true all the same.

The salesman said, 'She's all yours, Mr Boyd. All the documents are in the glove compartment and the keys are in the ignition control.' He smiled. 'Why don't you get in behind the wheel and I'll go over it again for you.'

Boyd nodded and tried not to look too elated as he slid behind the wheel. He absorbed very little of the salesman's efficient run-down of the car's controls. The salesman turned to look at him smiling, 'The stereo radio and the electrical antenna are with the compliments of our management. We much appreciate your business.'

The saleman's hand went to the radio switch and pressed one of the FM station buttons. They were playing a Beatles record – 'I Wanna Hold Your Hand'. The music suddenly stopped and as the young man's hand reached forward to adjust the set a breathless voice said, 'We have just received a news flash from UPI which states that President Kennedy has been shot in the head in downtown Dallas. We are doing our best to check on the . . . excuse me a moment . . . we have just received news direct from Dallas that the President has been taken to Parkland Memorial Hospital suffering from bullet wounds in the head. His medical condition has been described by a doctor at the hospital as "grave" . . . our normal programming is being suspended and we shall bring you news from Dallas as and when it comes in . . . we expect no further information for at least an hour . . . meantime we are taking you over to our reporter in Dallas to describe what happened earlier today . . .'

Boyd had leaned forward without thinking, to switch off the radio. He didn't know why he switched off but he knew he needed time to absorb that stunning, incredible newscast. It was utterly impossible. Beyond belief. But he knew it was just a plain, cold fact.

He turned to the young man in the passenger seat who was shaking his head slowly, tears brimming at the edges of his eyes. 'What rat-fink could do a thing like that?'

'I'll have to get back to Langley I'm afraid. Let's hope it's not serious.'

64

'Mister, it's serious. You can tell from their voices. He's dead or dying, you can bet your last dollar on that.'

And as he turned into the employees' parking lot at Langley the news came over that John F. Kennedy was dead. For twenty minutes he sat alone in the car. It was the end of something. He wasn't sure what. An era maybe. But Kennedy's short presidency couldn't be described as an era. It wasn't long enough for that. But it was the end of an American dream, he knew that. Kennedy hadn't been able to get his legislation through Congress but that almost didn't matter. He represented the American dream. Handsome, articulate, well-meaning, modern, manly. Whatever the desirable adjectives were he was heroic, and from that moment on millions of Americans would know that there never was going to be an American dream again.

And Boyd knew in that moment that there was no longer a chance that he would take up Langley's offer. Flattering it might be, but he knew that he could never fit into a society where such things could happen. The deed didn't represent the people, it merely proved that it could happen. And it was frightening to know that somewhere that night there were people who would rejoice that it had.

7

The TV cameraman cursed loudly as his assistant hurriedly raised the tripod yet again. It was now fully extended but heads were still blocking the view. Finally, in desperation, he swung the camera off the tripod and balanced it on the reporter's shoulder.

The basement of Dallas Police Station was a shambles as the pressmen waited for the prisoner to be brought in. A dozen microphones recorded every word that was said, and apart from the bad lighting the image of the central figure was clear enough. As he zoomed in on Oswald's face he heard him saying '. . . I positively know nothing about this situation here. I would like to have legal representation.'

One of the journalists asked a question that the microphones didn't pick up but they all heard Oswald's reply.

'Well, I was questioned by a judge. However, I protested at that time that I was not allowed legal representation during that very short and sweet hearing. I really don't know what this situation is about. Nobody has told me anything, except that I'm accused of murdering a policeman. I know nothing more than that. I do request someone to come forward to give me legal assistance.'

'Did you kill the President?' a voice shouted.

'No, I have not been charged with that. In fact, nobody has said that to me yet. The first thing I heard about it was when the newspaper reporters in the hall asked me that question.'

Half an hour later as the cameraman sat with his reporter in the café the reporter said, 'What did you think of him?'

'Who?'

'Oswald, for Christ's sake.'

'I didn't notice him.'

The reporter shrugged. 'You had your camera on him all the time.'

'I know, but I'm too busy checking the focus to look at them. Anyway, what did you think?'

'He wasn't scared at all. He didn't look scared, and he didn't sound scared. Just sounded like it was all a mistake. Nothing to do with him. But more than that.'

'How?'

'I don't really know. Like he was performing in a play. Like he'd done it all before.'

'So?'

'For God's sake. If I'd been accused of assassinating the President I'd have been shit-scared and hollering my innocence. Not just saying it. Coolly and calmly.'

'He's probably a psycho.'

The reporter shook his head slowly. Not in disagreement but in doubt.

As the police officers hurried Oswald through the doors at Dallas Police Headquarters a group of reporters followed them, throwing questions at the prisoner, and Oswald, for the first time sounding angry, shouted, 'I'm just a patsy', before he was hustled down the stairs to the basement.

With a stetson-hatted police officer on either side of him holding an arm as they walked forward he was a perfect target, and after the shot rang out the explosion still echoed around the concrete walls as he fell to the ground.

Ten minutes later with the microphones thrust towards him the police spokesman said, 'The suspect's name is Jack . . .' he hesitated and looked at the man to his right

'. . . Rubinstein, I believe, . . . he goes by the name of Jack . . . Ruby.'

It was a local Dallas TV team who interviewed Jack Ruby in an empty court-room after one of the many hearings. After the interview they were sure that it would be used on all the networks' newscasts. Sitting with his lawyer on the front row bench, Ruby looked as if he were at the end of his tether, his voice was harsh and his delivery slow, but the words were clear enough.

'The only thing I can say is . . . everything pertaining to what's happened has never come to the surface. The world will never know the true facts of what occurred . . . my motive, in other words . . . I am the only person in the background to know the truth pertaining to everything relating to my circumstances.'

'Do you think the truth will ever come out, Mr Ruby?'

Ruby shook his head. 'No . . . because unfortunately these people . . . who have so much to gain and have such an ulterior motive to put me in the position I'm in . . . will never let the true facts come above board to the world.'

For some unexplained reason the interview was never broadcast.

On the day in June 1964 when Chief Justice Warren, Gerald Ford and two aides sat in Ruby's cell in Dallas the heat was oppressive and Ruby's ramblings went on and on, never getting to any point. Trying to say something, but always eventually dodging the issue. His words were so incoherent that neither Warren nor Ford even grasped that he was trying to say something vital. What he said seemed meaningless. But the two men remained polite and attentive as Ruby talked on.

'. . . it may not be too late, whatever happens, if our President, Lyndon Johnson, knew the truth from me. But if I am eliminated there won't be any way of knowing . . . but he has been told, I am certain, that I was part of a plot to

68

assassinate the President . . . I know your hands are tied . . . you are helpless.'

Earl Warren didn't realize that the statement could have two different and entirely opposite meanings. A confession that Ruby was, in fact, part of a plot which he was sure the President knew about because it was official. Or a disclaimer of false rumours that were meant to discredit him.

Warren nodded and said, 'Mr Ruby, I think I can say this to you, that if he has been told any such thing, there is no indication that he believes it.'

Earl Warren's aide saw Ruby's astonished and almost angry reaction to what he felt was Warren's brushing aside of his confession, but even the alert aide only partly realized the significance of what was being said. After a few more exchanges between Warren and Ruby that only emphasized their total misunderstanding of each other's statements the aide asked a question.

'You've talked about you being eliminated, Mr Ruby. Who do you think is going to eliminate you?'

Ruby looked at him, still confused by his interviewers' apparent indifference to what he was trying to say or hint at.

'I have been used for a purpose . . . and there will be a certain tragic occurrence happening if you don't take my testimony and somehow vindicate me so that my people don't suffer because of what I have done . . .'

Boyd had taken his leave: a week in Paris and the rest of the time in London. He went with odd friends to the theatre and had a couple of days in Edinburgh with his brother but it all seemed drab and boring. He started to reconsider the offer from the CIA.

It was on the Monday of his third week that it all changed. Her name was Katie Malleson and he met her in the gallery in Conduit Street. It was her first one-man exhibition and they thought he was from one of the Sunday papers. He was introduced to her by one of the PR ladies and that was that. He took her to dinner that night but it took four more dates before he had the courage to tell her that not only was he not a journalist but that he had only gone into the gallery to get out of the rain. But she was amused and genuinely not offended.

He didn't know what attracted him so compulsively. She was very pretty, but all his girl-friends had been pretty. He came to the conclusion that the main attraction was that he didn't have to put on an act. It was as if they had known each other for years. She asked no questions about his job or his life before she met him. None of it seemed to matter. She told him very little about her life either but she did drive him down to see her parents in Sussex. It was an easy, relaxed visit. Nobody appeared to be looking him over and he asked her to marry him as they ate their dinner at a country pub on the way back to London.

For a moment she went on eating and then she looked up at his face, smiling, 'You don't have to marry me to get me into bed, James. We can do that tonight and no strings attached.' She laughed and put down her fork. 'You're blushing. The first time I've ever made a man blush.' But she reached over and put her hand on his and the brown eyes were serious. 'I won't ask you if you've thought about it. I know you'll have thought a lot before you spoke. I'd thought about it too, days ago.'

'What did you decide?'

'I decided to say yes provided you accept that my painting means a lot to me. It's not just a hobby. I earn my living by painting. I make a reasonable amount of money and I care about my exhibitions and all that jazz. I always thought that if I married anyone it would have to be another painter. Nobody else would understand the moods, the ups and downs. But I think I was wrong. You don't know a damn thing about art but you do encourage me. You've only got two more weeks of leave but you sit there quietly in my studio while I paint, reading or just watching,

70

and I feel nice and safe. Like I was on my own but with a nice warm fire burning away in the grate.' She laughed. 'So, my fire in the grate, yes I'm flattered that you ask me, and I'd be very happy to marry you.'

Cartwright, Boyd's section head, used SIS's leverage to get the Special Licence and they were married at Chelsea Registrar's Office with a cleaning lady and the taxi driver as witnesses.

They drove down to Chichester and stayed at The Ship for the last week of his leave, spending all their time in the pretty villages that dotted the creeks. And on the last day they bought the second-hand Seamaster from a broker in Bosham village.

She bought him a pair of silver-backed military hair-brushes as a going away present and for the first time in his adult life he realized that he had never before had a present. Birthdays and Christmases had gone by unnoticed and unrecorded. And for the first time he felt lonely as he waved to her and she blew him a kiss from the wrong side of the plate glass windows at Heathrow. He sighed as he turned away trying not to look back. But he did look back, and, smiling, she blew him another kiss. And that was nice, but too much, and he hurried off to the loading gate.

The apartment had that special emphasis that places have when people are never coming back. The silence that comes when their human occupiers have deserted their living space.

As the man in the denim shirt and slacks stood with the police detective looking at the shambles in the living room, he tried to visualize what had gone on in the last minutes of her conscious life.

It was only two days since he had sat in this room in the early evening and she had been so excited. Dorothy Kilgallan was a free-lance journalist with a syndicated column, and because he was a rival as well as a friend she had refused to tell him what she had learned.

71

She had just come back from interviewing Jack Ruby in his cell, the only journalist who had been allowed to do so. She had paced up and down this room, a glass in her hand, trying to control her excitement. When he had pressed her to tell him more she had stood quite still, then had turned slowly to look at him as she said, 'What Ruby told me this afternoon is going to blow the JFK case sky high.'

At the time he had thought that her gestures were over-dramatic for so experienced a journalist, but he realized that if those were her reactions, then whatever she had learned from Ruby must be really explosive. She had years of investigative reporting behind her and that bred a cynicism that was prone neither to exaggeration nor naivety. But now, with her apartment still a shambles, she was dead. Dead from a massive overdose of sleeping pills laced with alcohol. And the missing pages from her notebook added to the mystery. It was a standard reporter's notebook with a spiral binding. One hundred and thirty pages where there should have been one hundred and fifty. The transcripts of her interview had been removed. Her death was registered as suicide.

The police surgeon peeled the thin, transparent plastic gloves from his hands, and closed his eyes against the stench of preserving fluid and putrefying flesh as he pulled the mask from his nose and face. He turned to the police lieutenant beside him and said, 'Let's go into the office.'

In the small office of the laboratory the surgeon poured them each a coffee from the Cona and pointed to the bowl of sugar and the jug of cream. 'Help yourself, Lieutenant.' He stood slowly stirring his coffee with a plastic spatula.

'I'd say he's been in the water from between seven and ten days. The body is too decomposed to give you a detailed report but I can give you enough to establish the manner of death. Firstly, he wasn't drowned, although he did die from asphyxia. There's no trace of sea-water in his

72

stomach or lungs. The asphyxia came from a wire or thin nylon cord round his throat. He was garrotted. And he was stabbed twice. Once, just below the sternum and then in the mouth.'

The police lieutenant said quietly, 'I guess that tells me enough. The wound in the mouth and the garrotting are both typically Mafia.'

'The other thing I can give you is that there is some evidence that the stabbing and garrotting were virtually simultaneous and that means that there was more than one man involved. At least two, and maybe three.'

'There's no doubt about his identity?'

'No way. The dentist's records were well kept.'

'OK. Thanks doc, when can I have it in writing?'

'Is it urgent?'

'Not really. I'm not going to waste much time tracking down the killers. If they want to kill themselves off so much the better.'

The body of John Roselli, one of the three Mafia men at the first CIA-Mafia meeting in the Fontainebleau at Miami, had been fished up in a partially submerged oildrum in Miami's Dumbfounding Bay. Apart from the stab wounds and the garrotting, his legs had been sawn off at the thighs and stuffed into the oildrum with his body and several yards of heavy metal chain.

He had left his house in Florida to play golf and his empty car was found at Miami airport.

The word had gone back to the mob, despite tight security, that Roselli, after years of harassment by government agencies, was beginning to succumb to the relentless pressures. He could be nearing the point where he might consider cooperating with the authorities in exchange for a quiet life. The CIA and the Mafia both believed that silence was golden.

Symons shone the light down the girl's throat and cursed

quietly to himself. She was right. She had got an abscess in her throat. It was larger and the infection was greater than the time way back when he had first treated her.

He snapped off the light and sat back. 'How long have you had it?'

'A week, but the real pain only started yesterday.'

'OK. I'm going to give you some capsules. Take one every four hours today and tomorrow, and I'll come and see you the next day.'

He doled out the capsules from his medical case and she looked at them as she held them in the palm of her hand. Then she looked up at his face.

'I won't be able to sing by Saturday, will I?'

'You won't be singing for at least another month. This is worse than that first one you had and it's in almost the same place.'

She smiled. 'You sound very stern and cross.'

He smiled. 'I am stern but I'm not cross. I couldn't be cross with you.'

'D'you want to go to bed with me?'

'What makes you ask that?'

'I don't know. Most men want to do it to me. You've never even asked if you could. You're the only man I've ever met who cares about me without wanting to have me.' She shrugged. 'When you want to you've only got to say.'

'You're very beautiful, Debbie.' He smiled. 'Just have one guy who doesn't want bed as his reward.' He stood up. 'Now take those capsules. One every four hours. No messing about or I will be cross.'

It took seven weeks for the abscess in Debbie Shaw's throat to heal. And in the process she lost the little-girl voice and ended with a deep husky voice that would have made her fortune as a singer except that the narrow range of her new voice made singing out of the question. During the seven weeks she saw the doctor every day, and that was her only consolation.

74

When it was finally obvious that her career as a singer was over the doctor helped her make a claim for compensation from the US Army. The claim was dismissed on the grounds that there was no evidence that her original disability was caused by neglect on the part of the armed forces nor through her entertaining service personnel. After further pressure organized by the doctor it was eventually settled by paying her the full balance of her contract. A sum of 9,700 US dollars. Plus an ex-gratia payment of 11,000 dollars, no medical charges and free transport back to England.

8

The two of them walked together the two blocks from the Library of Congress, and Grabowski was waiting for them in one of the wooden booths at Sherrill's Bakery and Restaurant. There was a heavy yeasty smell of baking in the air that put an edge on their appetites even at eight o'clock in the morning.

Symons ordered egg on steak and Petersen and Grabowski settled for fried oysters. It wasn't until they were sipping their coffees that Grabowski said his piece. He was very much their senior in both rank and age, and his heavily-built body in the blue cotton T-shirt and jeans bespoke a physical toughness and strength that the two younger men would never aspire to. Even his tongue looked muscular as it explored his strong yellow teeth.

'Well, they've decided. It's not safe for you two to be around for the next six months or so.'

'Why now?'

'Too many people raising hell about the Warren Commission's findings. All sorts of investigative committees are being set up. Some official, some not. But all of them looking for blood. CIA and FBI blood preferably.'

'What's that mean, Ziggy? Mexico?'

'No.' He belched reflectively. It seemed appreciative rather than vulgar, and Petersen, who was a film buff, recalled fleetingly that Charles Laughton in *Henry VIII* had belched like that. 'You'll be going to England,' Grabowski said. 'You won't be so noticeable there.'

'What are we going to do?'

'Our people have rented a house for you up in the north near the border with Wales.'

'Wales isn't north, Ziggy. It's west.'

'What's the name of the other place then?'

'Scotland.'

'Yeah, that's it.'

'And what do we do?'

'They want you to do a report on all your work and thinking. The theoretical stuff with all those Kraut and Latin words, and all the practical stuff. When you've done that we'll see what else we can find you.'

'Sounds like white-washing stones at boot camp,' Petersen said, and he didn't look amused.

Grabowski shrugged his huge shoulders. 'That's what you're gonna do, my friends. Nobody's asking. It's an order.'

'Who's given the order, Ziggy? Was it Helms?'

Grabowski ignored the question. 'You'll get full overseas allowances. The accommodations and upkeep will be on the house, and it'll all count for your seniority.'

'When do we go?'

'Tonight. You're booked on a flight to Prestwick which they tell me is the nearest airport.'

'Jesus, Ziggy. I've got things to arrange. We both have.' Symons's face had lost its Boston cool but Grabowski had had twenty years of dealing with all sorts of men, and Ivy Leaguers were the easiest of the lot. So long as you didn't let them argue.

'We're going back to Langley now. You can both of you tell me all the things you want doing and I'll get them done. Neither of you goes back for anything.'

'What about clothes and passports?'

'You'll have an allowance for buying clothes out there

77

and you'll be having new passports. Canadian ones. New names, new IDs.'

Grabowski stood up, walked over to the counter and paid the bill. He smiled to himself as the two men followed him out. They were going to be no problem. They would do as they were told all right.

The only concession that had been made was to let them take a crate of text-books, half a dozen cans of film, and a few bundles of scientific papers. Grabowski had gone with them on the shuttle to New York so that their point of exit wasn't traceable to Washington. As they sat drinking in the departure lounge Grabowski handed over an envelope to each of them.

'You'll find details in there with two telephone numbers. The first of them is for routine communications but only when it's really necessary. The second is for a real emergency. I don't expect you to use that. You'll be contacted every two weeks and you'll be under surveillance most of the time.'

'Are there any restrictions on travel?'

'You'll find the ground rules in your envelopes. One thing is for sure: you don't talk to anyone about anything except social chit-chat. And you don't reveal your real identities or your status. Not to anybody. Not even the Queen of England.'

Symons risked a glance at Petersen's face and saw his colleague's irritation at Grabowski's banality. Symons wondered what sort of ranking Grabowski had. He seemed to have no official title and they had no idea who he reported to, but he had all the clout he needed, and they had both seen him at ease and using his authority on far senior agents to themselves. Somebody high up in the CIA seemed to use Ziggy Grabowski as his personal tracker dog, sniffing the air and herding the wayward back into the flock.

Grabowski walked across the tarmac with them and stood smiling, with his arms folded, until the last passenger was on board the jumbo and the doors had been fastened and the ramps pulled away. Symons could see him standing by the fuel bowsers, shading his eyes against the setting sun as the aircraft rolled forward along the feeder to the main runway.

The dawn was already glimmering six and a half hours later when they landed in Scotland. The Texan who met them as they passed through with their luggage was young, amiable and energetic. He had made arrangements for their wooden crate to go through customs and had arranged for a carrier to deliver it the next day.

It was a two-hour drive, the last hour giving glimpses of a heavy grey sea and a few farmhouses with their lights already on. The Texan wasn't a talker and Petersen, uncurious about the scenery, slept as Symons looked out of the car window.

As they passed an old castle built up high on a rock-face the Texan said, 'Bamburgh Castle. That's where Polanski filmed his *Macbeth*.' Symons didn't reply. Petersen was the film buff.

Symons saw a sign that said, 'Craster ½m', and the car swung left down a narrow lane, and then a couple of hundred yards later left again between two wrought-iron gates. The gravel drive sloped steeply upwards and at its crest it curved right and they saw the grey stone house. It was a typical eighteenth-century Northumberland gentleman's house. Not as large as a manor house but bigger than even a large farmhouse. It stood in a saucer-like depression with wide gravel paths in front of the house and its outbuildings. It had the dignity of nice proportions but it had been built less for beauty than to defy the long, northern, winter storms and the invaders from over the border.

79

The cover story for the two Americans was built on the truth. They were on sabbaticals, using the time, as Canadian medical historians, to do research on their subject regarding European medicine from the turn of the century. There was a gardener and a housekeeper, a married couple who lived in a converted flat over the stable block.

The Texan stayed with them for a week, driving them round the countryside, to the nearest town, Alnwick, and along the coast road that could take them up to Edinburgh. Their instructions allowed them to socialize with discretion. It was important that they didn't appear to be recluses. Recluses were always objects of curiosity in any community. They learned to drink the strong local beers at the pub in Craster and once a week they ate at The White Swan in Alnwick. From time to time, as the weeks passed, one or both of them were invited by local families to meals or picnics. They returned the hospitality at The White Swan. They had each bought second-hand cars, Petersen a white MG, and Symons a primose yellow Mini.

There were girls from local families whom they took to the cinema and for meals, but they were careful to keep them emotionally at arm's length. There was a pretty shop assistant from Seahouses who spent odd nights with Petersen and an even prettier barmaid from Alnwick who slept with Symons. The relationships were relaxed and financial, and in the rather puritan atmosphere of the area neither party had any interest in making the liaison known.

The BBC cameraman shook his head. 'There's a reflection from the oil-painting. Can't we take it away?'

'No way, or we'd just have a blank wall behind his head. We'll try moving the lights. Or maybe you can use a polarizer to cut it down.'

'I can't shift the polarizer, I've got to use it to mask the shine of his skin where he's had surgery.'

'OK.' The producer turned towards the lighting crew. 'Can you take the reflection off the painting, please?'

The lighting crew put up a cotton screen to soften the two main lights and most of the reflection disappeared, but the soft lighting seemed to emphasize the unnatural smoothness and cavities on the attorney's facial skin-grafts.

Another ten minutes of checking focus and zooming, and the producer nodded to the interviewer. He sat opposite the man behind the desk, his eye on the teleprompter as he gave the voice-over to match the head on the monitor screen.

'William Alexander, Assistant District Attorney of Dallas who attended the police interrogation of Lee Harvey Oswald.'

The producer jabbed his finger towards the second camera and a black and white photograph of Oswald came up on the screen. He gave it three seconds and then pointed at the interviewer who looked across at the attorney and said, 'What were your impressions at the interrogation, Mr Alexander?', and the producer prayed that the reflection in the attorney's spectacles wouldn't ruin the shot. The attorney hunched forward over his desk and the cameraman silently cursed him and shifted the focus.

'I was amazed that someone so young could have the self-control that he had. Almost as if he had anticipated the situation . . . it was almost as if he had been rehearsed or programmed to meet the situation that he found himself in . . . it was almost as if he anticipated every . . . question, every suggestion, every move, that the people in charge of him made.'

'Rehearsed by whom?'

The rather grim mouth of the attorney arranged itself into an acid smile as he said with a shake of the head, 'Who knows?'

The producer waved his hand, looking at his stop watch.

'OK, Michael. That gives us one minute fourteen, maybe fifteen seconds.' He put out his hand to the attorney. 'Thank you, sir, for your time, your help and the interview.'

'You're welcome. When will it be shown?'

The producer smiled. 'There'll be a lot of pressure not to show it at all. It'll take time. I'd say nine months.'

Jimmy Hoffa sat in the private suite adjoining his office in the large Teamsters Union building. The man with the black wavy hair poured them each a half glass of whisky, handed one of the glasses to Hoffa and sat down carefully in the chair alongside the union boss. He turned to Hoffa, his gentle, brown eyes smiling.

'I heard a story about you the other day, Jimmy. I wondered if it was true.'

'They're never true, pal. What was this one?'

'I heard that you were in Miami when JFK was shot and when you heard that your people had lowered the flag on this building you'd given them hell and told them to raise it again.'

Hoffa scratched his crotch and said, 'Yeah. That's true all right. And when those goddamed reporters started phoning me they asked for a comment and I told 'em that Bobby Kennedy was just another lawyer now. And the bastards wouldn't print it.' He turned his head to look at the dark man. 'What does Provenzano want?'

'He's got a proposition he thinks you'll go for.'

'So why all this crap about wanting me to go to Detroit for a meeting? Why doesn't he come here? He may be big but he ain't that big. He's just one of the Teamsters' officials as far as my book's concerned.'

The man smiled. 'You know better than that, Jimmy. He wants you to talk to the syndicate in Detroit. He's laid it all on for you. All you gotta do is say yes . . . or no.'

'Why the hurry then? Why tonight?'

82

'So's you can be back for the weekend. I'll drive you there and back.'

Hoffa looked at his watch, shrugged and stood up.

'OK. Let's go.'

It was past midnight when the car turned off Highway 75 and took the road to Trenton.

'Why you come off the highway, Louis?'

'The meeting's in a place we've got in Lincoln Park and it's quicker this way.'

Hoffa noticed the 'we've' and made a mental note to take the Italian down a notch or two when they got back to Washington.

'Somebody told me, Jimmy, that you were the contact between the CIA and the syndicate when they fixed to knock off John F. Is that so?'

'There were two of us. What are you stopping for?'

'I wanna phone at the gas-station over there to let 'em know we're on the way.'

Hoffa sat waiting in the car looking across to the lights of the McLouth Steel Corporation's huge complex. He looked at his watch. It was twenty minutes past midnight and the little squares said it was already the 30th of July.

When the Italian got back in the car he didn't speak or look at Hoffa, and ten minutes later he pulled into a deserted lay-by. Hoffa was sitting with his eyes closed but he wasn't asleep and the pressure of the silencer against his chest made him stir. He looked down, then, disbelieving, he looked at the Italian. 'For Christ's sake what . . .' And those were the last words Jimmy Hoffa ever spoke.

Half an hour later the car drove through the open gates of a scrapyard. Two men helped the Italian stuff Hoffa's body into the fifty-gallon oildrum. The big jib-crane swung down and its metal claws gripped the oildrum, biting into the metal swages, lifting it over the pyramids of rusting metal to the scrap-crusher. When the oildrum was released ten minutes later, from the press that could pulp a truck to a neat bale of metal in ten minutes, it was a quite small cube. That would normally have been the end of the matter but the men who had given the order wanted absolute finality and a truck took the bale to a smelting plant in River Rouge. There the Italian stood on the platform shielding his eyes from the white heat and watched the bale of metal drop into the molten metal of the furnace.

9

Maclaren left his car at what had once been the grand entrance to the estate and the big house, which was now no more than two gaunt stone pillars with an eroded coat of arms carved on a shield at eye-level. The big house had been bulldozed flat by the developers' men a week before the local authority appeal to make it a listed building was to be heard by the Ministry. The ensuing public outrage had been pointless apart from ensuring that the Lodge House and the Dower House could not be demolished. There had been no intention to demolish them. They could be done up and sold for a good price. Meanwhile the Dower House had been let. A young American diplomat had taken it on a twelve-month lease.

There were lights on downstairs in the house and one bedroom window showed a pale pink glow through the net curtains. Maclaren turned his back to the house to light a cigarette and held it cupped in his palm when he turned back to keep watch.

He had watched the house for two weeks, alternating the shifts with Sturgiss. The red Mustang was there. It was there almost every night except at the weekends when the girl's husband was at home. She worked in Woolworth's and her husband was a joiner on the night-shift at one of the big furniture factories in High Wycombe. But Maclaren guessed that she was earning more money in her sessions with the young American than she earned at Woolworth's. She was in her early twenties and it was her gossip with one of the girls at the store that had caused Maclaren and Sturgiss to be sent down. Her gossip had been with the girl on the sweet-counter who happened to be the girl-friend of a police-constable at Marlow police station. According to the girl her extra-marital boy-friend not only looked like James Bond but had told her that he was a real-life spy.

When Maclaren and Sturgiss first went down to Marlow and the house near the moorings at Temple, they had taken for granted that it was a waste of time. Just the usual bullshit that was meant to impress a girl enough to get her into bed. But when they saw the little dish aerial lashed to the tallest chimney they changed their minds. It wasn't big or particularly noticeable, but it was a piece of powerful high-technology that Cheltenham had confirmed as being suitable for both long-range transmission and receiving. What was also significant was that the aerial lead went down inside the chimney so that it couldn't be tapped from outside the house.

The American was in his late twenties, and he did have a vague resemblance to Bond in the days when Sean Connery first played the part. Except for shopping and eating he seldom went out, but whenever he went into the town he called for mail at the main Post Office. Maclaren had asked for a mail check but Century House hadn't responded either way. Neither would they agree to a break-in without more indication that it was necessary. Maclaren despised the old-maidish reaction. In the kind of work he normally carried out for SIS the only reason you needed for a break-in was that you wanted to do it.

Except for the rustling of disturbed wood-pigeons in the copse of willows and chestnuts, and a distant quack from a restless mallard, there was complete silence. From far away Maclaren could just make out the faint sounds of the traffic on Marlow Bridge. But as often happens just before midnight a slight breeze got up, stirring the branches of the trees and flapping the shrouds of pleasure boats moored on

86

the river bank on the far side of the house. As he looked up at the full moon the faint trails of cloud across its face were barely moving and the sky was almost clear.

It was just before one o'clock when he heard the sound of the car. It was coming up the lane from the road and he turned to look towards the gate. He was just in time to see the headlights fade into darkness. It was a small pick-up van, not a car, and it was still coming on, in the dark. He saw its outline as it navigated the pillars that had once held the wrought-iron gates and then the driver cut the engine, letting the van roll on until it was almost alongside the parked Mustang.

A man got out of the van and Maclaren pulled up his binoculars. But in the dim light he could only see that the man was big built. He watched him walk to the porch and try to turn the handle on the big white door. For a moment the man looked up at the first-floor windows and then walked to the corner of the house to be lost in the shadows.

Maclaren lowered the glasses and waited. Fifteen minutes had gone by when he heard the shouting, and a girl screaming, and five minutes later the front door was flung open, and in the bright light from inside the house he saw the girl, and the man from the van. He was holding her by her hair, her head thrown back to ease the pain, and she was whimpering as the man shoved her towards the van. She was wearing a light summer coat and Maclaren could see that she was naked except for the unbuttoned coat. She cried out as the man struck at her face as he bundled her into the passenger seat of the van. Moments later the car turned and backed, obviously deliberately, into the side of the Mustang, and then as its headlights came on he watched it head towards the gate pillars. Then it was bouncing down the pot-holed lane until eventually its red rear lights disappeared.

Looking back at the house, Maclaren saw that the big white door still stood open, the lights from the hallway sending an orange swath across the gravel drive on to the grass below the edge of the small copse. And gradually the silence settled back again. Maclaren turned his watch to the moon and saw that it was only half an hour since the van had appeared.

He waited another half hour but there was no sound from inside the house and the door was still wide open. He slid off his shoes and walked to the edge of the copse, across the gravel path to the steps that led to the door. At the door he brushed the soles of his socks and slid his shoes back on, all the while watching the stairs that he could see facing him on the far side of the hallway.

Slowly and quietly he walked inside. It was a big square hall with a stripped pine floor, and he didn't notice the small pool of blood until another drop splashed loudly on to the wooden boards. When he looked up he saw the man's head hanging over the side of the landing between two broken bannisters.

Maclaren walked up the thickly carpeted stairs to the landing and bent down beside the man's body. He knew from the bleeding that he wasn't dead, but the blow had exposed the blue-whiteness of his cheekbone and left a deep, open wound above the ear. There was not much blood from the skull wound but a trickle of colourless liquid was accumulating in the dent of the wound itself. The blood was coming from the cheek. Maclaren put his hand on the man's chest and turned back one eye-lid. Then he stood up and looked around. He wasn't dead yet but it wouldn't take long.

He tried all the doors until he found one that was locked and he guessed that that was the room that mattered. It had a double lock set in a shining brass plate, and the door didn't give as he braced his foot and shoved. He walked back to the bedroom with the light. It came from a pink-shaded bedside lamp that lay on its side on the floor. The girl's bra, panties and dress were still in a heap beside the bed, and a silk dressing gown hung from a chair by the window. A well-cut light grey suit was draped over a stool in front of a dressing table. There was a bunch of keys in the trousers' pocket and two brass keys on a ring in the jacket pocket.

When he had unlocked the door he switched on the light and walked inside. The room was almost bare except for a black Yaesu transceiver on a trestle table, its red digital display winking away, two telephones, two Revox tape-recorders and a double-drawer metal filing cabinet. A couple of cheap, folding wooden chairs were propped against a bare wall.

The transceiver was set at receive and as Maclaren flipped up the power supply switch the red digital read-out showed 15206 megacycles and an American was reading a news bulletin at dictation speed in basic English. It was a Voice of America broadcast. Flicking off the switch, Maclaren turned to the filing cabinet. Not only was it not locked but it didn't have locks, and Maclaren walked over to the window pulling aside the curtains. He knew there would be some form of security for the stuff in the room. A heavy angle-iron frame was screwed to the brickwork and the window frame to prevent the window from opening, a thin loom of wires sprayed out from a rubber suction pad in the centre of the window, and a slightly thicker wire ran down to a metal Klaxon alarm screwed to the floor.

There were no files in the top drawer, just a batch of one-time pads with its adhesive band still wrapped round it, and a micro-dot reader that looked as if it had never been used.

In the bottom drawer were five standard blue file covers, none of them very thick, and Maclaren lifted them out and opened one of the wooden chairs putting the files beside him on the floor. The first one was marked 'Personal' and it was a collection of letters from a doting mother, a whole string of girls from Texas to Teheran, notifications of dividends and correspondence with Chase Manhattan Bank. Maclaren skipped through the other four files before putting the personal file back in the cabinet. Then with the four files under his arm he walked back to look at the man's body. There was still blood oozing from the cheek wound but it was a darker red now, and beginning to congeal.

As he walked out of the house and back to his car he wondered how much to tell them. He decided then that the stuff in the files was too good to be lost in the archives of SIS. It was the kind of stuff that Carter would find better use for. The others would be scared to use it.

He dialled the emergency number from the call-box in Marlow High Street and asked for the police. He gave the Dower House address and reported a disturbance. When they asked for his name he hung up.

Maclaren met Carter in the drinking club off Brewer Street. Carter was already there when he arrived, sitting in the far corner, barely distinguishable in the dim lighting and the haze of cigar smoke. Although Carter had his suits made by a first-class tailor in Covent Garden, whatever he wore always looked a size too small. With shoulders, arms, chest and thighs like an all-in wrestler's it seemed incongruous that his round, moon face always looked so amiable, almost childlike. He waved Maclaren to the empty seat beside him and offered him a cigar from a leather case, still holding it out after Maclaren had declined.

'What's all the excitement about, sonny boy?'

Maclaren outlined what had happened on his surveillance without mentioning the contents of the files.

'Did he kick the bucket, the American?'

'I phoned the hospital. He's in their intensive care unit. They weren't saying much but they didn't sound hopeful. They've sent for his parents from San Antonio.'

Carter beamed. 'I like San Antonio. Best Angus cattle I've ever seen, and some nice little girls. So you think he's had it?'

'I'd say so.'

'So what's the rest of it? The files I suppose?'

'There's two CIA men stashed away in this country.'

'Two. For Christ's sake. Two hundred's more like it.'

'I mean two CIA men who aren't on the list. Canadian passports. No contact with Grosvenor Square, who've never heard of either of them.'

Carter drew on his cigar, his eyes half-closed against the smoke. He was looking straight ahead, his eyebrows raised as his mind went over the possibilities.

'What do you reckon they're doing here?'

'Hiding.'

'Who from?'

'Practically everybody.'

'Don't play games, boy. What's it all about?'

'They're both psychiatrists. They specialize in hypnotizing. And they're both CIA agents.'

'So why the excitement?'

'Have you ever heard of the MKULTRA programme?'

'No. What is it?'

'It's a CIA programme about the use of special drugs and hypnosis to control somebody's mind. So that they do whatever they're told to do but they never know what they've done. Or even that they've done anything. They don't know that they were hypnotized at all.'

Carter tapped out the long cylinder of ash in the cracked saucer that served as an ash-tray, turning to look at Maclaren as he lifted the cigar back to his mouth.

'I heard a rumour about this. Two years, maybe three years ago. One of the Mossad boys was talking about it when I was in Tel Aviv. How much truth is there in it?'

'It's a hundred per cent true. They've been doing it on scores of people for years.'

'You mean experimenting?'

'No. Actually doing it. Operationally.'

'What sort of things?'

'Everything from simple courier work to murder.'

91

Carter sniffed loudly and swallowed, his eyes on Maclaren's face.

'How can you be sure?'

'It's in those files. Code-names, the lot.'

'What are these guys doing here?'

'Like I said . . . hiding.'

'Who from?'

'According to the files – the FBI, the CIA, several congressional committees and a few independent investigators.'

'Why should that bunch be after them? They're on their side for Christ's sake.'

'Depends on what you've been up to.'

'Like what for instance?'

'Like hypnotizing people and using them as killers.'

'You mean they've actually done that?'

'Yes. According to the files they have.'

'Maybe the stuff in the files is just feasibility studies. Checking over what they'd like to do, but never got around to.'

Maclaren smiled. 'You ought to read the files, Nick.'

'Better pass them to one of the evaluation teams.'

'What, and give up one of the best pieces of luck we've ever had? We could use those guys ourselves.'

'For what?'

'Knocking off some of the central council of the IRA maybe. In Dublin. Either these two Americans cooperate with us or we blow them.'

Carter smiled. A slow, fat-cat smile. 'Now you're cookin' with gas, sunbeam.'

Maclaren waited for a moment and then said quietly: 'These two could do it for us.'

Carter sat in silence for several minutes and Maclaren knew better than to disturb his thoughts. Twice Carter leaned forward as if he were going to speak, and twice he leaned back again in his chair. Then, without looking at Maclaren, Carter said, 'Why should they?'

92

'So that we don't send copies of the files to *The Washington Post* and Reuters.'

'How definite is the file material?'

'Definite enough. Even as it stands it would finish the CIA for good and all.'

'Where are the files?'

'At my place.'

'You'd better go and get 'em. I'll come with you.'

'You'll use them, Nick? You won't let them rot?'

'I'll think about it. Have you made copies of 'em?'

'No. Not yet.'

'Right.' He stood up, surprisingly smoothly for his bulk. 'Let's go and find them.'

Carter read the file material carefully. Again and again. He motored down to the cottage he owned outside Folkestone and spent the weekend gardening. When he left on the Sunday evening the metal map-cylinder with the files inside was a couple of feet under some Ailsa Craig seed potatoes that were neatly earthed-up in three long rows in the vegetable patch.

On the Monday he bought a stand-by ticket at Heathrow and was in Washington mid-morning local time. He looked in his little notebook and asked the cab-driver to take him to The Brighton Hotel on California Street. After consulting his notebook again, he dialled the CIA number in Langley. He asked for Mr Grabowski. The telephone operator had no Mr Grabowski listed but she would pass him on to someone who maybe could help. Carter recognized the standard ploy and went patiently through several levels until a man with a cool, calm voice confirmed that there was no trace of a Mr Grabowski in any CIA division or department but if he left his name and telephone number they would go on checking and if they were successful they would call him back. Carter gave him the hotel number.

An hour later the British Embassy called him. He hadn't given them or anyone else his number at the hotel and he smiled as they asked if they could be of help. He declined the offer, smiling to himself as he waited for their next move. And then it came. A US agency had enquired of the embassy about his status. Could he help them? He told them that he was Foreign Office but merely on holiday. They thanked him politely and rang off. He guessed it would take them less than ten minutes to find his name on the FO list. Then maybe another ten minutes to contact the CIA.

The man with the cool, calm voice called back in sixteen minutes with the good news. They had traced Mr Grabowski and were putting him through.

He didn't say much to Grabowski but it was enough to make him agree that he would call on Mr Carter that evening about eight.

Despite their natural caution and experience Grabowski and Carter sized each other up favourably in the first ten minutes of social chit-chat. They did similar jobs. They were of a kind. Their outward appearance and the image they both projected were of brute force and energy, but they were both not only shrewd but perceptive, and Grabowski found no negative vibes coming from the Englishman. They sat there slowly sipping their whiskies, probing gently for basic information.

'By the way, Mr Carter, how'd you get hold of my name?'

'The usual way, out of a file.'

'You mean you've got my name on one of your SIS files, for God's sake?'

'I'm sure we have, but that wasn't where I saw it. As a matter of fact it was an American file. A CIA file.'

'Our people don't have my name on file over there. I can tell you that right now.'

'Did you have a young guy named Deeming?'

94

Grabowski shrugged and shook his head. 'Not that I know of.'

'He died about a week ago. Multiple injuries to the skull. Was doing surveillance on two CIA fellows and reporting to you.'

Carter saw the recognition dawn on Grabowski's face. He would have plenty of other irons in the fire that could make him not recall the name, especially from an unexpected source. But he obviously recognized the circumstances of his man's death. It was several moments before Grabowski spoke and Carter made no move to hurry him. Finally Grabowski said, 'We're treading around on thin ice, Mr Carter. For both our sakes we'd better watch where we're putting our feet.'

'Maybe I could get us off the ice altogether.'

'I'd appreciate that if it was possible.'

'We found his files. The police know nothing about them. At the moment only three people know what's in them. And one of the three only knows part of the scenario. But before I go on I'd like an honest answer to a question.' Carter paused and stared at Grabowski. 'If I have any doubts about whether you tell me the truth I shan't make my suggestion to relieve the situation. What I propose would require absolute frankness between us. What do you feel about that?'

Grabowski shifted his backside in the chair. 'Mr Carter, we're both in the same business. I already assume that if all you had in mind was to cause trouble I shouldn't be sitting here now. You could have thrown your little bomb in the direction of Langley and that would be that.' Grabowski sighed. 'So ask your question. If I can answer at all I'll answer truthfully. If I would be going too far by telling the truth, then I'll say so, and leave you to do whatever you choose to do.'

Carter nodded. 'I've taken some precautions about the documents. If anybody fancied the idea of doing a "wet-job" on me then the bomb would go off in hours. I thought I should mention that.'

Grabowski raised his eyebrows but said nothing, and Carter asked his question.

'Are your responsibilities connected with what I can only refer to as operations outside normal CIA operations?'

Grabowski shrugged. 'We might as well say it as it is. Yes. My responsibilities are with operations that the top echelons of CIA could never officially approve but are necessary when the chips are on the table. And in some cases the top echelons don't even know what my people are doing.'

'Would you be personally sacrificed if any of it came to light?'

'You betcha. A lot of heads would roll, but mine would roll first. And in this particular case I'd end in jail. No doubt about that. And I guess I'd be there to the end of my days.'

'OK, Mr Grabowski. We can talk. My responsibilities are much the same as yours. In other words, I and my people do the dirty work that wouldn't be admitted to by my chiefs. And sometimes I don't even ask first, I just get on with it, because, for better or worse, I think it has to be done.

'Which brings me to the point of my visit. I want to use the services of your two chaps up north for a few months.'

'How many months?'

'At least six, maybe a year.'

'You'd give them protection and cover in that time?'

Carter nodded. 'Better than they've had so far.'

'Are you prepared to discuss what you'll use them for?'

'Sure. You've already got a British subject . . . a girl . . . under control. I want to use her in Northern Ireland against the IRA. And I want them to find me a man . . . a soldier . . . who I can use in Germany.'

'What happens to the documents you picked up?'

96

'I'll hand them back to you when we're finished.' He half-smiled. 'One original and two copies. All in safe hands.'

'Tell me about Deeming. How did you get on to him?'

'He was screwing the wife of a local man who found out and beat him up. Your boy was shooting a James Bond line with her to get her into bed, and she talked to a girl-friend who told her boy-friend, a local policeman. We were just doing a routine surveillance.'

'Why wasn't the husband prosecuted?'

'Nobody knew what had happened except the wife and her husband . . . and us of course . . . so nobody had any interest in letting it blow up. I'd guess the husband didn't intend to kill him, just beat the hell out of him and went too far.'

'When do you want my guys to start?'

'Soon as you can fix it.'

'They call me Ziggy. What do they call you?'

'My name's Tom but they call me Nick. I hate it, but I'm stuck with it.'

'Let me use your phone here and I'll get us both plane seats for tomorrow. I'll fly back with you. Unless you've got anything else to do in Washington.'

'That's fine. I'll give you my ticket details.'

10

It was in mid-March 1969 that the car drew up outside the house and Symons walked out to see who it was. It was Grabowski looking strangely respectable in a neat blue suit and a Hardy Amies tie, with black brogues and a white shirt.

Grabowski barely touched Symons's offered hand, sweeping past him into the house as if he not only owned it but knew his way around it. Inside the big beamed hall he stood waiting impatiently for Symons to close the outer door.

'Where's your friend?'

'He's upstairs, typing.'

'Have you got a secure room where we can talk?'

'Yes. Our workroom where Pete's working.'

Petersen was typing on a portable on the table and he didn't look up as Grabowski walked into the room. Symons coughed a warning and as Petersen looked up from his typing he stared at Grabowski with disbelief. 'Jesus God . . . angels and ministers of grace defend us, be thou a spirit of health or goblin damned etcetera, etcetera. What have we done to deserve this?'

Grabowski ignored the comment and Petersen, and glanced around the sparsely furnished room, picked the only comfortable chair, pulled it towards him and sat down, his briefcase beside him.

'I've got mail for both of you. I'll give it you later, after we've talked.'

Petersen grinned. 'You been steamin' it open, Grab?'

Grabowski wasn't amused but he shuffled his backside more comfortably into the chair.

'I've got work for you two. Langley thinks it's time you started earning your corn.'

Neither of them responded and he turned to look at Symons.

'You had a girl . . . a singer . . . she was used by you for MKULTRA. Remember?'

Symons nodded but said nothing.

'You're gonna use her again.'

'She's not a United States national and she doesn't live in the States.'

'I know all that. She lives in London. You and Mortensen were using her as a courier just before you came over here. Yes?'

'Yes.'

'We want to use her again.'

'What for?'

'Same again. As a stake-out and as a courier.'

'Is this for Bill Mortensen again?'

'No. We've got ourselves a problem. She's the solution. Or part of it.'

'What's the problem?'

'The Brits. SIS know you're over here. They want to know why.'

'You didn't tell them, for God's sake?'

'Of course we didn't. But the guy who spotted you knows what your speciality is and he wants a piece of the action.'

'What's that mean?'

'He wants to use you. Both of you. And if we play ball then he plays ball and says nothing. If not he'll tell the brass at Century House.'

'He'll probably tell them anyway.'

'That wouldn't matter. They've no idea why you're here, and they'd never put it together. They'd just raise hell that

99

we've got two CIA men in this country who they don't know about.'

'Who's this SIS guy?'

'Maclaren. He's bringing in another fellow. Sturgiss.'

'Have you checked on them?'

'You betcha. I'll give you a summary that you can keep. Maclaren's an old hand. A dirty-tricks man. I'd say he's pretty good at it. Very rough. Sturgiss is in his thirties. Another rough boy. Not as experienced as Maclaren but a real bastard.' Grabowski tapped the side of his head. 'I'd put him down as a psycho. But I leave that sort of thing to you boys.'

Symons said, 'When do we go back Stateside?'

Grabowski bent his arm and scratched slowly at the back of his neck and both Symons and Petersen wondered if it was a diversionary gesture or a geniune itch.

'A month or two.'

'That girl's going to come apart if there's too much pressure. The screws were coming loose last time we used her.'

'Then what happens?'

'She goes in the bin.'

'Would she talk?'

'No. She doesn't know anything. It's wiped each time so there's nothing for her to tell. If I told her when she's normal what she's done under hypnosis she wouldn't believe me. For her it's never happened. She could only talk under hypnosis. And you'd need the code which she only knows at another level. And there are safety controls I can build in if she's operating for the Brits.'

'Like what?'

'It's better you don't know, Grab.'

Grabowski shrugged. 'Maclaren and Sturgiss are coming up tomorrow to brief you on how they want to use her. I'll stay until it's all settled.'

*   *   *

100

Grabowski seemed to know both Maclaren and Sturgiss quite well. He introduced them with no more background than to say they were SIS and highly respected by CIA HQ at Langley.

Maclaren was tall and gangling with a raw, red face that was all bumps and cavities and looked as if it had been scrubbed over-enthusiastically. Sturgiss was small and sinewy, and although he was the younger of the two his red hair was sparse like a halo round his freckled bald head. He looked like one of those champion jockeys with a young man's lean body and an old man's creased face and stony eyes.

The two Americans recognized them at once as typical of the kind of thugs that most intelligence organizations keep in their closets for special operations where ruthlessness is the main characteristic needed. Even Grabowski, for all his attempted *bonhomie*, didn't look entirely at home with the two Britishers. Finally Grabowski gave up on the broken-backed pleasantries and suggested that they sit around the table.

'Our friends here have asked if we could assist them, and Langley have agreed. It's more consultation than assistance but . . .' Grabowski shrugged his shoulders and waved a hand dismissively '. . . on the other hand we're aware that there has to be some actual participation. So it's . . . let's say . . . a wide brief.' He turned to Maclaren. 'You give an outline of what you want, Mac.'

The Scot raised his eyebrows as if more was being asked of him than he could be expected to deliver.

'We heard you've got one of your zombies here we could use.'

The two Americans didn't respond and Grabowski leaped into his role of honest broker.

'These guys have been shown the routine records so they've got the basic background. We haven't discussed what use we might or might not have made of your existing

101

client but they know the . . . what do you call it . . . the potential.'

It was Symons who answered. 'She wouldn't respond to anyone but me. That was the whole point of the programme.'

Grabowski nodded. 'I know that. They want you to operate her for us just like you did over the other side.'

Symons reached in his pocket for his cigarettes, lit one slowly, and only after he exhaled did he turn to look at Grabowski.

'I told you, Ziggy, she's going to come apart at the seams if she's put under pressure for too long.'

Maclaren interrupted as Grabowski leaned forward to reply.

'We need her right now, Symons. So let's cut out the bullshit. Either you can do it or you can't. Which is it?'

Symons deliberately avoided looking at Maclaren, as if he had no significance.

'What kind of mission did you have in mind, Ziggy?'

'They . . . we want to use her in Northern Ireland against the IRA.'

'To do what?'

Grabowski nodded to Maclaren who could barely keep the anger from his voice.

'To wipe out certain IRA men. And one or two other bad friends.'

Symons raised his eyebrows. 'Can't you just shoot them?'

'If that was the answer we'd have done it, sunshine. There are a lot of reasons why we need to do it this way.'

'Don't call me sunshine, mister. I'm not impressed. What are the reasons?'

'That's our business not yours.'

Symons nodded, and for a moment Maclaren thought it was in agreement, until Symons spoke.

'In that case, Mr Maclaren, I suggest you get yourself

back to London and get on with it.'

There were flecks of saliva on Maclaren's lips as the words burst out. He meant to wag his finger to emphasize his words but it ended up as a shaking fist.

'You stupid bastard. We can put you in the nick inside an hour on what we know about you. We can finish the bloody CIA for good and we can . . .'

'Maclaren!' Grabowski's voice was loud and angry. 'Cool it, Maclaren, or I'll phone Nick Carter right now and get him to fly up. You're not here to give orders or to lay down the law. If anyone's going to do that it's me. That's the arrangement Carter and I have made. If you want cooperation you'd better calm down right now.'

Maclaren shrugged and leaned back in his chair, his eyes hard with anger.

'You tell them, then. You know the scenario.'

Grabowski stood up. 'Let's have a drink and leave the planning for tomorrow.' He looked at Petersen. 'You got some liquor stashed away someplace, Pete?'

They had a few drinks and at least the surface antagonism faded, but the tensions were all too obviously still there when the two SIS men opted for bed and Petersen showed them to their rooms. When he came back to their workroom the three Americans sat in silence for several minutes before Grabowski started mending the fences.

'Why did you provoke him, Tony? It was deliberate. I watched you doing it. It's crazy.'

Symons lit another cigarette. 'I tell you what, Ziggy. That sonofabitch is dangerous. He's a psychopath. Straight out of a text-book. So's his little red-haired pal, sitting there all silent, clenching his fists and grinding his jaws. Where the hell did you find them?'

'I didn't. They found you. They were carrying out the surveillance of Deeming's house and they found the files on you two. Nick Carter, their boss, gave me the option. We co-operate or they blow you two and the whole CIA sky high.'

Symons shrugged. 'So get some of our guys over to knock 'em off.'

Grabowski sighed, his hand cupping his chin as he slowly shook his head. 'Sometimes you guys make me feel very old.' He was a shrewd operator and he knew he had won when Symons laughed softly.

'Have they told you what they want us to do?'

'Not in detail. And I don't want to know.'

'Why not?'

'I've got enough trouble trying to keep the lid on what happened back home. More, I don't need.'

'Who's making trouble there?'

'Congressional committeemen, judges, half a dozen independent committees, the media, you name it. It's the most popular blood-sport Washington ever had . . . and you don't even need to go out in the rain. Fifty assassination theories, and every one a winner.'

Petersen stretched out his long legs. 'Tell us what the two Brits want us to do.'

'There are two key IRA leaders . . . one in Belfast and the other in Dublin. They want to use the girl to eliminate them both.'

'Why don't they shoot them themselves?'

'There's several reasons. The most important is that Dublin and London have been talking for months to try and solve their problems in Northern Ireland. It's an almost impossible task anyway. An Irish Prime Minister who spoke out for Northern Ireland deciding its own destiny would have his arse out in the snow in a matter of hours. And a British Prime Minister who even vaguely hinted that there might some good in a united Ireland would be starting a civil war.

'When the two prime ministers met last year they looked at the whole bag of tricks all over again and reckoned there was only one way out . . . to make Northern Ireland an independent state with its independence guaranteed by both Dublin and London.'

Symons yawned. 'How would that help . . . the Irish would still want a united Ireland and the people in the north wouldn't have it in a million years. I don't see what difference it makes.'

'That's why you're not on Capitol Hill, buddy. The difference is that London would be out of it. The Irish hate the Brits and they enjoy hating them. It's their national sport. The idea of negotiating with the Brits about anything is a signal for raking up all the old hatreds. And the Northern Ireland lot detest London almost as much. So it would change the sides of the triangle. It would be independent Irishmen negotiating with independent Irishmen. Given time they could work something out.

'So why the wet-jobs on the IRA men?'

'Dublin and London feel that with those two out of the way they could get maybe two, three months without murders so that when the Independent Northern Ireland Bill comes up in the House of Commons and the Dail it could stand a sporting chance of being discussed. There could be one more job to do, on one of the so-called Loyalist leaders, but they'll decide that when the first two targets have been hit.'

'So again, Ziggy, why don't they just shoot those two?'

'So that London, and the Army, or even the Loyalists, can't be accused. The two IRA men are die-hard gorillas; as much agin Dublin as London. It would take months for the IRA to mount a real campaign with them out of the way.'

Petersen sat with his head back, turning it slightly to look at Grabowski.

'You know . . . the Irish are always supposed to be able to charm the birds off the trees . . . why for God's sake do they murder and cripple people instead of trying the charm?'

Grabowski shrugged. 'Maybe like you just said . . . they

105

do it for God's sake. For the Belfast Irish, God's a Brit and the Pope's the whore of Rome. For the southern Irish they don't spend much time worrying about God. They've got priests and their fellow in the Vatican to worry about God for them.'

Symons stood up, stretching carefully. 'When do they want to start?'

'Soon as you can make it.'

'Maybe you can get your pal Carter to make clear that we're in charge of controlling the girl. It's medical and scientific not bang-bang stuff.'

'I'll talk to him on the phone tomorrow before we get started.'

Donald Hardie Maclaren folded his clothes carefully and neatly, arranging them on the two chairs as if for a kit inspection. For a few minutes he stood at the uncurtained window. There was no light from a house or a building as far as he could see. Just a faint glow on the horizon that could be from the sea or the moonlight on the far-away hills. Beyond those hills was the Scottish border and across the Forth was Methil, the small town where he was born. His father and mother would be fast asleep in their separate beds in their separate rooms.

His father's family had owned the chemist's shop at the turn of the century, several Maclarens had been town councillors, and at least two had been magistrates. His father was a magistrate. He could remember being taken to the court to see his father handing out justice and advice to the grey figures in the dock. His father was much respected by the townspeople. Hard on offenders of course, but that was what the law was all about, and what they deserved.

His mother was on a dozen committees and was liked even more than his father. She was known for her good works and energy.

106

Maclaren had hated them both for most of his life. Certainly all his life that he could remember. He could still feel anger at 6.15 any evening. The time when his father came home from the shop. The time when the day with his mother was cut short and he no longer mattered. Lying upstairs in his bed, hearing their low voices and sometimes his mother's laugh, he had sweated with rage and frustration. Twice he had run away from home. The first time, when he was six and a half, the town had turned out to search for him. They had found him in the hut on the golf links. The second time was a year later, and he had gone down to the docks and the dock police had taken him home. He had heard his father tell the policeman that it was just an attention-getting expedition, and he had decided then and there to kill his father when he was big enough and old enough. He still thought about it sometimes.

The girls at the school had been scared of him. He was a bully. Most boys were scared of him too, and whenever he was involved in a fight it always went far beyond the usual schoolboy horse-play. He hurt people when he could. He in his turn was hated. Not only for his cruelty but also because he was always the cleverest boy in his class. He had won a scholarship to George Heriot's School in Edinburgh, and had won a university place with only minimum effort.

Twice he had gone on mad spending sprees in Edinburgh, pledging his father's credit. The money had gone on clothes and girls. Girls found him strangely attractive until he got them into bed. Once was always enough. In some cases too much.

He had achieved a double-first in French and German and when a perceptive senior member of the faculty had introduced him to one of their former honours graduates who had suggested a career in the Foreign Office, he had accepted the offer immediately.

There had been several internal FO selection boards. The

107

first had indicated some doubts about his suitability for the diplomatic service and he had been posted to SIS. After two years he had been moved to one side, out of the mainstream of SIS's operation. It was then he had started work for Nick Carter.

He had mixed feelings about Carter. Almost like the feelings he had for his father. He respected him for his experience and courage, but there were times when he went out of his way to antagonize Carter. And when he was taken to task those pale blue eyes looked at him as if they knew his innermost secrets. Knew the pleasure he got when his fist thudded into flesh until it met bone. And the pleasure that was almost ecstasy that he felt at the fear in a victim's eyes. He didn't want Carter to know those things. He wanted Carter to admire him, and he wasn't sure whether Carter approved or disapproved his private zest for violence. He wasn't even certain that Carter had noticed it.

Arnold Fergus Sturgiss could have been the monozygotic twin of Maclaren except for his physical appearance. And his background.

Sturgiss was only a couple or so inches over five foot. Born and raised in Govan, within sight and sound of the football crowds in Ibrox Park, in one of the tenement blocks off Shieldhall Road, he was typical of his roots. Social workers who came with their various sociology degrees and a wild enthusiasm to put the world to rights were sent early on to the Govan tenements. It brought them back to earth in a matter of weeks. The very conscientious and loving were driven to nervous breakdowns, and the more politically inclined would experience their first doubts as to whether Marxism could actually work if human beings had to be involved.

108

His father had died in a foundry accident in Possil when the boy was nine, and his mother had done her best for the boy until her basically frail body had succumbed to the long hours of grinding work that had earned her just enough to keep their heads above water. When there was only her minute widow's pension and Social Security benefits to live on she had eventually given up the struggle. She took to her bed, and at eleven years old the boy became their only bread-winner. Devoted to his mother he treated the rest of the world as his enemies. He fought, stole and bullied for food and cash. Working for money was too time-consuming and ill-rewarded. Just once he had taken money for having sex with a man from Bearsden and when the agony was over he had left the man unconscious. He had taken his wallet, cheque-book, and even his clothes.

At school he was admired for his courage by both teachers and pupils but he was no scholar. His mind was never on his books, and teachers gave up expecting homework from him. They knew his circumstances and knew that so far as school was concerned he was doomed.

A friendly neighbour had got him a labourer's job at the foundry where his father had worked, and died. He was fifteen then, and his mother was bedridden. Pressed by the doctor to go into the isolation hospital to see if they couldn't cure her TB she had adamantly and tearfully refused. She died a couple of months before his eighteenth birthday.

He sold their few sticks of furniture, and with twelve pounds in his Post Office Savings book he joined the army. Everything about him suited the army. His aggression, his guts, and his liking for every aspect of the military life. A sergeant by the time he was twenty he saw the notice on the company board for volunteers for a Field Security parachute unit and he applied.

109

After the parachute course he was sent down to the Intelligence Corps depot in Kent where he completed the course in three months. His first posting was to Hong Kong, and after that, Berlin and Hamburg. It was the SIS detachment in Hamburg who noticed him, and after some routine checking on his background he was transferred to their establishment. He made no protest when he was given the more violent subjects to handle when the interrogators were in a hurry for information. There were odd occasions when they left some minor interrogation to Sturgiss and were surprised that just being street-smart was sometimes more effective than the usual grinding down by multiple interrogation. Despite the fact that he was an established field-agent for SIS he wasn't really part of the group. Nothing had ever been said, but when they invited him to one of their parties or picnics they obviously didn't expect him to accept. They admired him for his guts, but they were embarrassed by his lack of even the elementary social graces. He was neither hurt nor angered by their attitude. The world was still his enemy. And they were part of it.

When Carter interviewed him he was 26, and for the first time in his life another human being made him feel wanted. Carter was big and tough, and he talked with Sturgiss about his background and SIS experience for a whole weekend. Carter was looking for another man for his small group who carried out SIS's borderline assignments. The borderline between mere illegality, which they were well used to, and outrage.

Sturgiss had heard nothing after the weekend for almost three months, and then he had been told to make his way to an address just outside Stratford on Avon. A house set in its own grounds. The house had once been a parsonage, but its windows were now double-glazed and barred. The double-glazing was not to keep noise out but to keep it in. That house, Carter and the other four men, were the

110

nearest thing Sturgiss had ever had to a home and family.

Sturgiss's team-mate had been Maclaren right from the first days. They were not friends but they worked together well enough, both indifferent to the other's approval or disapproval.

11

Symons sat in the army dentist's waiting-room with the men and NCOs who were there for treatment. The privates had all gravitated to the bench against the far wall leaving the bentwood chairs for the five NCOs. There was very little talking, certainly not enough to help him decide, but there was one who looked a possible. A corporal. Fair-haired and fresh-faced, his nose and forehead sprinkled with freckles so that he looked even younger than he was.

In the small office next to the surgery Symons looked through the cards. The corporal was in his last year of service. Twenty-four, physically fit, in charge of the stores on an infantry base in Yorkshire. He had an abscess on the root of one of his front teeth. There was an X-ray clipped to his record card and he'd been given a full term of antibiotic. Allergic to penicillin, he had been prescribed erythromycin and he was now coming back for the clearing-up operations. He turned to Maclaren. 'This one might be suitable, but I'll need to speak to the dentist.'

Maclaren reached for the record card and read it, his lips moving silently as they formed the words he was reading. He handed it back without comment, and opened the door to the surgery and nodded to the young captain who came over to the door.

'My colleague wants to talk to you, captain.'

The captain looked at Symons, his eyebrows raised in question.

'What is it you want?'

112

Symons handed over the card. 'What do you have to do to him today?'

The dentist read the card and then looked up at Symons. 'I'll have to take another X-ray to check that the infection is cleared up. It almost certainly will be. Then I have to cut a flap in the gum, clean out the cavity and sterilize it. Then I stitch up the flap.'

'What kind of anaesthetic will you use?'

'Local. It'll have to be four or five big shots because it will take quite a time.'

'Will he be conscious all the time?'

'Yes. But he'll feel no pain until after the effect of the anaesthetic wears off. He'll be drowsy and I'll give him pain-killers. I have to pull up his lip so there will be quite extensive local pain including the lip and the nose.'

'Could I try an experiment for the post-operative pain?'

'What kind of experiment?'

'Hypnosis instead of pain-killer.'

'I'd have to ask the DDMS at Corps before I could do that. But it sounds interesting.'

Maclaren said, 'Leave him to last and I'll get the permission from Corps before you start.'

'What's all this in aid of? Are you two doctors?'

Symons said. 'I am. I'm a psychiatrist in the Canadian army.'

The captain smiled. 'Pleased to meet you. We've had lots of discussions about whether hypnosis is effective for dental operations that take a long time to perform or where the post-operative pain is abnormally high. I'd be interested in the results.'

Maclaren cut in. 'I'll get Corps to phone you in the surgery, and when you've finished with the corporal I'd like you to send him across to Hut Seven. We'll wait for him there. We'll send a report on him through Corps HQ.'

'I'll be very interested. I really will.' He looked at Symons. 'It really does work, does it?'

Symons nodded. 'It has so far.'

Symons was on his own in the small room in Hut Seven. It was normally used as a living room for senior officers recuperating from serious operations. The furniture was modern and comfortable and there were rows of books, a colour TV and hi-fi equipment. He looked at the soldier.

'It's Corporal Walker isn't it?'

'Yes, sir.'

'The treatment all done?'

'Got to come back next week to have the stitches out.'

Symons smiled. 'It's not easy to talk is it?'

'It's my lip. Feels all swollen and numb.'

'Sit down, corporal.' Symons pointed to the low chair and Walker sat down carefully.

'Tell me what the dentist did?'

'It was an abscess on my jaw.' He pointed to the front of his mouth.

'Just relax. Put your head back and tell me what it feels like. Close your eyes and that will help.'

'He just drilled a lot.'

'Do you feel drowsy?'

'I do a bit.'

'Close your eyes. That's right. Now relax. I'm going to relax you even more. I'm going to count to ten and then you'll be deeply relaxed. One, two . . . nice and easy . . . three, four . . . deeper and deeper . . . six, seven, eight . . . nice deep breaths . . . nine, ten . . . that's it. Now you're asleep. Can you hear me, George?'

Walker nodded.

'Your name's George Walker, yes?'

'Yes.'

'Have you got a steady girl-friend?'

'No.'

'Tell me about your parents.'

'My dad works on the railway. Mom's just a housewife.'

114

'You live with them when you're not in the army?'

'Yes.'

'Where do you live?'

'Chester Road, Stockport.'

'When you leave here you won't feel any pain where your abscess was. No pain at all in your mouth. No pain at all.' Symons paused. 'Do you read books at all?'

'Yes. Quite a lot.'

'Who's your favourite author?'

'Dickens.'

'Would you like to be able to write like Dickens?'

'Yes.'

'I tell you what. When we talk together like this your name will be Dickens. You'll really be Mr Dickens. How about that?'

'OK.'

'And whenever I call you Dickens you'll do whatever I say. OK?'

'Yes.'

'I'm going to bring you back now. When I count from ten to one you'll be wide awake. You won't remember anything we've talked about but you'll take a book from the bookshelf when I say the word "careful" and you'll give the book to me. Understood?'

'Yes.'

'Right. Ten, nine . . . you're coming awake . . . eight, seven, six . . . that's fine . . . you're feeling great . . . five, four, three . . . your eyes are opening . . . two, one. You're feeling good . . . How do you feel, corporal?'

'I feel fine.'

'What were we talking about?'

'My tooth.'

'It will be tender. So be careful what you eat. No toast or hard things.'

Walker nodded, stood up, walked over to the bookshelf, removed a book and walked back with it, handing it to Symons.

'You'll need something to read I expect.'

'Thanks. How about you call in and see me tomorrow at about noon? I'll fix it with your CSM.'

'OK.'

When Walker had left Symons looked at the title of the book as he slid it back into place on the shelf. It was *Brideshead Revisited*.

There were daily sessions with Walker until Symons was satisfied that he was fully under control and the memory block solidly established. And after three weeks Maclaren, Sturgiss and Symons took him down to the static caravan on the perimeter of the SAS camp in Hereford.

It took only ten days to get Walker down to the next level. At that level he was an SAS sergeant and they gave him short courses on the firing range and a few hours' practice on the assault courses. Sturgiss was responsible for the training and it was done when the camp was between intakes and there was only a skeleton staff for routine cooking and cleaning. Symons and Maclaren watched the last two days' training. He didn't have to be anywhere near the real SAS level. It would all be close-up work and mainly in a confined space.

Symons took readings of Walker's body and brain functions in his role of Dickens and as Sergeant Madden of SAS, and he made detailed notes of his extensive chats with Walker in his two hypnotic states. Six weeks from the first interview in Hut Seven Walker was ready for Maclaren and Sturgiss to use.

It was a new model Merc and Maclaren drove it with professional skill, taking no risks but using the power of its engine and the ratios of its gearbox to keep them moving fast. He deliberately avoided the direct motorway route under the Elbe, preferring the old route that took them through Wilhelmsburg. There was a hold-up when they approached the bridge over the Lower Elbe where an articulated lorry had jack-knifed half-across the centre verge, but they were on the Hamburg city boundary between Harburg and Ehestorf before seven.

Walker sat with Sturgiss in the back seat and Symons was in front with Maclaren. Walker was already in level one hypnosis and when they spoke to him they addressed him as Mr Dickens. He had been Dickens from the fourth session in Hut Seven, and Symons was concerned at the long state of hypnosis that the SIS operation required. He consoled himself that in a few more days he could bring Walker back to his normal state for a week or two until the next operation.

The grey Merc pulled into the driveway that was signposted 'Bauernhof Leidermann' and headed up the roadway to the house. Despite calling itself a farm it wasn't a farm, and had never been a farm. Until it had been bought through several intermediaries by SIS it had been a small-holding that supplied fruit and fresh vegetables for many of the top Hamburg hotels. But a year's neglect had left an acre of waist-high weeds and four good-sized glasshouses with bindweed and Creeping Jenny where tomatoes and early lettuce had once provided a handsome profit. Maclaren and Sturgiss were both wearing British army battle-dress with Grenadier Guards flashes.

They ate together and then Symons walked with Walker and the two SIS men to the brick building that had once housed the boilers for the glasshouses. It was divided into two now by a breeze block wall with a metal door at the right-hand side. In the middle of the room was a small wooden table. Plain and solidly built it was bolted to the concrete floor with angle-iron clamps. There were three heavy wooden chairs, two of which were also clamped to the floor. And a man in a roll-neck sweater and khaki slacks stood swinging a bunch of heavy keys from his hand.

117

Maclaren nodded to the man who turned and unlocked the metal door, beckoning them inside. Two men stumbled out from the darkness inside the back room screwing up their eyes against the not very bright light over the table. Sturgiss pointed silently to the two chairs and the men sat down clumsily. They were both wearing crumpled battle-dress, the jackets unbuttoned and the khaki shirts torn and stained.

Symons stood in the corner alone, leaning back against the wall, his eyes on the two soldiers.

Maclaren was wearing a captain's three pips and Sturgiss the single pip of a second-lieutenant. Maclaren stood in front of the two men.

'Are you ready to talk now?'

Neither man responded. Maclaren addressed the man on the left. Ginger-haired, sweaty-faced and about twenty years old.

'I'll start with you again, Fox. How did you pay her?'

The man named Fox shook his head, and Sturgiss moved silently to stand behind him.

'I'll ask you again. How did you pay her?'

Almost before the man could have responded Sturgiss' hand had grasped his hair and wrenched his head back until the man was gasping, reaching up in vain to free his hair from Sturgiss's grasp. Sturgiss smiled and pulled the head back to what seemed an impossible angle and the man gave a strangled cry.

'You gonna talk, Fox?'

The man tried to nod and held up one hand. Sturgiss released his head and the man put up both hands to rub his neck.

'How did you pay her then, Fox?'

'Cigarettes from NAAFI.'

'How many?'

'Two hundred. A carton.'

'What brand?'

118

'It didn't matter. Any kind would do.'

'What brand did you usually bring?'

Fox hesitated. 'Generally Benson and Hedges.'

'How much did you pay for a carton?'

'I don't remember.'

'Oh come off it, soldier. You mean to say you screwed her without checking how much it cost you.'

'It wasn't much. I didn't bother.'

'That wasn't what she told me.'

'What did she say?'

'She said you always screwed her all night, and you don't get that these days for two hundred ciggies.'

'It wasn't just screwing. She was my girl-friend.'

'Where did you meet her?'

'I told your other chap, I met her in a bar.'

'How long had you been in Berlin when you met her?'

'Two months.'

'Had you screwed any other Kraut birds?'

'No.'

'What was the first document you gave her?'

'I never gave her a document.'

'Was it the GHQ phone list?'

'I never gave her any document.'

'I've got a list of what you gave her, sunbeam.'

Fox shrugged. 'She made a mistake. It wasn't me.'

Maclaren took a deep breath. 'I haven't got time to play games with you, my friend. Either you gave her the documents or your mate gave them to her. Was it him?'

'How should I know?'

'Because you slept in the same billet. You've been mates all through your service. And you both screwed the same Kraut girl . . . were you gonna marry her?'

'No way. I'm not interested in marrying anybody.'

Maclaren looked at the other man.'

'So it was you who was gonna marry her, Mason.'

The man shrugged and shook his head. Maclaren

119

shouted. 'Was it you or him was gonna marry that Kraut bitch.'

'Neither of us.'

Maclaren turned away impatiently and then turned back again. 'I've had enough of you two bastards.' He turned. 'Mr Dickens.' Maclaren pointed at Fox and Walker raised the Luger and pointed it at Fox's chest. Maclaren looked at Mason.

'You talk, Mason, right now, or he gets it. I'll give you to five. One . . . two . . . three . . . four . . . five.' Maclaren nodded at Walker who fired two shots into Fox's chest. The impact jerked the soldier's body violently. Then his body arched until it slid sideways off the seat. Maclaren glanced briefly at the body on the floor and turned to look at Mason.

'Are you ready to talk now, or do you want the same?'

Mason's face was frozen and he whispered, 'You just killed him . . . you can't do that . . . there's regulations. Queen's Regs . . . I don't believe it . . . it's . . .' And he closed his eyes and whispered 'Oh God . . . save me . . . please God save me.'

Maclaren's voice was harsh. 'Are you going to talk, Mason. I'll count to five. One . . . two . . .'

'For Christ's sake what do you want to know?'

'Was it you gave her the documents?'

'Yes.' Mason sighed. 'Yes it was me.'

'Why?'

'I wanted to marry her.'

'What did you give her?'

'Anything she wanted that I could lay hands on.'

'Like what?'

'The order of battle, Two Corps deployment and unit strength, our radio schedules, names of officers, billet addresses. I can't remember exactly.'

'You knew she was East German?'

Mason nodded. 'Not at first. After about two weeks.'

120

'How long have you been providing this stuff?'

'About a year.'

'Did you know she was working for the KGB?'

'I guessed it must be something like that. I didn't know who exactly.'

'What reason did she give for wanting the information?'

'She said that they'd let her and her family come over to West Berlin and then we could be married.'

'You believed her?'

'Yes.'

'You didn't think it might be sensible to report it to one of your officers?'

Mason shrugged and sat silent, trembling visibly, his hands clutching his knees.

'Did she tell you who she passed the information to?'

'She said it was a man named Boris.'

'Boris who?'

'I don't know.'

'Where did you meet her to hand over the stuff?'

'There's a hotel. She booked us a room.'

'What's the name of the hotel?'

'Pension Lobau. It's near Check-point Charlie.'

'Is that where you screwed her?'

'Yes.'

'Did you ever go into East Berlin?'

'No. Never.'

'You bloody liar. We've got photos of you over there.'

The sound of Maclaren's closed fist on the man's nose and mouth was sickening. His hands went up to his face and he rocked up and down with pain, blood seeping through his fingers.

Maclaren nodded to Sturgiss. 'Get her.'

There was only the sound of Mason's groaning in the room and then the door burst open. Sturgiss was struggling with a girl. Her hands were tied behind her back, her body twisting and lunging as she fought to get free of Sturgiss's

121

hands on her breasts. As Sturgiss kicked the door to with his foot his right hand went up, taking a thick swatch of her hair, pulling back her head until she was looking up at the ceiling. He pushed her forward until she was standing by Maclaren and facing Mason.

Mason looked up at the girl, his mouth swollen and bloody, the massive bruise across his nose and cheek already forming. He tried to smile at her but the muscles around his mouth barely moved, and he closed his eyes.

Maclaren said, 'Look at her, Mason, and listen. Learn the lesson even if it's too late.' He turned to the girl. 'What's your name?'

She shook her head and Maclaren nodded to Walker who levelled the Luger at Mason's chest just as he had done to Fox.

'If you don't talk, little girl, he's going to end up on the floor like the other one. *Verstehen?*'

As he turned to look at the girl she spat in his face and he laughed, hawked and spat back. 'Are you going to let your sweetheart die for the KGB, Ushi?'

The girl nodded in defiance and tears rolled down Mason's face. Maclaren nodded to Walker who fired twice. Mason's body jerked twice and as he tried to stagger to his feet the chair went backwards taking his body with it.

Despite her defiance the girl looked shocked. Her mouth opening and closing, her head shaking slowly in disbelief.

'You just killed him . . . you liked it. You're worse than they say . . . animals.'

Mason grinned. 'Ursula Breitmann. Aged twenty. Address, Flat twelve number seventy-four Gorlindestrasse, East Berlin. Opposite the cemetery. Courier and informant for Yuri Simenov. KGB overseas detachment seven three nine. Yes?'

The girl shrugged. 'If you know – why you asking?'

'We want to know a lot more, sweetheart.'

'You get nothing from me.'

122

'Are you sure?'

'Very sure.'

Maclaren pointed to Sturgiss. 'I'll hand you over to my friend.' Sturgiss grinned and his hands went up to cup the girl's breasts and he lifted her so that her feet were off the floor. He carried her writhing and kicking into the dark backroom. Maclaren followed them, standing in the doorway watching, and Symons heard the girl's muffled shouts and Sturgiss's obscenities. Then Maclaren said 'OK. Bring her back.'

The girl was half-naked as Sturgiss bundled her back into the room. Maclaren stood looking at the red marks coming up on the girl's naked breasts. Her eyes were closed and she hung limply, enfolded in Sturgiss's strong arms. Maclaren nodded and Sturgiss put her on one of the fixed chairs, her arms still tied behind her back.

When she opened her eyes Maclaren said, 'Do you want some more, baby, or are you gonna talk?'

The girl bowed her head, nodding.

'Did he give you codes?'

She nodded.

'What codes?'

'NATO second level and BAOR operational.'

'What else?'

'He got us service manuals for F-111.'

'How did he get those?'

'He fixed for me to have sex with US airman.'

'What else?'

'He get me many NATO documents. I not read them.'

'What kind of documents?'

'Of communications and monitoring, Red Alert procedures. I don't remember more.'

'Who directed you?'

'Yuri. Yuri Simenov.'

'Where did you meet him to be briefed?'

'I don't understand . . . what is briefed.'

'Where did he meet you to tell you what to do?'

'Sometimes at my place, sometimes at MfS.'

'In Normannenallee?'

'Yes.'

'What rank is he?'

'Captain. He is not KGB. He is GRU.'

'How much did they pay you?'

'I got my flat and one thousand marks a month. Sometimes extra if I do well.'

'Who else did you have in West Berlin?'

'Fox and Mason and one other.'

'Who was the other?'

'A sergeant in Military Police.'

'Did he work at Check-point Charlie?'

'Yes.'

'That's how you got in and out, yes?'

'Yes.'

'Would you work for us?'

She shook her head. 'No.'

'Why not?'

'I love Yuri. He's going to marry me.'

Maclaren smiled. 'He's already married. Got a wife in Kiev.'

'I know, he is going to divorce her.'

'How long have you known him?'

'Two years three months.'

'You know his wife is three months pregnant?'

'I don't believe. He loves only me.'

'Must be screwing his wife all the same. We could pay you well if you worked for us. You'd have their money and ours.'

'I do it for Yuri. Is not only the money.'

'What else can you remember?'

'My head aches. I am very tired.'

Maclaren nodded to Sturgiss who smiled, and Maclaren said, 'Not longer than an hour.'

Maclaren turned to Symons and Walker. 'Let's go back to the house.'

Back at the house the man in civilian clothes who had unlocked the back room in the outbuilding made them coffee and then went back to the kitchen.

As they sat around drinking Symons said to Maclaren, 'Did you get what you want?'

'More or less.'

'Why didn't you ask for the MP's name and the US airman's name?'

'No point. We know it already. They've been dealt with. Both of them.'

'What's going to happen to the girl?'

Maclaren smiled. 'Sturgiss will have his fun and then we'll bung her in with the other two.'

'Won't the two soldiers be reported AWOL?'

'No. We've covered all that.'

'How?'

'You're a nosy sod, Symons. We shall put out a story that they've defected to the East Germans with the girl. It'll give the Russkis something to work out.' Maclaren turned his head to watch as Walker signalled that he wanted the toilet and the man with the keys took him out of the room. 'What do you tell your soldier friend to make him do what you tell him?'

'I hypnotize him.'

'I know. But how do you make him shoot the buggers? He's not the shooting kind.'

'That's why he was chosen, so that nobody would ever believe him if he came apart when I'm not around. I told him that they were spies trying to help the Russians take over the UK and we were all relying on him saving us. They were desperate men. He has to save us all.'

'And he believes all that crap?'

'Of course.'

'Tell me about the girl.'

125

'She's the same. She does what I tell her to do when she's hypnotized.'

'And neither of them know what they've done?'

'No. They're programmed to forget it all.'

'That means you could screw the girl and she'd never know.'

'Yes.'

'And you could do this with any girl?'

'Ninety-nine out of a hundred.'

'Jesus. You must have a fantastic time.' He looked at Symons' face. 'When we were looking for a soldier why did you go to the dentist's surgery?'

'Because in a dentist's waiting room people are under mild stress. You can assess them more easily and most people have an injection and they are drowsy and relaxed. Easy to influence.'

Maclaren nodded, as if he had learned something he might be able to use himself some day.

'We've got to find another squaddie. He's being discharged next month.'

'Maybe we should try a civilian, they are just as suitable.'

'No. We'd rather keep it in the army. We can cover up for them. We know the rules and regulations. We've got a better hold on them.'

12

The receptionist looked at the card and handed it back to him, pointing down the corridor.

'Go down to the end of the corridor, Mr Walker, turn left and the third office along on the right is marked Personnel. They'll be expecting you. Ask for Mr Patel.'

George Walker knocked on the door and walked inside the office. An Indian with thick-rimmed glasses pointed, smiling, to the chair at his desk.

'Mr Walker?'

'Yes.'

'You got the company brochure I sent you?'

'Yes. Thank you.'

'Anything you didn't understand?'

'No. I don't think so.'

'Any questions on the company employment policy?'

'No. I don't think so.'

Patel smiled, opened a drawer and took out a printed form, pushing it across the desk. 'I'd like you to fill that in and then we'll talk. It's a standard form. Just a few basics.'

The young man reached inside his jacket and took out a ball-point as he read the form. And as Patel watched, Walker filled in the details on the first page. Name, Christian names, address, date of birth, education, qualifications, and finally hobbies and interests.

He turned over the page and the heading said 'Previous Employment'. Slowly and carefully he filled in the details of the part-time job he had had before he joined the army and pushed the form back across the desk.

Patel checked the details on the first page and then turned the form over. He looked up, smiling.

'You haven't covered the last four years, Mr Walker. Generally people can't remember the first bit when they left school. Let me fill it in for you. Right now . . . let's work backwards from now. What were you doing last year? How many jobs?'

George Walker sat without answering and after a few moments Patel said, 'How many jobs, Mr Walker? How many lines do we need to use on the form?'

Walker was looking past Patel towards the window and he was trembling.

Patel said quietly, 'Are you OK, Mr Walker? Are you all right?'

And then Walker was shaking, sweat pouring down his face. Patel was sure then that he knew what the problem was.

'Have you been serving a prison sentence, Mr Walker?'

Walker shook his head violently, but didn't speak.

'The company has a liberal attitude to such problems, Mr Walker. We would liaise with your probation officer without anything going on your file.'

Even as Patel was finishing Walker vomited, and the Indian reached for his internal phone.

'Get the nurse up at once, Judy. Quickly.'

George Walker was nearly 26. He had done well at school and at the grammar school. He had got one 'A' level and four 'O' levels, and his parents were proud of his achievements. Both in their different ways.

His father was a ticket-clerk at Stockport railway station, five minutes' walk from the row of terraced houses where they had lived for twenty years. His father was not a communicative man, not even with his wife. But that was not in any way abnormal for men born and bred in that part of the country. Southerners often interpreted the silence as surliness, but in fact it was an inborn reticence overlain with shyness. Men like Harry Walker had little to say, and their upbringing and environment had taught them that talking was dangerous. Talking could lose men jobs; and talking could make men look fools. In Stockport and Manchester silence was equated with dignity. Chatter was for women. When his father had been told the exam results when he came home that evening he had nodded his approval, and the only outward sign of his internal emotion was leaving the *Evening News* unread and his meal uneaten. He had spent most of the evening tidying up the small wooden shack in the tiny garden.

Mrs Walker had made no attempt to hide her pleasure. She and her only son had always been close. Close enough for her to understand why he chose to join the army for a four-year enlistment with the hope of getting a commission. His talents and enthusiasms were latent and unformed and he needed to experience the world outside. She would have liked to experience it herself.

When he came out of the army she was surprised that he failed so many interviews that had looked so promising. Patience was a well-developed virtue in the Walker family, but she was shocked that morning when she took him his cup of tea in bed and saw the tears on his cheeks.

Being a calm woman she opened the curtains to let in the sunshine and then she sat on the edge of the bed, her hand placed gently on the cover, touching his foot. When he eventually turned to face her she was shocked by the pallor of his face and the tortured look in his eyes.

'What is it, son,' she said softly, 'tell me what's the matter.'

'I don't really know, mom, I just don't know.'

'Are you worried about not getting those jobs?'

He sighed. 'That's part of it.'

'What's the other part, boy?'

He shook his head slowly. 'I have nightmares.'

'What about?'

'About killing people.'

'You mean when you were in the army?'

'I think so. I'm not sure.'

'Tell me what happens in your dreams.'

For long moments he was silent, looking vacantly at the wallpaper beside his head. And when he spoke she could barely hear him.

'It's in a barn . . . there's a wooden table . . . an army issue table with papers and maps on it. And two men tied to chairs. There were two officers in battle dress. One of them told the two men if they didn't talk they would be shot . . . the one with ginger hair spits at the officer who tells me to shoot him. And when I shoot him there's stuff comes out of his chest, like spaghetti and blood and . . .' His eyes closed, and his head fell back on the pillow and the woman realized that he was actually asleep.

It was almost an hour before his eyes opened. She wished that she could hold back and wait, but her tension and worry were too much.

'Where was this place?'

'What place?'

'Where you killed this man in your dream. Was it a place you know?'

'I don't know. I think so.'

'But you were in Bradford for a year and then you were at the depot place where you were in the stores. It must be one of those places.'

'No. I can remember signposts on a motorway. They were in German.'

'Did your unit go to Germany? Maybe one of those NATO exercises?'

'No. I never left this country.'

'Have you seen a film like this or seen it on TV?'

'I don't think so. I just don't know.'

'Maybe we should write to the War Office. Maybe they could help.'

He shook his head violently. 'I don't want to know, mom. I want to forget it.'

'That's the first sensible thing you've said, my boy. Maybe you should see the doctor. He always asks after you. He could give you a tonic. That's what you need.'

George Walker found a job, working on the forecourt of a local garage, and in six months he had the nightmare only twice.

It was when he came home one evening and the two letters were waiting for him that he was finally driven to consult the family doctor. One letter was his weekly football pools coupon and the other was in the standard buff envelope overprinted 'WAR OFFICE'. His hands trembled as he opened the letter in the privacy of his bedroom. It was only two lines and a formal confirmation that he had served his full time and had been demobilized at Catterick Camp in the previous August.

His father came into his bedroom in the early hours of the morning. Roused by his son's screams and his complaint of acute stomach pains, he dissolved an Alka-Seltzer in warm water and watched as his son drank it down. The next day Mrs Walker went down to the call-box in the High Street and asked the doctor to call. Before he went up to see her son she told the doctor all that she could remember about his failure to get a real job and the story of the nightmares.

When he talked with the young man he knew at once that he needed help that was beyond a general practitioner's expertise. George Walker had suffered some kind of shock and only a psychiatrist could help him. He prescribed some mild tranquillizers and didn't probe too deeply into the problem. His questions were more to show his concern than to establish a diagnosis, and he told George Walker that he

131

was arranging for him to see a specialist.

Armed with a sealed letter from the doctor Walker went to his appointment at the hospital in Manchester. He was surprised and uneasy when he was directed at the gate to follow the blue signs to the Psychiatric and Neural Research Department.

When he was shown into the interview room he saw that the doctor was young. Not more than thirty-five. Doctors were generally father figures where he lived. The doctor was casually dressed in a blue shirt and jeans but there was nothing casual about his approach. He read the GP's letter, put it to one side and leaned back in his chair.

'How long were you in the army?'

'Four years and one month.'

'Did you like service life?'

Walker shrugged. 'It was OK.'

'What was your rank when you came out?'

'Corporal.'

'What were you in?'

'I don't understand?'

'Were you signals, transport or what?'

'I was infantry. And when I was promoted I worked in the depot stores.'

'How did you get on with the other men?'

'OK.' He shrugged. 'It's hard to tell.'

'Anybody you particularly disliked?'

'No.'

'Any quarrels at all?'

'No.'

'Any charges laid against you?'

'No, none.'

'Were you glad to be out?'

'I suppose so.'

'Why?'

'I wanted to earn some money.'

'Do you earn more now?'

'A bit more.'

'You applied for several jobs. I understand you had all the necessary qualifications but you didn't get them. Why?'

'I don't know.'

The doctor noticed the beads of sweat that broke out on the young man's face.

'You've been having nightmares. Tell me about them.'

He listened without comment as Walker haltingly described his dreams, making no attempt to prompt him in the gaps of silence or the searching for words. When Walker finished the doctor was silent for a moment.

'Can you come again on Friday at the same time?'

'Yes. Providing the boss doesn't object.'

'D'you want me to give you a medical note for him?'

'No. He'll be OK.'

Walker lay back on the couch uneasily and as Dr Ansell looked at his notes he said, without looking at Walker, 'Just relax, George.'

Then the doctor put his hand on Walker's wrist. Without counting he could tell that his pulse was fast, and he wondered for a moment if maybe Walker had been hypnotized before.

'Have you ever been hypnotized, George?'

'No, doc.'

'Well I'm going to relax you so that you can talk more easily. You don't mind that, do you?'

Walker shook his head.

'Close your eyes . . . that's right . . . now relax . . . good . . . just relax. When I count from ten you're going to be completely relaxed and perfectly comfortable. Ten . . . eyes closed . . . nine, eight . . . deeper and deeper . . . seven, six, five . . . just nod if you can hear me . . . good . . . four, three . . . two, one and zero . . . Can you still hear me?'

Walker nodded, and the doctor checked the blood-pressure reading on the instrument panel as he spoke. 'Let's talk

133

about your dream, George. Just tell me what you can remember.' He saw the needle swing on the dial and stay well above the normal reading.

'Where did it happen, George? Where was the room?'

'The road sign said Hamburg. But outside in the country. A big house near the woods.'

'Who was there?'

'Captain Ames and Lieutenant Leclerc, and Mason and Fox.'

'The officers were British Army officers, were they?'

'They were both Grenadier Guards.'

'Who else was there?'

'There were two soldiers . . . prisoners.'

'Why were the two men prisoners?'

'Because of Mason's girl-friend.'

'Go on.'

'She was a Kraut. They said she was working for the East Germans and one of them was giving her documents.'

'What sort of documents?'

'Orders of battle and NATO sitreps.'

'What's a sitrep?'

'A situation report.'

'Who told you to kill him?'

'Ames.'

'What did he say?'

Walker sighed and Ansell saw the beads of sweat forming on the forehead and round the mouth. He said softly, 'Tell me what he said.'

'He called me Mr Dickens and told me to kill Fox.'

'And did you?'

'Yes.'

'How did you kill him?'

'With a gun. A Luger.'

'Why did he call you Mr Dickens?'

'That's my name.'

'But your name's Walker. George Walker.'

'No. It's Dickens.'

'Then what happened?'

'The aeroplane.'

'Where did it go to?'

'US air force base in Norfolk.'

'Where in Norfolk?'

'I don't know. But always fried egg and bacon.'

Ansell sat silent for several minutes, and then went through the ritual to bring Walker out of hypnosis. As his eyes flickered open Ansell said, 'How do you feel, George?'

'I feel good. Kind of lighter, somehow.'

'Good. I want you to come back to see me again next week. Friday, same time.'

'OK.'

13

As the small group of Concorde passengers filed out on to the tarmac at Dulles International Airport Boyd turned and waved to the two men standing at the observation windows. His time with the CIA was over. Schultz and Friedlander had been his closest colleagues, and he counted them as more than colleagues, they were friends. Men he admired for their professional skills and experience, but even more for their judgement. He knew that he would miss them both.

As usual the Concorde was only two-thirds full and the roomy seating gave space for him to stretch out his long legs and sleep.

At Heathrow Boyd showed his passport at the immigration desk and the officer smiled and nodded as he handed it back. He had spotted the tell-tale 'S' that preceded the passport number. He showed the cover of his passport to the customs officer who waved him through. And as he went through the doors there she was. The beautiful Kate, smiling, almost laughing, because she was so pleased to have him back.

'I'm sorry we're late, honey. There were headwinds.'

She looked up at his face, eyebrows raised. 'What's all this honey business. Who's been teaching you to call her honey?'

He smiled. 'Let's go grab a drink before we go home.'

'Where are your cases?'

'They're by the carousel. We'll pick them up later.'

When he had ordered their drinks he sat on the bar stool, smiling as he looked at her. 'It's wonderful to be back with you, kid. I missed you so much after you'd gone.'

'Did you sell the lease of the apartment?'

'You bet. My relief bought it. I made five hundred bucks.'

'You're an old softie. You told me it was worth at least another thousand when I was over with you, and that was three months ago.'

He looked down at his drink and then back at her face. 'Doesn't matter. We've always got your painting.'

She opened her handbag and handed him an envelope. 'They brought that round and asked me to give it to you.'

He hesitated for a moment and then slid the letter into his jacket pocket. She smiled. 'Read it. You know you want to.'

It was very brief. No words of welcome. Just asking that he phone Arkwright as soon as possible. He folded it, put it back into the envelope and stuffed it into his pocket.

'Why don't we eat here? The food's not bad if we go for the plain things.'

'Let's do that.' She smiled.

When they were back at Hampstead he phoned Arkwright. The duty officer gave him another number and Arkwright asked if he could attend a meeting the next day at three in the afternoon.

'It's a Sunday, for God's sake.'

He could hear the smile of satisfaction in Arkwright's languid tones. 'We're heathens over here, James. You must have forgotten.'

'I've got two weeks' leave. I'm not on duty.'

'It'll only be an hour. Blame Cartwright not me.'

'Where can I get hold of him?'

'Right at this moment he's airborne, chum. From Hong Kong. See you tomorrow.' And Arkwright hung up.

But not even Arkwright could spoil his pleasure at being home. There was a pile of mail on his desk but he wasn't curious, it could wait. There were new curtains in the sitting room and half a dozen vases crammed full of Sweet William, his favourite flower; and a crayon portrait of Katie on the wall over the settee. It was signed Leslie Grosvenor, and as he looked at the gooseberry-green eyes, and the whiteness of the teeth behind the full sensual lips, he felt a fleeting twinge of jealousy. The bastard had painted a bedroom face. It was true and authentic, but how did he know that she looked like that when she was making love?

She came into the room naked, brushing her long dark hair.

'D'you like it, Jimmy?'

'It's beautiful. Who's the lucky man?'

'How do you mean?'

'Who's the artist?'

She laughed. 'I can't believe it. You're jealous, aren't you?'

'A bit.'

'Leslie's a girl. She's coming to tea tomorrow with her husband. He plays fiddle in the Philharmonic.'

'Sounds interesting.'

She put her arms around his neck and kissed him gently. 'I love you so much.'

Boyd got on well with Cartwright. They were nothing like each other in character or temperament but they had both managed to avoid that totally implacable immersion in their jobs that most SIS men suffered from. Divorce was par for the course, and most of the marriages that survived, survived because the couple concerned had found some *modus vivendi* that only the most cynical or naïve observer could call a normal marriage.

138

The breakdowns were seldom indicative of any unusual failure on the part of the people concerned, but there can be few forms of employment more likely to guarantee disaster than a job where the husband is prohibited from telling his wife how he spends his days and nights, and that makes sudden, unannounced trips overseas frequent events. And when the training and experience make subterfuge, suspicion and lying into virtues that could preserve a man's life, it's not easy to be a good husband. Add to this that most of the men were self-confident, and sure of themselves, traits which attracted many young women. And on the other side take account of the fact that this kind of man generally chooses attractive women, and the apparent neglect, secretiveness and jealousies are magnified grossly in a marriage which would have had the usual teething troubles even in normal life. Add up all this and you have a well proven recipe for emotional disaster.

Boyd had kept his work at arms-length so far as his marriage was concerned. Despite signing the Official Secrets Act he had told Katie roughly what he did before he asked her to marry him. Not all that much, but enough to show that the hazards would not be solely of his making. It would be wrong to say that they trusted each other completely, but only because it never entered their minds to be suspicious of each other. If there had been grounds for jealousy they were both of a temperament that would have shown it, openly and destructively. It was perhaps more difficult for the man, who was trained to trust nobody and to be suspicious of everyone.

Cartwright had never married and he had preserved his independence by music. With a natural violin-playing talent and a catholic taste in music he was welcome at jazz sessions in Islington pubs, and in trios and quartets whose tastes were more inclined towards Beethoven and Schubert. He had girl-friends, but he didn't inhale.

Cartwright was Boyd's section head. A section that had no traditional role and which only handled those problems that regularly came up which didn't fit into the normal MI6 structure.

Cartwright was waiting for him in the reception lobby of Century House, a courtesy that was typical of the man. As they went up to the seventeenth floor he asked after Katie and told Boyd briefly of his trip to Hong Kong.

'We've been getting a run of defectors from the Chinese Intelligence Service in the past two months. All coming through Hong Kong, and our people were getting bogged down trying to sort the sheep from the goats.'

'How do you sort them out?'

'Well, we start by assuming that they're all planted on us. The Chinese aren't natural defectors, you know. They don't like living outside China. And they're not interested in doing exchanges of captured intelligence agents. If one of their chaps get caught they just see it that he's fallen down on the job and that's it. In this particular case it turned out that it was a check that Peking were doing to try out our narcotics people. We sent them all back and closed the frontier for a week just to show we didn't approve. They'll find some other way to get the heroin through, but that's not our problem, thank God.'

'Why are they so active in drugs? Is it because Peking needs foreign currencies?'

'Partly that, but mainly it's ideological. They want to help the decline of the decadent West. And now that the Americans have clamped down on Turkey the Chinese want to fill in the gaps.'

Cartwright ignored his desk and pointed to the two armchairs.

'I apologize for dragging you back off leave but I shan't take up much of your time. I've got a little *douceur* for Katie.'

140

He fished around in his pocket and pulled out a small box wrapped in tissue paper. As he handed it to Boyd he said, 'Don't open it. It's a jade brooch to go with those lovely green eyes of hers.' He paused. 'She must be glad to have you back.'

'I'm glad to be back myself, Ken.'

'I've got an enquiry that should keep you in this country for some time. It could be a sheer waste of time but I'd like you to give it a whirl until you can confirm that it's a nonsense.'

'What is it? KGB?'

'No. I don't think so.' He laughed. 'And that's probably the only interesting aspect. There's no real indication of *anyone* being involved. Let me give you the basics. There's a file but it doesn't tell you much.' He waved his hand in the general direction of his desk. 'There's no great urgency but I'd like you to read the stuff and let it wash around your mind while you're on leave. We had a report from the Provost Marshal's office that a psychiatrist up North had a patient with hallucinations about his time in the army. There was a lot of detail involving killings ordered by army officers, but the fact is that the chap had a perfectly routine job in a depot in the UK. The killings were supposed to be in Germany but the fellow was never out of this country. Not even in civilian life. Despite all this the psychiatrist is worried. The chap isn't complaining and he seems an honest, unimaginative fellow, who is obviously not aware of what he's saying under hypnosis. He has nightmares but he doesn't remember much until he's under hypnosis. Then he seems to remember more each session. The doctor spoke to the Military Police at Northern Command, and SIB did a check or two on some of the names and drew a blank. A report went down the routine channels to the Provost Marshal and he's passed it to us.' He smiled. 'And now I'm passing it to you.'

Boyd smiled. 'Well, at least it's the first time I've been

asked to investigate somebody's dreams.'

'Nightmares, James. Not dreams. And the psychiatrist thinks they're real.' He stood up, reaching for the file and handing it to Boyd. 'Have a quick read and phone me if you want anything done before you come back. I'll leave you in peace.'

There were only four pages in the file and Boyd read them carefully, three times. Then he sat for a few minutes, thinking, before he put the file back on Cartwright's desk.

The second-hand 27-foot Seamaster had served them well. They kept it in the yacht basin at Chichester but spent most of their time at Itchenor and Bosham. It could creep around the coast in winds that were under Force 3 but it was really a boat for creeks and rivers, and the furthest they had ventured was to Portsmouth. An experience they never wanted to repeat. In the sea-lanes, with Royal Navy frigates and ocean-going liners, you needed to be a real seaman and Boyd made no such claims.

Their two weeks had only three more days to go, but the autumn sun and the sea air had done them both good. They had dropped anchor in one of the side creeks, and the tall reeds, sedges and hair grass were so high that they could see only the blue sky as they lay on the aft deck sunbathing with their eyes closed, with only the slapping of the incoming tide against the hull to disturb them.

'D'you know what you'll be doing now you're back, sweetie?'

'More or less. I'll be in the UK anyway.'

'Exciting?'

'No. Routine.'

'I'm glad of that.'

'Thanks, pal.'

'Do you *like* what you do?'

'Most of it.'

'What don't you like?'

142

'Being away from you.'

'What else?'

'The bits I can't talk about.'

'Do people get hurt?'

'Sometimes. Mainly they go in the nick.'

'Would you hurt people?'

'If it was necessary I would. I'd rather it was them than me.'

'Is that how you got the scar on your shoulder?'

'What is all this, kid?' he said, turning his head to look at her. 'Are you worried about something?'

'Not really. But I worry about you.'

'I can look after myself, Katie. They don't send us like lambs to the slaughter.'

'It isn't just that. I read things sometimes in the paper and I wonder if they're to do with you. Or if you do such things.'

'What sort of things?'

'Men who are dragged out of rivers or found dead in back-alleys, and hints that they were spies. I can't somehow imagine you in those scenarios.'

'They don't often happen.'

'Maybe not, but you seem too honest and . . . something or other . . . to be mixed up in things like that.'

'It's only being a kind of policeman.'

'Policemen don't kill the criminals.' She paused. 'Have you killed people, Jimmy?'

He sat up rubbing his eyelids. 'God, this sun-oil really stings.'

She reached out her hand to his leg. 'I'm sorry, love. I'll shut up. I shouldn't have gone on like that.'

He shrugged. 'It's not like you, Katie. But I understand. I'd be the same if our roles were reversed. I'd be much worse, I'm sure. Let's go round to Itchenor and have a drink. They'll be open by the time we get there.'

143

As they sat in the pub an hour later in the hubbub of chatter about dinghies and stabilizers, radar and gin-palaces, he smiled as he saw her normal animation return, and was vaguely annoyed that his mind went back so frequently to the ex-soldier who had nightmares.

14

Back in London Debbie Shaw started her own management agency in a small suite of offices in Wardour Street. She soon found that her pretty face and attractive personality combined successfully with her tough business sense to give her a virtual monopoly over supplying dancers, singers and 'personality' girls for overseas tours. Her girls went all over the world, and she quickly built a reputation for obtaining good terms and good bookings for her clients. Debbie Shaw's girls were never stranded in Teheran by absconding operators, nor did they have to hustle drinks in German nightclubs after the act. If they wanted to earn more money by obliging men it was up to them.

She had several men-friends. None of the relationships was too serious. One was a radio announcer working for the BBC's World Services at Bush House. One was a crime reporter on one of the London evening papers; and the other was an older man who had a show-biz act and performed in clubs and provincial variety theatres. She slept with all three of them from time to time but none of them could take the privilege for granted.

It was seven-thirty on a summer evening as she locked her office door when she noticed the man at the far end of the corridor. He was knocking on the insurance agent's door. The insurance agent always left promptly at five-fifteen. As the man heard her footsteps he turned and as she got to him she said, 'Mr Nugent went some time ago.'

'Is he here every day, miss?'

'He seems to be. Try him tomorrow.'

The man's eyes narrowed as he looked at her face.

'Say, don't I know you?'

'I don't think so.'

'You ever been to the States, honey?'

'Yes. As a matter of fact I have.'

He looked over her shoulder at the gold lettering on the glass panel of her office door.

'Debbie Shaw. My God. Where was it now?' He screwed up his eyes. 'Texas. Fort Bliss, El Paso, Texas. Way, way back and you sang.' He smiled. 'Yes?'

She smiled too. 'I'm afraid you're right. You've got a good memory.'

He grinned. 'I have for pretty girls. Say is that really your outfit there? Debbie Shaw Management?'

'Yes.'

'Well, well. How're you making out? I bet you're real good at your job.'

She smiled. 'I get by. How about you?'

He laughed softly. 'Me? I'm still in the army. Still the same old routine. Say, how about I take you for a drink or a meal some place. You tell me what's the real best place in this town.'

'I'm afraid I can't. I've got a business meeting at eight. I'm going to be late as it is.'

'Too bad. I'll walk you downstairs.'

At the street door he said, 'Can I contact you some other time, honey?'

'Of course you can.'

She waved to a cruising taxi and as she sat back in the seat she wondered if the big American remembered that he'd slept with her after she'd sung in the officer's mess that night in El Paso. At least he had remembered her face and her name. She hadn't recognized him at first, and she still had no idea of his name.

*   *   *

It was exactly a week later when he called at her office just after lunch and he'd brought her a bottle of expensive perfume.

'Any chance of that date tonight, Debbie?'

She shook her head. 'You'll have to give me notice. By the way, I can't remember your name.'

'Bill. Bill Mortensen. Full colonel US army, at your service. And rarin' to go.'

'Next time phone me in advance and we'll make a proper date.'

'I'll sure do that, honey.' He paused, looking at her face. 'Could I ask you a favour?'

She smiled. 'Try me.'

'Can I leave a letter here to be picked up? It's kinda special. Security stuff.'

'OK.'

He handed it over and she looked at the envelope. There was no name or address on it. She stood up as the light flashed on her internal telephone.

'I'll have to throw you out. I've got a client waiting outside.'

'And I really can call you, honey?'

'Of course you can.'

A man called for the letter the next day and the colonel phoned her two days later to make a date.

She had never been to the Connaught before. Show-biz people preferred somewhere more lively. She liked the food but found the place dreary. No laughing and chatting at other people's tables.

They were sipping coffee in the far corner of the residents' lounge when he put the question.

'That letter you held for me, we really appreciated your help.'

She shrugged. 'It was nothing. Who's "we" by the way?'

'I work for the CIA, honey. We sometimes have

147

problems about confidential material. You helped us solve one of our problems.'

'Sounds very exciting and hush-hush.'

'Would you help us again?'

'It depends what you want.'

'I've got a small package I want delivered personally to New York. We'd pay you, honey.'

'I couldn't spare the time, Bill.'

'We'd fly you Concorde both ways. There and back in a day. Could be a Saturday or a Sunday if that's easier.'

She pursed her lips. 'Sounds interesting. How much do I get?'

'A hundred and fifty dollars in cash.'

'When do you want this done?'

'As soon as you can make it.'

'OK. I'll do it on Saturday and I can sleep on Sunday.'

The colonel smiled. 'I'll fix for you to meet an old admirer of yours while you're in New York.'

'Who's that?'

'Remember the doctor, the guy who played piano for you that night in the mess after your act?'

'Yes.'

'He'd just love to say hello again.'

'Me too. I'll look forward to that.'

He offered to take her on to a nightclub but instead she took him to a pub near Piccadilly Circus where they sang old music-hall songs and then he taxied her back to her flat off Buckingham Palace Road. She didn't invite him in but she didn't object when his hands explored her breasts as he kissed her good-night.

Symons was waiting for her at Kennedy, standing by the immigration desk and waving her past the immigration officer. It was then that she realized that he must be CIA too. She wondered for a moment what a doctor was doing

148

in an intelligence agency.

She handed over the packet and he reached for her canvas hold-all, taking her arm as he led her to a side door and a waiting car. He sat in the driver's seat looking at her face.

'You know, you're even prettier than you were way back, honey. You really are.'

She smiled. 'And you're a lot smoother than you used to be.'

He laughed and started the car. 'You've got six hours in New York and I'm not going to tire you out. First we're going to Saks and you're going to buy a nice dress on the company's account. Then we eat in a nice suite overlooking Central Park. After that we'll see how the time has gone and maybe go down to the Village for a drink.'

'Sounds nice . . . doctor?'

He laughed. 'I'm not your doctor now, so you can call me . . . what shall you call me? How about Joe Spellman?'

He glanced at her face and he saw the momentary frown and then she smiled. 'OK Joe. You're the boss.'

She chose an Italian dress, black, formal and elegant. He drove her up to the park, past the lake, and then he turned off half-way up the park to cross over the avenue and swing into the basement car-park of a residential apartment block.

A waiter served the meal in the elegant suite. Israeli melon, smoked salmon, a T-bone steak and a trolley of tempting *patisserie*. The only drink she was offered was orange juice and tomato juice.

When the waiter had cleared away, she sat back in the comfortable arm-chair. Symons leaned forward and put his hand gently on her knee, saying softly, 'Nancy. Nancy Rawlins . . . Nancy Rawlins.' And he held his breath until her eyes closed and her mouth opened as she breathed deeply and steadily. ·

149

'Can you hear me, Nancy?'

'Yes.'

'Have you told anyone about this trip, Nancy?'

'No.'

'Not even your boy-friend?'

'I don't understand.'

'Do you have a steady boy-friend?'

'No.'

'Tell me about when you were a little girl.'

She sighed. 'I didn't like it. I hated them both . . . he was always touching me and she knew. She beat me. Said I was a whore . . .'

'How old were you when she said that?'

'Ten, maybe eleven. She was always saying it.'

'Go on.'

'I was unhappy all the time . . . it's making me cry. I never think about it now.'

'Is there anyone you really trust in your life?'

'I trust you.'

'Good girl. Do you like Bill Mortensen?'

'He's OK.'

'Listen very carefully, Nancy. When Bill tells you to do something I want you to do it. Whatever it is I want you to drop everything and do what he asks. Do you understand?'

'Yes.'

'Tell me your name.'

'Nancy Rawlins.'

'What other girl's name do you like?'

'Lara.'

'That's a nice name. Why do you like that?'

'*Dr Zhivago*. I liked that film. Her name was Lara. There were daffodils in front of the house. But they came and took her away.'

'I'm going to count to ten and then you'll be Lara. Do you understand?'

'Yes.'

'One, two . . . go to sleep . . . three, four . . . deeper and deeper . . . that's right . . . five, six . . . seven, eight . . . you're feeling great . . . nine, ten. And now you're Lara. Can you hear me?'

'Yes.'

'What's your name?'

'Lara.'

'What's my name?'

'Joe Spellman.'

'Do you like me, Lara?'

'Yes. I like you a lot.'

'And you'll always do what I tell you to do?'

'Yes.'

'Would you kill someone if I told you to? Somebody evil.'

'Yes. Of course.'

'Do you like being Lara?'

'Yes.'

'When I want you to be Lara I shall say a special number to you. Eight nine zero. When I say eight nine zero you'll be Lara. You understand?'

'Yes.'

'Say the number to me.'

'Eight nine zero.'

'Now I'm going to wake you up. I'm going to count from ten to one and when you hear me say one you'll be awake and you'll be Nancy again.'

He put her through the ritual, checked that she said that her name was Nancy. Put her back again to Lara to check that it had held, then brought her back twice until she was Debbie Shaw again. As her eyes fluttered open she yawned and stretched. 'It was a lovely meal, Joe. Really lovely.'

He bought her a couple of magazines at Kennedy and waited until Concorde took off. He boarded the scheduled flight to Prestwick two hours later. Grabowski and Mortensen had reckoned it was worth the risk of him being in New York for a couple of days rather than let her have any idea that he was based in England.

15

He stood for a moment at the cottage door, his hands in the pockets of his towelling bath-robe as he looked up at the grey sky. It was the first skylark he had heard that year and it was barely the end of January. But it was mild enough to walk down to the front gate and see if the boy had delivered the Sunday papers.

The Sunday Times was there. Three sections and the comic. But no *Observer*. 'Britain protests to S. Africa over petrol supplies to Rhodesia' the headline said. He wondered what Alan Watkins would have had to say about that. And then he saw it. There were small droplets of dew on the spiky fur around its neck, and it had obviously been run over by a car in the night. Its guts had burst from its open belly, and as he bent slowly to lift it from the edge of the road the cat's body was stiff, and lighter than he expected. The girls would be upset if they saw it.

He sacrificed the *Business News* as a shroud and walked over to the small cedar-wood toolshed. The ground was hard and, with only slippers on his feet, the digging was uncomfortable and inexpert. At about eighteen inches deep he stopped, unwrapped the corpse and laid it in the rough grave. The hole was too short and it was when he was adjusting the position of the cat's head that his fingers disturbed the thin filament of wire. His eyes followed it to the thick fur at the cat's neck and as he pulled on it gently the filament loosened and then caught for a moment. With his right hand he diffidently parted the dank fur and saw the

153

gaping wound in the cat's skull. A jagged sliver of broken bone was holding back a small plastic ball about the size of a large marble. As he tugged at the filament the ball came free and swung gently on the end of the thin wire.

Slowly he wiped the ball free of the blood and tissue clinging to it. It was made of a clear plastic that gave slightly to the pressure of his fingers and as he turned it to the light he saw the cluster of what looked like tiny, various coloured pin-heads embedded inside it. He stood up, turned to look at the cottage, and after a moment's hesitation walked back to the open door. Everyone was still asleep upstairs and he spoke quietly when he asked the emergencies operator for the police.

'Police. Can I help you?'

'A cat was run over near my cottage. When I was burying it I noticed it had some kind of device in its head.'

There was a pause at the police end.

'What d'you mean, a device? What kind of device?'

'I don't know. It looks like something scientific.'

'Can I have your name and address, sir?'

'My name's Phillip Cruickshank and my address is Lindens, Sandy Lane, Petchford.'

'Somebody'll come out, sir.'

'How long will they be?'

'Not long, sir. Five or ten minutes.'

The man in the white jacket sat alongside the table, his glasses pushed up on to his forehead.

'There's nothing more I can say, Tony, unless I cut the damn thing up.'

'There's no indication of what it does?'

'Not a sausage. I assume that it's from some animal research laboratory. The components are obviously highly miniaturized electronics but I've never seen anything like them before. Even the plastic covering isn't any material I've come across before.' The man looked at his colleague.

154

'There's only one sensible thing you can do, Tony.'

'What's that?'

'Send it to Special Branch. Either that or just send it to Victoria Street and let the Yard forensic people sort it out.'

'Why Special Branch?'

'Because there are two devices inside, and my guess is that one of them must be a radio. That's what the filament is for. It's probably an aerial of some kind.'

It was handed over to the senior Special Branch officer at Newcastle who was ordered to take it personally to New Scotland Yard.

The device was photographed from every angle, with black and white, infra-red and colour film, and finally, before it was opened, a technician produced a hologram for reference. The cutting open of the device was filmed, and it took almost two hours to remove the outer sheath without damaging the components.

Despite two months of careful examination it was not possible to determine the function of the device. Photographs were circulated to the Royal College of Surgeons, the Royal College of Veterinary Surgeons, commercial and government laboratories and two or three university physics research laboratories. No components were identified, and suggestions about the device's function were no more than speculation. The material of the outer sheath was identified, by spectography, as a derivative of an inert material manufactured by a Swiss drug company for use where capsules taken by mouth in research experiments needed to be recovered. A four-line summary was passed to Regional Special Branch offices, MI6, the CIA in Washington, the BfV in Bonn and the SDECE in Paris. The summaries were acknowledged but there was no additional information in response. Only the CIA asked to be put on the circulation list for any subsequent information.

The three of them, the girl, Symons and Maclaren flew in to

155

Ireland on a TWA flight from Prestwick to New York via Shannon. Symons, with a US passport, hired a car from Ryan's and they were in Dublin in mid-afternoon. They booked in separately at the Hibernian.

Maclaren had taken a suite and that evening they ate together. After the waiter had cleared away Maclaren went into his bedroom and left Symons alone with the girl. He lifted the slim leather briefcase on to his lap and took out a fat, brown envelope, placing it carefully by his chair as he snapped closed the briefcase and moved it off the table.

Symons turned to face the girl, his eyes on hers. 'How do you feel, Nancy?'

'I'm ready for bed. It was a lovely meal.'

'Why don't you close your eyes for a few minutes?'

She laughed. 'I'd just go to sleep.'

'I'll wake you up. Just rest your eyes . . . that's it. When I count to ten you'll be asleep but you'll still hear me. One, two . . . three, four . . . good . . . five . . . six . . . seven . . . deeper and deeper . . . eight, nine . . . ten.' He paused for a few seconds and said softly, 'Can you hear me?'

The girl nodded and Symons said, 'Eight, nine, zero. And now you're Lara. Beautiful Lara. And you hate what they're doing to the man you love. The house in the snow and then the Spring and the daffodils. Do you remember?'

'I can hear the tune. The lovely tune, and the bells on the horses' harness when we had to go away and leave him . . .' She sighed softly.

'Look at these photographs, Lara. Look at this man. He's your enemy. And your husband's enemy. He's the man who will split you all up. This is where he lives. In this house. Remember this house. Tomorrow you'll go to that house and ask to see him. You'll give him this letter and tell him to read it right away. And as soon as he opens it you'll shoot him with this gun. In his face and his chest. You know how to shoot. You'll fire twice and then run down the path to the car. This man will be in the car. His name is

156

Ames. He'll bring you to me and you will have saved us all.'

The long row of Victorian terraced houses looked grim despite the sunshine. As the car pulled up at the corner of the road Symons got out of the car with the girl and as they walked together he said, 'Lara, you know what to do?' The girl nodded and Symons walked back down the street, ignoring the parked car.

There was a dusty privet hedge in the small front garden, marking the boundary with its neighbour, and a cement path led up to the door. She knocked on the door and stood back as she had been told to do. So that they could see that it was only a girl.

The man who opened the door was holding a half-eaten bacon sandwich in his hand. Dark-haired and red-faced he seemed younger than he had looked in the photographs.

'Mr. Rafferty?'

'That's me.'

'I was told to give you this letter They want me to take back an answer.'

The man put the last of the sandwich in his mouth, wiped his hands on his shirt and started to tear open the envelope. The first shot took him full in the face, jerking back his head. His hands were reaching out for the support of the wall when the second shot, in his chest, knocked him off his feet.

The door of the car was already open and the engine running, and Maclaren pulled the girl inside as he let in the clutch. They left the car outside St Saviour's Church and walked a hundred yards down the road to where Symons was waiting for them in the hire car. Maclaren took the wheel and Symons scrambled in the back with the girl. He turned to her quickly.

'Close your eyes Lara . . . I'll count from one to ten and you'll feel real good. One, two . . . coming up . . . three, four . . . five . . . waking slowly . . . six, seven, eight . . .

157

deep breaths . . . nine . . . ten. Can you hear me?'

'Yes,' she whispered. Maclaren reached over with one arm and took her handbag as he watched the road ahead. Driving with one hand he removed the gun and passed the bag back to Symons.

'You're nice and relaxed . . . you don't remember anything about today or yesterday evening . . . you're Nancy Rawlins . . . and you're on holiday. D'you understand?'

'Yes. I like being on holiday.'

'Tell me your name.'

'I'm Nancy Rawlins and I'm on holiday.'

'Good girl. Now I'll wake you up again.'

16

Percy House could only be reached by the rough dirt road from the metalled road that eventually wound its way half-way up the Cheviot Hills. From the bedroom windows you could see the deserted beach and the sea where it foamed and crashed against the strange outcrop of granite rocks that jutted out from the shore for almost two hundred yards. Local historians sometimes claimed that the outcrop was man-made, a sighting line from the big house to Holy Island. Geologists dismissed the theory as totally unfounded, but the annual debate on the subject at Alnwick Local History Society was always the liveliest night in their winter programme.

Symons and Petersen sat in one of the workrooms watching the screen. They were both in casual clothes. Blue denim shirts and trousers, their feet in solid walking shoes. As the black and white film flickered to an end on the screen and the tail of the film came free from the sprocket Symons switched off the projector and used a torch to walk over to the main light switch.

He made his way back to the armchair, sat down and leaned back looking at Petersen.

'D'you trust them, Pete?'

'You mean all of them?'

'Yep.'

Petersen yawned and stretched his arms and legs.

'They're too deeply involved to try any fancy games.'

'I don't know. I wouldn't trust that bastard Maclaren.'

'Why him particularly?'

'He's always probing around. Have I had any practical experience that it works at different levels? How did the CIA pay me? Always back in the past. Away from what we're doing now.'

'They're scared that it could leak that we're doing it for them.'

'Let's have another look at the film.'

When the lights were out and the focus readjusted on the projector they both sat watching the screen.

The camera angle was low and the lens slowly followed the white lines on what looked like a parquet floor. The lines were straight, branching off at right angles, left and right, in a convoluted pattern that eventually led back to the starting point. When the cat came into the frame it was barely discernible at first. It followed the lines, sometimes sitting at some random point on the line then moving on. Eventually it returned to the starting point. At that point the film stock changed to black and white and there was the hum of a sound-track as code numbers changed on the screen.

As the next sequence came up the cat was walking slowly across a flower border towards a small brick-built cottage. Along the front of the cottage was a narrow border of herbaceous flowers with frost-burned leaves and dry, faded blooms on woody stalks. At the door of the cottage the cat hesitated, looked up at a slightly open window and jumped easily up to the wooden sill. For a moment the lens zoomed in on to the cat, so that the film was momentarily over exposed. The camera cut to the interior of a room. Two men sat talking and the sound-track changed so that the men's words were audible but the speech degraded with an uneven pulse and a regular variation in volume. One of the men talking reached out his hand to the cat, which sniffed it tentatively and then jumped up on to his lap. From then until the film ran out both men's speech was clear and only slightly degraded by intermittent static.

As the film slapped free of the sprockets it flapped round on the spool until Symons reached over and switched off the projector. He said softly, 'I wonder what the hell happened to that bloody cat.'

When their guests had left, Boyd and Katie had one last drink before going to bed and as they sat relaxed on the settee she said, 'Why were you so cross with Tom Frazer?'

'He's a bit of a creep when he's had a couple of whiskies.'

'How did he know that you work for MI6?'

'He works at the Ministry that supplies government departments with furniture and carpets and that sort of stuff. When we moved from Queen Anne's Gate he saw me at Century House when they were making an inventory. He wasn't sure that I worked there. He was just fishing.'

'You were rather nasty with him, darling.'

'I ignored him twice, my love. He should have taken the hint, not gone on.'

'But I think a lot of people would like to know what the difference is between MI5 and MI6.'

'Well they must carry on wanting, so far as I'm concerned.'

She smiled at him. 'Would you tell me?'

'Oh, honey. You're not really interested, are you?'

'Yes.'

'Why?'

'I'm just curious. It's interesting.'

'It's not really interesting. But anyway . . . MI5 is responsible for this country's security. They keep tabs on foreign intelligence agents, subversives . . . that sort of stuff. They don't arrest people themselves. Special Branch, which is part of the normal police force under the Commissioner, do all the actual arrests.

'MI6 are responsible for getting intelligence from other countries.' He shrugged. 'That's all it is. But even that's not for publication.'

161

She laughed. 'But the Russians must know all about it already.'

'Maybe.'

'So why can't *we* know? The public.'

'Why should we confirm anything for the other side?'

'It might stop people criticizing what you do.'

'The ones who criticize don't know what we do. And if they do know and still criticize it's generally because they've got some ulterior motive.'

'You mean they're on the other side?'

'Most of them.'

'But some MPs criticize.'

'So?'

'You mean that those MPs are working for the Russians?'

'Not all of them. Some just want to bring the country to a state of anarchy and revolution. So that they can take over.'

'And it's your job to find out who they are and stop them?'

'No that's Five's job. My lot find out what we want to know about other governments and their intelligence services.'

'I can't imagine you doing that, somehow.'

He leaned over and kissed her gently. 'OK Mata Hari, here endeth the first lesson. And the last one too.'

Slowly she pulled back her head and her green eyes looked at his face. 'We could live quite well off my paintings.'

He smiled. 'I'd rather like being a kept man, sweetie.'

'I mean it, Jimmy.'

'Why should we?'

She said softly. 'Have you ever killed anybody?'

'No comment.' He yawned, but it wasn't very convincing. 'It's time for bed, love. I've got an early start tomorrow.'

'I'm being silly, James. Aren't I?'

'No. You're being kind and caring and I think about you

162

and those virtues very often when I'm away.'

'Honestly?'

'Honestly. Come on, it's past midnight.'

Debbie Shaw was walking through Berwick Market towards Wardour Street and she had to stop. It was like a series of slides in her mind. The big white house on the side of the hill and the hot sunshine. And the man with her in the car, kissing her, trying to get his hand up her skirt, and the car turning into the big gates of the white house. Then a passer-by was asking her if she was all right and the last slide just faded away and she was back in Berwick Market by the second-hand bookstall.

It had happened twice before. Once when she was getting into bed and the second time in a cinema. The first time only lasted for a few seconds and the street signs and shop signs were all in Chinese. Then the cabin on the boat. The beautiful white panels all splashed with blood and the two Americans looking at the man lying on the table. And the sign at the airport said Kai Tak and she found out later that that means Hong Kong.

The second time, in the cinema, had been bad. She had handed over the envelope as soon as she got to the house and when they read it they were angry. The two men had held her and the woman had burned the backs of her hands with a lighted cigarette. They kept asking questions in terrible English and she couldn't understand what they were saying. The next day they had untied her, all smiles. They said there had been a mistake. A doctor had come to treat the big yellow blisters on her hands and she had refused to let him near her, screaming and fighting until he left her alone. She had asked them what language they were speaking and they smiled and said their language was Farsi. She had never heard of such a language.

Ansell was annoyed at the cool reception his report had

received from the military. He had wrestled with his conscience before sending it, and had rationalized his decision as being inevitable because if he raised the issue with his patient, Walker would probably be in a position to claim some sort of disability pension from the War Office. He was merely anticipating the authorities being informed. When he had the call from Boyd he was relieved that his report had not been completely ignored, and he agreed to see him unofficially, off the record, and away from the hospital. He suggested they meet at his home in Wilmslow.

Ansell noticed the official file that Boyd took out of his briefcase.

'I thought the soldiers were taking their normal stance towards psychiatrists as one step worse than witch-doctors.'

Boyd smiled. 'The army employs at least a couple of hundred psychiatrists itself. Most of them field-rank or above. We're not quite the Philistines the media make us out to be. Not that we mind too much what outsiders think.'

'That puts me in my place.'

'I didn't mean that, doctor. And we're quite genuinely grateful that you decided to notify us.'

'How much have they told you?'

'I've read your report and I've read the report by the Military Police. They weren't able to trace any officers of those names operating in Germany from 1945 onwards. That's about all I know.'

'There's one thing I know now that I didn't know when I contacted the army. My patient has definitely been hypnotized before. He says he hasn't, and that probably means that he's been hypnotized surreptitiously.'

'Is that possible? I thought you could only be hypnotized if you wanted to be and you co-operated.'

'That used to be the thinking, but it isn't so. And the old theory that nobody under hypnosis could be made to do something that he or she found repugnant when they were conscious has also gone by the board.'

'Would it be possible for you to ask him questions for me?'

'Depends what they are but there's no practical problem.'

'Could I be there to hear his answers?'

Ansell shook his head. 'No. I'm afraid not.'

'Not even if he agreed?'

'Ah well. That's different, but I couldn't agree to any deception. He'd have to know who you are.'

'When are you seeing him again?'

'Tomorrow at three.'

'Can I make out a list of questions tonight, and let you have them in the morning at the hospital?'

'OK.'

'Just one more question. Have you any idea as to who might have hypnotized him before, and why they would have done it?'

Ansell raised his eyebrows. 'Have you any ideas yourself?'

'Half an idea.'

'Can I hear it?'

'The likely person could be someone in the army. But I don't see how they would do it. Or why.'

Ansell nodded. 'I won't add to that.' He stood up. 'Where are you staying?'

'I'm staying with friends. I've got a car outside. Can I see you about four tomorrow?'

'Make it six and I'll have finished my clinic.'

Boyd hesitated. 'Would it be possible to have your session taped?'

'They're all taped anyway. But I wouldn't be keen to let you hear them. Not at this stage anyway.'

'We could talk about that, maybe?'

Ansell smiled. 'Maybe.'

Ansell glanced at Boyd's typed list of questions and went

over the last two again.

'Tell me again, George, what Ames looked like.'

'Quite tall . . . nearly six foot . . . well-built, strong . . . red face and light brown eyes . . . black hair smarmed down . . . a Brylcreem type . . . spots on the back of his hands . . . pug nose and he'd always got a five o'clock shadow . . . a smooth bastard.'

'Did you ever see him apart from this one place?'

Ansell suddenly noticed the sweat on Walker's face. An instant response to his last question. And Walker was panting. There was something odd about this reaction. Why should he be so disturbed?

'Was he an officer at your depot?'

Walker shook his head slowly. 'No more. No more to say.'

Ansell took a risk he knew he shouldn't take and he said softly, 'It's not only Dickens, is it? There's the other one. What do they say to Dickens to find the other man?' And as he saw Walker's body stiffen as if he were having a fit Ansell said quickly, 'That's fine . . . you're coming back . . . four, five . . . nice and easy . . . six, seven . . . your eyes are opening . . . eight, nine . . . ten . . . good . . . good.'

As Walker struggled to sit up he shook his head, smiling. 'You don't like the Kennedys, do you?'

Ansell held his breath and then quietly exhaled. 'What makes you think that, George?'

'Think what?'

'That I don't like the Kennedys.'

Walker frowned and Ansell saw his pupils contracting. 'I don't know what you mean, doc. Are we finished?'

'How do you feel?'

'OK. But my neck feels kind of stiff.'

'Move it gently, from left to right and then up and down.'

He watched Walker moving his head, his right hand massaging his neck muscles.

'Is that better?'

'A bit.'

'Could you come again tomorrow?'

'I'm playing football tomorrow. It's Saturday tomorrow, isn't it?'

'Yes. How about Monday after work?'

'OK. But I'm feeling much better. You're doing me good, doc.'

'I'm glad. I'll see you on Monday.'

Ansell sat for a long time at his desk before he looked at his watch. It was ten to six. The man Boyd would be pleased, but for himself he felt ashamed. For a second or two he had been on the wrong side. Maybe it had done no harm. Only time would tell. And if it had, no one would be any the wiser. Only he himself, and the man who might start having a brand new nightmare.

When his phone rang it was the reception office to say that his visitor had arrived. He asked for one of the porters to bring him over.

He waved Boyd to the chair on the other side of his desk.

'I've got a problem, Mr Boyd. I'm not sure I can co-operate with you any more.'

'Can you tell me why?'

'If I get satisfactory answers to a couple of questions I'll tell you why I might have to withdraw.'

Boyd shrugged. 'Ask away then.'

'I don't know which order to put them in so I'll ask them both together. Who the hell are you? And why are you interested now when you weren't when I originally reported it?'

'I'm an intelligence officer, Dr Ansell.'

'That can mean anything or nothing. It's not an answer.'

'It's all I can tell you, doctor, so let me answer the other question. You sent a report which made its slow progress through the usual channels to my section of the intelligence services. We think you were right to do so. You're obviously concerned as to what has been happening to this

167

man. Whether he's hallucinating, or malingering, or is genuinely disturbed. It would help you, and maybe him too, to know the truth. I've been ordered to find out the truth. If I can. I need all the help you can give me.'

'Have you got any kind of identity card I could see?'

Boyd fished in his pocket and pulled out the identity card that was used for the general public. Ansell looked at it carefully and handed it back. For a few moments he looked down at his empty desk top and then he lifted his head and looked across at Boyd.

'I hope I'm not making a terrible mistake, Mr Boyd.' And he turned in his chair, reached out and switched on the Technics tape-recorder. It was almost twenty minutes later when he turned to switch it off.

'It's not much help to you, Mr Boyd, but maybe what I'm going to tell you can help. That man has not only been hypnotized before, but he's been hypnotized many, many times, by a professional. He has no realization that he's been hypnotized.' He paused. 'And what is more he has been hypnotized at two levels. The second, deeper level showed up briefly in that session. And he's also . . . and it's significant . . . been given a post-hypnotic block. Do you understand what that is?'

'No.'

'It means that nobody except the original hypnotist can get into the second level. He has been hypnotized to forget that he's been hypnotized. No normal psychiatrist would have any need to do that. It's highly dangerous. It also explains why the poor fellow never got any of the decent jobs he applied for. He has been hypnotized to forget a whole year of his life in the army, so when he has to fill in an application form covering what he had been doing in that twelve months he can't do it. Literally can't do it. This man has been grossly abused. And abused by a highly competent psychiatrist.'

'Have you any idea as to why this should be done?'

168

'There's the obvious suggestion that he was hypnotized by someone during his army service.'

'For what purpose?'

'God knows. Maybe you could hazard a guess better than I can.'

'Is there any way for you to get to the second level of hypnosis?'

'Only by luck. Skill can't do it. The key to that level will be some code-word. Without that it's locked in his brain.'

'What about a pentathol injection?'

'It would make no difference. He doesn't even know that he was hypnotized at all. I doubt if he would believe it if I told him.'

'How can you find the code-word?'

'He gave a clue.'

'What was it?'

'He said, "You don't like the Kennedys", or words to that effect. He was fully conscious when he said that. When I asked him what he meant he didn't know what I was talking about. It had already gone. I suspect that the code-word is in that sentence or is something to do with it.'

'You'd be guessing?'

'Exactly. So is it worth it? Wouldn't it be better to let sleeping dogs lie?'

'From my point of view it has to be done.'

'Even if it could end by doing this man even more damage than has been done already?'

'Yes.'

'Don't underestimate even his present condition. He is a deeply disturbed man. There's little I can do for him now that I know about the second level. I could just be opening Pandora's box.'

'My answer still has to be – go ahead and try.'

'That means you feel you have a very good reason to want to pursue this?'

'Yes.'

'May I ask what it is?'

'I wouldn't be prepared to discuss it. I wouldn't be allowed to anyway.'

'It seems to me that we both suspect the same scenario.'

'I'm sure we do.'

'If what we both suspect is true, would this man be able to claim some disability pension?'

'No.'

'Why not?'

'He wouldn't be able to prove anything.'

'You mean your evidence would be withheld?'

'It wouldn't exist. It would be highly classified.'

'What makes you think it's that important?'

'My training and my experience,' Boyd said softly.

'And if I refuse?'

'I couldn't discuss what would happen if you refuse. We should have to make other arrangements.'

'Sounds ominous.'

Boyd didn't reply.

'Tell me what you want.'

'I want enough information to find out who hypnotized him and why.'

'Nothing more?'

'Maybe.'

'Are you married, Mr Boyd?'

'Yes.'

'Any children?'

'No. Why do you ask?'

'To see how much of a stake you've got in humanity.'

'What about you?'

Ansell smiled. 'No wife. No children. But a soft spot for the wounded. Especially the mentally wounded.'

Boyd said softly, 'Maybe Walker isn't the only one with this problem.'

'I've already thought of that. Let me take you for a drink in our bar and it will give me time to think.'

170

'OK.'

They had their drinks, and as they walked back to Ansell's consulting room he said, 'It's going to take a lot of sessions you know, and the odds are against me being successful.'

'Somebody's going to have to try to do it. I'd rather it was you.'

'Why?'

'You care about him, so he's as protected as he can be, and I think you understand my problems too.'

'Would you like to come in tomorrow and you can hear all the tapes.'

'I would.' Boyd sighed. 'Would you be prepared to sign the Official Secrets Act if it were considered necessary by my people in London?'

'Under no circumstances. I'm a doctor not a civil servant. They take it as it is or they can forget the whole thing.'

Boyd smiled. 'Let's see how it goes.'

17

Stephen Randall had always hated his name being abbreviated to Steve but, as his agent had pointed out, Randall alone took up a lot of space on the posters outside theatres. Put in Stephen as well and all the other acts and their agents would raise hell. He had never been top of the bill but he was always second principal, the last act before the interval.

For years he had done the magic act. Doves, rabbits, cards, and disappearing girl assistants in coffins and sedan chairs, but he had gradually realized that he couldn't compete any longer. There were the world's top magicians on TV. Men whose equipment cost thousands of pounds. New tricks, new hardware and a slicker style. Steve Randall hated the need for change. For one thing it meant he would no longer have the pretty girl assistants. They earned good money but all they had to do was clear away the ribbons and livestock and lie in the coffin, so they took it for granted that part of their duties was to spend an hour or two each day in their boss's bed. Most show-girls were subject to what the trade refers to as 'management privileges' and Steve Randall was both good-looking and charming. They all liked him, and several had quite genuinely fallen in love with him. He gave them a good time and was easy-going, and it was all too easy to end up having to open your legs for some skinflint comedian who was all smiles on stage and a foul-mouthed lout when the lights went out.

Steve Randall's main problem was what to do as an

172

alternative, and it was his agent who suggested a mind-reading act. But not an old-fashioned act. Something slick and modern and involving the audience. Randall had protested that he knew nothing about mind-reading and his agent sent him to a man in Pimlico who could teach him.

The old man taught him the basics of stage hypnotism and memorizing and how to assess quickly people who would be easy subjects, and then he taught him the memory act of names and numbers and all the rest of it. His agent hired a professional script-writer to put together an act and Steve Randall's name was back on the posters. The memory part was absolutely genuine, so was the hypnotism, but it was elementary and superficial. Show-biz rather than serious hypnotism. But it was a good act. Good enough to get him twice on TV.

Steven Randall met Debbie Shaw when he was looking for a girl to join him in his act and he had gone to her agency. But although she was aware that the charm was natural and genuine she was experienced enough to surmise that 'management privileges' were going to be the assistant's principal contribution. She told him so, tactfully but firmly; and, smiling, he hadn't denied it. She also advised him not to have an assistant, not even a man. It could look like collusion and rob his act of its authenticity. He recognized the shrewd mind behind the pretty face and invited her out to dinner that night. And to his surprise, and hers, she accepted.

He took her to the Savoy after she had watched his performance at The Talk of the Town and she enjoyed the meal and was amused by the man. It had been a long time since anyone had made her laugh. She invited him back to her flat for coffee and made quite clear that the only thing beyond the coffee would be a whisky or a brandy, and he would have to be very good to get either.

He *had* been very good and she realized that he had probably never needed to persuade very hard to get the girls

173

into his bed. And as they were sipping their whiskies she made the point.

'You shouldn't need to take advantage of your pretty girl assistants, Steve. Just a few words and your charm should be enough.'

He smiled. 'You don't understand, sweetie. If they're in the act the taxman pays. All of it. Clothes, flowers, meals – the lot.'

She laughed for long minutes as she realized that behind that elegant debonair façade there was a sort of innocent shrewdness that she found tolerable and amusing. And, as if to prove their mutual points, she let him stay the night.

Of the several men she went out with the only one she really cared for was Steve Randall. The others were intelligent and amusing but she was well aware that what they really wanted was her lithe young body. She let them make love to her from time to time but Steve Randall was the only man she let stay the night.

He seldom bought her presents or flowers as the others did regularly. But he gave her something that she valued far more. A feeling of security and being cared for. He remembered things that she told him. Little things. Her likes and dislikes, and her modest pleasures. When the others took her out for the day it was to well-known out-of-town hotels and restaurants. The Compleat Angler at Marlow, Skindles at Maidenhead. But Randall took her to the Zoo and the museums. Children's places. But children's places that had not been part of her grim childhood. He was twelve years older than she, and in some ways he seemed older still, but when she was happy they seemed much the same age. When they made love he was as avid for her body as the others, and no more exciting or arousing than the others, but somehow the sex was more in perspective. It mattered, it was enjoyed, but it wasn't the crown jewels of their relationship. After almost a year she came to realize where the difference lay. Steven Randall

174

was the only real friend she had ever had. Man or woman. They took each other for granted. Not in a negative way. It was their mutual liking and reliability that they took for granted. Nothing had to be excused or explained. Sometimes, after he had left, she thought about him and wished that she had had a brother like him, or a father.

He had taken her that particular day to see *My Fair Lady* at the local cinema. They ate after the show and went back to her flat. It was a Saturday and he was staying with her for the weekend. She went to her bedroom to change and came back in his bath-robe. A well-worn white towelling bath-robe that hung on her like a shroud, and she smiled as she sat down beside him. He poured them both a whisky and reached forward to switch on the TV.

On the screen a man and a woman were walking slowly together across a ramshackle courtyard. Randall leaned forward, turned up the sound and leaned back.

'I came here to find my husband. The one who was reported killed,' the woman said.

'Strelnikov. I met him.'

'Met him.' She looked disbelieving.

'Yes.'

The woman looked away from the man and they walked slowly forward together. And then came the gentle loving music. Strings and balalaikas, and 'Lara's Theme' from Zhivago. He watched as they sat on a bench under a tree, and leaves scattered before the wind across the pathway. He reached out to find Debbie's hand, still looking at the screen. His hand touched her leg, and he felt its coldness before he turned to look at her.

She was trembling as if she had an ague, her mouth gasping for breath, her eyes wide with fear.

'What is it, Debbie? What's the matter?'

She shook her head.

'Let me call a doctor.'

And then she screamed. 'No. No. No.'

175

And the scream seemed to release the tension. She bowed her head, her hands to her face, his arm around her. Then slowly she lifted her head and said, 'Switch it off. Please.'

'Switch what off?'

'The TV.'

He leaned forward and switched off the set and moved back beside her on the settee. He took her hand, holding it gently in both of his. For a long time he just sat there, holding her hand without speaking, until she eventually turned her face to look at him. 'I'm sorry, Steve. I was stupid.'

'Tell me. What was the matter?'

She sighed a deep, deep sigh. 'I don't really know.'

'Did you feel ill?'

'No. I was just frightened.'

'Frightened of what?'

She kissed him gently 'Take me to bed and love me.'

He shook his head. 'I want to know what frightened you.'

'It was a kind of dream.'

'What was it about?'

'I'm not sure. It was just like . . . I don't know how to explain . . . like a few seconds in a film that shouldn't be there . . . a bit that's nothing to do with the film.'

'What did you see?'

'A row of houses. Old-fashioned houses. And a man at an open door. There was a red hole over his nose, between his eyes.'

'Go on.'

'He fell down. Somebody had shot him.'

'Was it someone you know?'

'I don't know. I don't think so. And yet I did.'

'And that was all of it?'

'Yes.'

'What particular bit frightened you?'

'It was me who shot him.'

He smiled at her and kissed her cheek. 'That shows it was only a dream.'

'But I wasn't asleep.'

'It could be a day-dream.'

She turned and looked at him. 'It wasn't, Steve. Why should I day-dream about killing a man I don't know?'

'Maybe he's someone from way-back. Someone your conscious mind has long forgotten.'

She shook her head. 'It was real, Steve. It happened.'

'Now that's being silly, sweetie. Pretty girls don't go around shooting men they don't know. What did he look like?'

'Big, red-faced. Like a farmer or someone who spends all his time out of doors.'

'What were you thinking about before this day-dream?'

'I was trying to think who the girl was in the film they made of *Oklahoma*.'

'Gloria Grahame.' He smiled. 'Let's tuck you up in bed so that you can have a good night's sleep.'

He helped her to bed, plumped up the soft pillows for her head, switched out the main light so that only the shaded light from the bedside lamp was on her face. 'I'm going to get you a nice warm drink.'

He came back five minutes later with a tall glass on a tray. 'Here you are, sweetheart. Hot chocolate as made by the Waldorf Astoria, New York. The best in the world.'

She smiled and took the glass, blowing on the creamy foam that covered the top of it. She drank half of it and put the glass back on the bedside table.

'That was lovely, Steve. Do you want to make love?'

'Of course I do. But we're not going to. I want you to rest and relax.'

He saw her heavy eyelids close and he said, 'Good girl. Just relax.' And his long fingers gently stroked her brow. 'Try and sleep.'

She said very softly, 'I sometimes wonder what's in your letters and packages.'

177

'What letters?'

'The ones I take for you.'

'I don't understand, Debbie.'

'I'm not Debbie. I'm Nancy. You've forgotten.' She laughed softly. 'What's your *real* name? It's not really Joe Spellman, is it?'

'Are you asleep? Can you hear me?'

'Of course I can. Your voice sounds . . .'

She cried out, opening her eyes. 'Where am I? Where am I? I'm frightened.' She was looking around the room as if she had never seen it before and then she pulled aside the bedcovers and swung her legs to the floor.

He said very quietly, 'Lie back, sweetie. Lie back and rest.' And he did the first part of his act, passing his hand across her face, touching her forehead gently with his finger tips, and slowly she relaxed, her breathing deep and even. And then she slept.

She was quite normal when she woke the next day. He made no mention of what had happened. Neither did she.

He phoned the old man in Pimlico who said he couldn't help but gave him the address of a psychiatrist in Welbeck Street. He made an appointment for two o'clock that day.

It was a bright cheerful consulting room and the consultant seemed brisk and informal.

'Tell me your problem, Mr Randall.'

'It isn't my problem. It's a close friend of mine. I think she's seriously ill and doesn't know it.'

'And you'd like her to make an appointment to see me?'

'No. She wouldn't come. Like I said, she doesn't know that she's ill.'

'I can't treat or diagnose the problem without seeing her.'

'I thought I could tell you what's happening.'

'I'm afraid not. I can't, and wouldn't, discuss a third party's problems with you.'

'Can I ask why not?'

'First of all it's bad practice. Your observations could be wrong or misleading. Secondly you might have some ulterior motive. It has been known for wives to suggest that their husbands should be certified just because they were bored with them. There are all sorts of good reasons for not discussing one person's medical problems with another.'

'What can I do to help her then?'

'It's very simple. You get her to see her general practitioner, and if he decides it's necessary he will make arrangements for her to see an appropriate consultant.'

'She hasn't got a GP. She never has had one. And she refuses to go to one.'

'Maybe she doesn't need one, Mr Randall.'

The consultant stood up, holding out his hand. As he took it Randall said, 'She's been hypnotized without her knowing.'

'What makes you think that?'

'She thought yesterday that she was somebody else. Somebody with a different name.'

'People do have such thoughts, Mr Randall. It's not uncommon. It doesn't necessarily mean that she's been hypnotized.'

'It does. I know. I'm a hypnotist.'

'What do you mean – you're a hypnotist?'

'Just that. I'm on the stage. I do a hypnosis act. I can recognize the signs. But I can't help her. I'm not a doctor.'

'Sit down, Mr Randall.'

As Randall sat down the consultant took out a pen and reached for a writing block.

'Tell me what's worrying you.'

Randall told him everything that had happened and when he had finished the consultant pushed his notes to one side.

'Are you this girl's lover?'

'I suppose you could call it that. I sleep with her, if that's

179

what you mean. And I care for her too.'

'I'm sure you do, Mr Randall. Do you want her to marry you?'

'I've thought about it from time to time. I'm not sure.'

'Does she want to marry you?'

'I should think the same applies. She likes me. She may have thought about marriage but we've never discussed it.'

'Is she wealthy?'

'She's got a small business. A show-biz agency. I'd guess she makes a good living out of it. But I wouldn't see her as wealthy.'

'And how about you? Are you wealthy?'

Randall smiled. 'I get by. I'm not top of the bill but I'm usually second on the billings . . . I'm OK.'

'Do you know why I asked those questions?'

'I can only guess. You were trying to find out if my motives were money or some such thing.'

'Do you belong to a club?'

'I'm a member of Gerry's Club in Shaftesbury Avenue.'

'I meant a proper club. Whites. The Atheneum. Somewhere like that.'

Randall smiled. 'I'm afraid not.'

'What's your favourite restaurant where you take the girl?'

Randall shrugged. 'The Savoy, I suppose. The Grill Room.'

'Suppose you took her there on . . .' He reached for his diary and turned over the page. '. . . on Thursday evening. And I happened to walk in. You ask me over for a drink at your table and introduce me as a man who used to be your doctor. And we'll take it from there.'

'I'd be very happy to do that. Thursday then. About eight.'

The consultant stood up. 'You'll get a bill from my office for today's consultation and for the time at the Savoy. Is that OK?'

180

'Of course.'

He phoned the consultant on the Friday morning but he wasn't available. But he had left a message with the receptionist suggesting an appointment at four that afternoon. Randall told her he would be there.

The consultant was wearing a blue denim open-necked shirt and a pair of drill slacks. There was a bulging golf bag propped up in the corner of the room.

'Sit down, Mr Randall. Excuse the kit but I've been down to Wentworth.' He looked across his desk at Randall as if he were collecting his thoughts.

'I think you're right, Mr Randall. I think the girl has been subjected to hypnosis. But I need an absolutely truthful answer from you before I decide what to do.'

'Ask me the question.'

'The whole truth and nothing but the truth?'

'So help me God.'

'Have you ever hypnotized this girl yourself? In fun, as a demonstration of your act, as a party turn. In any way?'

'No. I've never even discussed my act with her. She's seen me perform in a theatre, but that's all.'

'Fine. I'm going to suggest that she sees a consultant at one of our research hospitals. He specializes in hypnotic complications and I think from what you've told me that she's not only been unwittingly hypnotized but has been given what we call a post-hypnotic block so that she can't remember anything about her time in hypnosis.' He paused and then said quietly, 'I think your young lady is going to come apart at the seams unless she has treatment. What she's experiencing now is a kind of leakage. And it could get worse. She's going to need a lot of hand-holding.'

'She'll refuse to see any doctor.'

'It's up to you to persuade her. Nobody else can. But I'll dictate a note to my secretary for you. Feel perfectly free to show it to her if you think it will help. Let me know when you've succeeded and I'll fix an appointment in a matter of hours.' The consultant stood up. 'Try hard, Mr Randall. She needs help. Professional help as well as yours.'

'What did you learn from our meeting?'

The man smiled. 'That you are an honest man, genuinely concerned, without ulterior motives, and that she is a nice, outwardly normal girl.'

'But what made you feel she needed help?'

'What you told me about what happened that evening before you came to see me. There were clues there that you couldn't have made up. I was only concerned about motives. Seeing you together dispelled my doubts. You're a friend, and she needs one.'

Each time Randall suggested that the girl should see a doctor it led to an outburst of anger that shocked them both.

Then the girl had one of her 'day-dreams' when they were in a restaurant. They had to leave, and he went back with her to her flat. She recovered but she was deathly pale and every few minutes she shivered violently and complained of feeling cold. After one of these spells he risked offending her.

'Who's Joe Spellman, Debbie?'

'Washington 547-9077.'

'Is that his telephone number?'

'It's the number to ring.'

'Who is he?'

'He's my doctor.'

'You said you hadn't got a doctor.'

'He's my doctor.'

'How can you have a doctor in Washington when you live in London?'

'He's my doctor.'

He took a deep breath. 'Something's wrong, my love. Very wrong.' He took the consultant's note from his pocket

182

and handed it to her. She read it slowly and he saw the tears on her cheeks as she looked up at his face.

'He thinks I'm mental, doesn't he? He wants to certify me and have me put away.'

'No, he doesn't. He thinks you've been hypnotized without knowing it and that it's causing your problems.'

'But I haven't *been* hypnotized. Ever. I don't believe in it. I'm not the kind who'd go for it. It's crazy.'

'Just see the man he recommends. I'll come with you. Nobody's going to hurt you. They want to help.'

'Was it you, Steve?'

'Was what me?'

'Was it you hypnotized me?'

'Of course it wasn't. I've no reason to.'

'You swear it?'

'Yes.'

'On the Bible.'

'Yes if you've got one.'

'I haven't . . . what shall I do, Steve? Help me.'

'Let me phone now and make an appointment for tomorrow.'

'And you'll come with me?'

'Of course.'

'OK.' She put her hand on his knee. 'I think I love you, Steve.'

'I think I love you too, sweetie.'

18

Boyd sat for two days in an empty room next to Ansell's consulting room, listening to the tapes of all the psychiatrist's sessions with Walker. Playing some parts several times as he made notes. When he eventually left he gave Ansell two London numbers where he could be contacted. Ansell wasn't due to see Walker again for several days.

Cartwright had not been available when Boyd got back to London. It was two days before they could meet. Some instinct made Boyd suggest that they do so away from the office and they made it the bridge over the lake in St James's Park. A frequent meeting place for SIS officers. As they leaned on the rails the mallard drakes were giving the ducks a hard time. It wasn't officially Spring on the calendar but it was Spring in St James's Park.

'How did you get on?'

'There's something going on, but I'm not sure what it is.' And Boyd outlined what he had learned.

'This doctor fellow, Ansell, do you want him leaned on from above?'

'Not at the moment. Let's wait and see.'

'And what do you think it's all about?'

'I think someone's being very naughty.'

'Who?'

'The soldiers is my guess.'

'What for? Why are they doing it?'

'God knows. What's the percentage in giving a man nightmares?'

184

'Is it worth the time finding out? Is it even our business?'
'I've got a feeling it is. On both counts.'
'Why?'
Boyd shrugged. 'Instinct. Experience. Nothing more.'
'OK. Do you need any help?'
'No. It's just a ferreting job. I need to do it myself in case
I miss anything.'
'Take care.'
'I will.'

Boyd checked through George Walker's file at War Office
Records. Walker had joined the army in November 1962
and had been demobilized in December 1966. At no time
had he been posted anywhere overseas and his unit had
never operated in Germany. His service had been exemplary
and he had never faced even a minor charge. He had been in
hospital for two days with blistered feet during his basic
infantry recruit training, and had been given light duties for
four days on one occasion for an abscess on a tooth. He had
been given a normal dose of antibiotic and the tooth had
later been extracted using only local anaesthetic.

Walker's service had been at Catterick Camp in Yorkshire,
the Green Jackets' depot at Winchester and at his regiment's
depot just outside Bradford. Boyd noted the dates when
Walker had been given leave, including a number of
weekend passes.

The Army computer printed out the details of twenty-five
commissioned officers named Ames but none named
Leclerc.

Debbie's appointment at the hospital was for nine o'clock
and Randall was shown into a small waiting room. At
intervals he was brought cups of tea but when it was one
o'clock he became anxious. When it got to three o'clock he
went outside to the reception desk and asked how much
longer it would be, pointing out that he had to be at the

theatre by eight o'clock. The receptionist dialled a number and asked how much longer he would have to wait. She listened and then hung up.

'Mr Salmon is coming out to see you, sir. If you'd go back to the waiting room he'll be there in a few minutes.'

Mr Salmon came in almost immediately. A tall, calm man in his fifties. His glasses were pushed up on to his forehead.

'Mr Randall isn't it? Do sit down.'

'How is she?'

'Ah. That's what I came to talk to you about. We'll have to keep her in for a day or two. Now don't be alarmed. I know you promised to stay with her and take her home. She told me all about that.' He smiled. 'You're obviously very important to her. Talked a lot about you.'

'Why does she have to stay?'

'Now don't worry on that score. I explained to her before we started that she might have to stay for a day or two. She didn't mind so long as you didn't mind.'

'You haven't told me why she has to stay.'

'Let me just say this. It's going to take some sorting out. All a bit tangled up if you know what I mean. But we've given her a relaxing drug that means she has to have proper medical supervision.'

'Can I see her before I go?'

'She's asleep at the moment. It's better not to disturb her. Now a message or two.'

Salmon pulled down his glasses and took a scrap of paper from his pocket.

'Ah yes. She sends you her love and says not to worry. And she asks if you can bring her pale-blue nightie, her dressing gown and bedroom slippers. And asks if you would check with her assistant at the office that all is OK. And that's it.'

'I'll come tomorrow with her things.'

'Good. Do you know the way out? Along the passage

186

then turn right where it says "Laundry".'

For the first time in his life Steve Randall was lonely and depressed. His nightly act seemed to exhaust him and he knew that he had lost his bounce. His usual amiable patter with his volunteers and his audience seemed desperately flat. He had never thought before about hypnosis as being more than an entertainment or maybe a cure for smoking or drinking. The girl had been in hospital over a month now. He had gone there every day but not been allowed to see her. And when it became obvious that that would continue he went only every three days. Salmon had explained that she was physically well, not distressed in any way and they were slowly and carefully unravelling the tangle in her mind.

He was lonely because he missed her, but he was depressed because it made him realize how vulnerable and unprotected she was. No parents, no family, not even a distant relative. He was all she had. But he had no standing in law. He was just a friend. He could enquire, but he couldn't demand to be told. He wasn't a husband. And it brought home to him that he was exactly the same. One cousin, God knows how many times removed. Last heard of in Belfast when he was a child. It had never got him down before. His life was too full and too interesting to give it a thought. But he was giving it a lot of thought now.

He spent his mornings at her agency. Helping where he could to keep things going smoothly. In the afternoon he slept or visited the hospital. At night he had the theatre, and on very bad days he brought home a bottle of whisky. He had moved into the girl's flat because it was a small consolation to be surrounded by her things.

It was one of the bad nights that he dialled the Washington number. It rang only twice before the receiver was picked up.

'CIA Langley, can I help you?'

187

For a moment he was so shocked that he couldn't speak, and the voice at the other end said again, 'CIA Langley. Can I help you?'

'I want to speak to Joe Spellman.'

'Who? . . . ah yes. One moment please.'

There were some clicks and a long pause and then a man's voice.

'Can I help you?'

'I want to speak to Joe Spellman.'

There was a pause and then the phone was hung up. He dialled the number again. It rang for almost a minute before a voice cut in. 'International operator, White Plains, can I help you?'

'I want Washington 547-9077.'

'Have you dialled the number?'

'Yes.'

'And what happened?'

'Someone answered but I was cut off.'

'Hold the line. I'll try again for you.'

There was about thirty seconds pause and the girl came back again.

'Would you repeat the number please.'

'Washington 547-9077.'

'I'm sorry, sir. I've checked. There's no such number listed. Do you know the name of the party you're calling?'

'Yes. CIA at Langley.'

'Let me check for you.'

She was back quite quickly. 'That number's not listed for CIA Langley or their office in downtown Washington. I can give you their general enquiries number at Langley if that would help.'

'No thanks. Thank you for trying.'

'You're welcome.'

Randall put down the phone. He didn't sleep that night.

*　　　*　　　*

It was on Boyd's fourth day back that he got the call from Ansell. The doctor didn't want to talk on the phone and suggested that he should fly up to Manchester as soon as possible.

Ansell seemed very nervous when they met in the foyer of The Midland. Not like psychiatrists are supposed to look; and as they walked into the residents' lounge Boyd, without thinking, put his hand on Ansell's shoulder. 'Let me get you a drink.'

The doctor shook his head. 'I'd rather get rid of my little pack of trouble first.'

They sat in the furthest corner in the big leather armchairs and Ansell leaned forward as he started to speak.

'The good bit first. I've found out roughly where this bloody house is supposed to be. It's not Hamburg. It's just outside Hamburg. A place called Harburg. The house is at the edge of a wood and it's been taken over by the army. You can hear the full description on the tapes. I'd say it's enough for you to trace it.'

'What's the bad news?'

'In the first level of hypnosis he calls himself Dickens. He's told me quite a lot about Dickens. Dickens is a hoodlum. A heavy for a gang of villains somewhere in London. I think it's in Shepherd's Bush or near there. But while I was trying to get down to the second level I tried a whole series of words to do with Dickens characters that might be the code into the second level. None of them worked but for a few moments he changed completely and he was talking about being a sergeant in Special Air Services. He was on a firing range somewhere very hot. Sounded more like Africa than England. It sounded to me like there might be even a third level of hypnosis. And this worries me stiff. It's the equivalent of digging around with a scalpel in somebody's brain with a Dunlop touring map for a guide. This chap is in a real mess.'

189

'Does that mean you have to stop?'

'I was considering it, so I phoned around a few research institutes where I know people personally. To see what they knew about multi-level hypnosis. I tried four different places. Three said it was theoretically possible but had never been done. Or they had never heard of it being done. The other one had not only heard about it but had a case of two-level hypnosis right now. I asked them to read me some typical extracts from their notes. And what they read me was straight out of a nightmare. I'll be having nightmares myself before long. The patient was going on about a Captain Ames but this time it was not in Germany but Dublin.'

'What was the chap's name? Had he been in the army?'

'It wasn't a chap, my friend. It was a woman. Thirty-one years old and runs a theatrical agency. Used to be in show-biz herself. You've probably heard of her. Debbie Shaw.'

'Wasn't she a dancer or something? Exotic dancer, whatever that is.'

'She was originally a stripper. Then she was an entertainer. A singer. Was in a touring company that went to the States and various places, putting on shows for American troops.'

'Why is she in hospital?'

'From what I can gather she's got a post-hypnotic leak that's giving her nightmares.'

'Explain to me again what a post-hypnotic leak is.'

'How much do you know about hypnosis?'

Boyd shrugged. 'Virtually nothing.'

'Well, most people can be hypnotized quite easily. It's often referred to as being asleep but the subject is never asleep. They can hear the hypnotist and, of course, they can respond. When somebody is under hypnosis they no longer initiate activity. They do what they are told to do. They accept uncritically what they are told. They stroke cats that aren't there. They can be easily regressed into their

190

childhood. And they can be made to forget what has happened under hypnosis including the fact that they were hypnotized. This is called post-hypnotic amnesia.

'It's possible to make a special feature of ensuring that the subject doesn't remember either the hypnosis or what happened under hypnosis. That's called a post-hypnotic block. Under certain conditions a second or two of hypnotic experience can seep through. That's what we call leaking.'

Boyd nodded. 'And what causes the leaking?'

'Nobody has established that. There's some indication that severe stress or certain types of illness can cause a leak but it's not been scientifically established as yet.'

'What actually happens when they leak?'

Ansell frowned and paused. 'It's hard to explain. It's a bit like the clutch on a car slipping. That's not a bad analogy. Take a man who drives to work every day. Along the same route, day after day. One day he'll look around and he won't see where he is. Suddenly he doesn't recognize what he sees. It's all grown so familiar that it doesn't register any more. He's looked at it every day but he hasn't seen it. Suddenly he sees it and doesn't recognize it. When a hypnotic experience leaks it's a bit like that. For a second or so you're in the wrong place doing something you know you've never done. Then it goes and you're back to normal.' Ansell smiled. 'That's about the best I can do. I've never experienced it.'

'Is it dangerous, or harmful?'

'It depends on what you experience. If it was reasonably normal, then it's maybe disturbing. No more than that. But if the hypnotic experience was horrific then you can have real problems.'

'What kind of problems?'

'I don't know enough to say, but I should imagine that disorientation could develop, a kind of schizophrenia. And depending on the character of the person concerned, you could end up with violent aggression or a complete retreat from reality. Hiding away from a reality that has become frightening.'

'Not good.'

'You're right, my friend. Not good.'

Randall got off the bus in Victoria Street and put up his umbrella. It was only a short walk to the big glass building but it was one of those drenching summer cloudbursts that could soak you in seconds.

He walked through the entrance and was immediately stopped by a policeman.

'Can I help you, sir?'

'I want to speak to a Special Branch officer.'

'Just take a seat, sir. I'll see what we can do.'

Randall was shown to a seat beside a well-grown *monstera deliciosa* and he sat there waiting as the police constable phoned from a sound-proofed plastic hood. And the small video camera in the shadows of the foyer ceiling recorded him on tape.

It was fifteen minutes before a uniformed policewoman escorted him to one of the lifts and up to the fifth floor. There was no name, just a number, on the office door that she opened for him.

The youngish man at the small teak desk stood up. 'Good morning. Would you take a seat?'

There was only one seat by the desk and when Randall had sat down the young man said. 'My name's Cavendish. I understand you wanted to see a Special Branch officer.'

'Are you Special Branch?'

'Yes. Can I have your name first.'

The SB man noted down the routine details and then closed his notebook.

'What is it you wanted?'

'I wanted to report something odd that's happened.'

The SB officer sighed inwardly and wondered whether it would be UFOs or the Bermuda Triangle.

'Please go ahead, Mr Randall.'

Steve Randall went through the whole story of Debbie and the previous night's telephone call.

'Can you remember the telephone number Mr Randall?'

'Yes. It was Washington 547-9077.'

'D'you know if Miss Shaw has ever been in the USA?'

'Yes, she was a singer and entertainer over there.'

'When was this?'

'I don't exactly know. I would guess she came back about eighteen months or two years ago.'

'Where does she work?'

'She's got her own business. A show-biz agency.'

'What hospital is she in?'

'Claunton Road Hospital in Tooting.'

'The name of the doctor?'

'Salmon. Mr Salmon.'

The SB man looked up from his notebook.

'Thank you for telling us, Mr Randall.'

'Will you be looking into it? Checking on it?'

'I should think that's possible.'

'Can you let me know what it's all about?'

'I don't think we could do that. You're not her next of kin or guardian you see.'

'But surely . . . after I've told you this.'

The man got up from his small desk.

'Let's wait and see, shall we. The number might have been given her as a hoax or something like that.'

'But in that case why . . .'

'. . . we'll look into it carefully, Mr Randall. Don't worry.'

Randall wondered, as he waited for a bus, why people

always said, 'Don't worry,' when you obviously were worried, and had good cause to be. He wondered if he had done right in telling them. Or could it make it even worse for Debbie?

19

Boyd sat reading the Joint Intelligence summary as he waited for the computer to print out the details he had asked for. There was always a section at the end with odds and ends of information from various sources that were not connected with any particular operation or related to a specific intelligence area. He read it half-heartedly until the bottom of the second page.

ITEM 43. PRAGUE. Apartment No. 17 at 27 Letenska has been positively identified as being occupied by Major KRETSKI KGB. OC communications Moscow–Prague. It is also occupied by his mistress Maria HASAK. See JICS 451/Item 19.

ITEM 44. Information requested by CIA regarding present whereabouts of James PARKINSON. a.k.a. Johnny PALMER. Ex-employee of AIR INDIA in their Paris office.

ITEM 45. Information requested from Hamburg office of BfV regarding signals traffic in code on 15,322 MHz. Tuesdays and Thursdays 21.04 hours from area English Channel believed Isle of Wight. Through liaison Bonn only.

ITEM 46. Information requested on British subject Deborah SHAW. Informant claims she was given special CIA telephone number whilst under hypnosis. Information to SB direct at NSY.

Boyd reached for the telephone and dialled SB liaison.

Boyd called in at Century House on the way home and phoned Ansell in Manchester. Ansell had left the hospital and was on his way home. Ten minutes later Boyd tried the Wilmslow number.

'Ansell here.'

'This is Boyd. Did you get any more information on the girl?'

'Yes. She's held under the Mental Health Act 1959 Section 72. That means that she's no longer a voluntary patient. They can keep her in there as long as they want. And nobody, parents, husband, can get her out. Only the Home Secretary himself could get her released.'

'How do they do that?'

'Two doctors certify that she is mentally ill and needs to be held in a mental institution for her own safety and the safety of the general public.'

'You mean two doctors can just put somebody in a mental hospital and nobody can appeal?'

'Nobody can appeal. But in the first place somebody would have to make the application for her to be detained.'

'And who could do that?'

'If she was an offender, a magistrates' court or another court could issue an order. Or some other official or official body could apply.'

'Is there any indication of who applied in this case?'

'Yes. The application was made by the Home Secretary's Office.'

'What's it got to do with him?'

'That's just the official channels. The Home Office could offer a dozen reasons that would be accepted. There's something wrong with all this you know, Jimmy. It stinks.'

'Of what?'

196

'Of you and your people. The establishment. A cover-up. Something sinister.'

'It's not me or my people, I assure you. I desperately want to talk to her and the hospital have point blank refused to let me talk to her or even see her.'

'That's all very well, but this girl went in there as a voluntary patient. No Section 72. No nothing. She could walk out any time she wanted. I hear about her. They're going to send me all the medical notes. And I tell *you*, my friend. And two days later I get the notes. And the next day – the very next day – she's a Section 72 patient. It's too much to swallow, Jimmy. Either you're playing games or someone else is. But I ain't going to join. Just count me out.'

'Can I see the notes?'

There was a long pause. 'I suppose so. If I refuse you'll get them some other way. But there's very little in them for you, it's mostly medical tests.'

'Can you send me a copy to my home address?'

'If that's what you want.'

'How's George Walker?'

'No, you don't get me helping on that one. There's not going to be any Section 72 dropped on him. Only over my dead body.'

'Ansell, I'm investigating what's happened to your patient. Believe me, we're both on the same side. And that means the establishment is on our side. If you can find out more about who ordered the detaining of the girl I'll look into it.'

For a few moments there was silence at the other end and then Ansell said, 'I can tell you who ordered it, Boyd. Salmon and the other doctor were leaned on. Heavily. Virtually threatened. The application was from the Foreign Office. A guy named Carter signed it. It was passed to the Home Office and they just rubber-stamped it through the system. Do you get the message now? Either the left hand doesn't know what the right hand's up to, or you're playing games with me as well as with the girl.'

'I assure you it's not me playing games, Ansell. I'll start checking on it.'

'You didn't sound surprised.'

'Nothing surprises me, Ansell. Not any more. But I still need your cooperation.'

'I'll send you a copy of the medical notes. After that I'll need a lot of persuading.'

For two days Boyd tried to check discreetly on what operation Carter's units were working on. He was able to trace a section operating in Cairo and two in the Far East who had been there for over six months, but Carter himself was 'not available' officially, and that meant that further checking, however subtle, would certainly be reported to the top. The top brass were never too happy about most of Carter's operations but SIS couldn't operate successfully without them, and they gave him whatever protection and security was possible. The Deputy Under Secretary had once responded to the distaste expressed by a Prime Minister for Carter's thugs, as being the distaste of those who complained about abattoirs but still relished a good steak.

Slowly and painstakingly he wrote down a list of the basic information he had accumulated about Walker and Debbie Shaw. He listed separately the loose ends of information that seemed to lead nowhere and finally he wrote out a column headed 'What I want to know'. There was no entry under that column. He had no idea of where it was all going or what he wanted to know. He was just stumbling around in a strange, misty wood, bumping into a tree now and again. For the sake of routine he wrote – 'Who and why?'

He knew what his next move had to be, but he hesitated about taking it. It could open it up so wide that the whole thing would get out of hand. But instinct and experience

198

told him that it was already out of hand. Maybe phoning Schultz would cut it back to size.

Boyd had compared notes with Mercer at Special Branch Liaison. Their information was overlapping except for Randall's details of the alleged CIA number which Boyd took down.

He checked in his own notebook for the CIA at Langley and reached for the phone.

He dialled carefully and when the Langley telephone operator replied he asked for extension 2971.

'Schultz.'

'Hi, Otto . . . Boyd . . . SIS.'

'Hi Jimmy. Where are you?'

'I'm in London.'

'Are you coming over?'

'No. But I need some information, off the record.'

'Go ahead.'

'I've got two cases I'm investigating. Both concern people who could possibly have been used under hypnosis for intelligence work. One of them's a girl. Her name's Debbie Shaw. She was given a phone number to ring in Washington if she ever needed a doctor, and was told to ask for a Joe Spellman. The number was Washington 547-9077. Her boy-friend dialled this number and whoever replied said it was CIA Langley. When he asked for Joe Spellman he was put through to a man, and when he asked again for Joe Spellman they hung up. He dialled the number again and after some palaver with the White Plains operator she said there was no such number listed and it certainly wasn't CIA Langley or the office on Pennsylvania Avenue. Could you do a check on that number for me?'

'Sure. Any chance it was a wrong number he dialled?'

'Could be, but I don't think so.'

'I'll see what I can ferret out.'

'Otto . . . can you keep this to yourself?'

199

'Sure. What's bugging you?'

'I don't know. Just a feeling in my bones.'

'OK. How's the beautiful Katie?'

'Fine. You and yours OK?'

'They're fine. I'll come back to you.'

It was three days before Schultz called back and Boyd could hear the hesitation in his voice.

'Is that you, Jimmy?'

'Yes. It's me, Otto.'

'That query you raised with me. How far d'you want to go with it?'

'I don't understand.'

'Let's say it's kind of complex.'

'That means the number was for real.'

'It's for real all right. But it's not in my area.'

'Can you pass me on to whoever's responsible?'

'There's problems involved in doing that.'

'Like what?'

'Like trouble.'

'For you or for me?'

'Both of us, I guess.'

'I'm being dumb, Otto. I haven't got the message.'

'Let me ask you a question. Are you going to carry on these investigations no matter what?'

'Of course.'

'What if you were told to lay off?'

'Nobody's going to suggest that, Otto.'

'Don't be too sure. The ice is very thin at this end. Maybe I should come over and talk with you. How about that?'

'That would be fine. Are you sure it's necessary?'

'I'm sure all right. When can you fit me in?'

'As soon as you can make it.'

'Tomorrow?'

'Yes.'

'OK. I'll be on Concorde. Can you meet me in?'

'I'll be there.'

'See you.'

He stood watching as Schultz came through Immigration and Customs. He looked more like a farmer than a senior officer of the CIA. His family were farmers, or had been until oil came to Olney, when their five hundred acres, modest by Texan standards, became the next best thing to a gold-mine. They still ran several hundred steers on the land but it was more from cussedness than necessity. Otto, the eldest of three sons, had practised as a lawyer in Austin for three years before he was lured into the CIA.

Then Schultz was waving to him as he came through the glass doors to the reception area.

'It's good to see you, Jimmy.'

'Good to see you too. I've got the car outside.'

'Is it parked OK?'

'Yes. Why?'

'I'd like to have a talk with you here before we get on to an official basis.'

'Let's have a meal in the restaurant.'

'Whatever you say.'

Despite his curiosity Boyd waited until they had got to the coffee before he got down to business.

'Tell me what all the song and dance is about, Otto?'

'This part's just between you and me. Off the record completely. Not to be repeated, or I'll swear I never said a word out of place.'

'Sounds grim.'

Schultz nodded. 'Maybe you've hit the right word there, pal. Anyway let me give you the picture. I checked on your number. Very discreetly, and got nowhere. It didn't exist. I dialled it myself and it didn't answer or even ring. So I probed a bit deeper.' Schultz paused to light a cigar. 'D'you ever meet a guy named Grabowski while you were over with us?'

'I remember the name but I'm not sure if I met him. It rings a bell. I've got an idea he was an observer down at Camp Peary when I was there on a visit.'

'That's the guy. Well now, Grabowski is CIA and a senior man. About the same level as me. But he's got a lot more clout than I've got. In certain directions anyway. And that's because of his job. Although he's as official as I am he works outside the official area. I hate the description "dirty tricks" but that's Grabowski's job. He protects his heavies from outsiders. Including protecting them from the FBI and State Police. He supervises what they do. If CIA top brass want something doing that's unconstitutional or illegal they just nod to Grabowski. He's a kind of cut-out. If anything came out it's Grabowski who'd get chopped. Nobody higher up could be blamed because they didn't give him any orders to do anything naughty. He's a kind of fuse. He blows but the circuit stays intact. OK?'

Boyd nodded without speaking.

'Your Washington telephone number is one that's used by Grabowski's mob. One of many all round the country. I did some checking with a pal of mine in communications and in fact it's one of a couple of dozen numbers that aren't even controlled by the CIA. They are controlled by a special high-security team from Fort George Meade. The National Security Agency. These numbers have all sorts of uses that vary from time to time depending on what's going on behind the scenes with Grabowski. I spent twenty-eight solid hours checking what your particular number was used for.' Schultz paused and then looked at Boyd's face. 'I wish I hadn't.'

Boyd waited for him to go on but he didn't, he just looked morosely at the cigar he was stubbing out in the ash-tray.

'You'd better tell me, Otto.'

Schultz looked up, and his sigh was deep and heart-felt. 'Now remember what I'm saying. I can't prove this; and

202

if I could I'd end up in the river. That number was a last resort contact for the Mafia in the six months before John F. Kennedy was assassinated. A last resort contact with the CIA. There's no record I can find of the traffic on that line, but there is a phone-log in the archives that shows that, last resort or not, it was in constant use from June 1963 rising to a peak in November of that year, after the President was killed. Then the number lay more or less dormant until early May in 1968. Bobbie Kennedy was killed in LA in June 1968, since when that particular number has hardly carried a couple of dozen calls.' Schultz pursed his big lips. 'Are you getting the drift of all this, my friend?'

'No. Not for my problem anyway.'

'I'm coming to your bit. With an emergency number as important as that the technicians put in a switching device. It has a list of numbers in sequence of importance that incoming calls are switched to if there is nobody manning the main number. Anybody on that line has a separate telephone that responds to that number only. You can't make outgoing calls on it even, so that it's always free. It was obvious by now that I wasn't going to get anywhere with a straight enquiry so I called in some old, old debts that were owing me and I got the list of all those alternative numbers. Their actual normal phone numbers.

'The first number was Grabowski. The second was one of Grabowski's senior men named Costello. The third was a CIA doctor named Symons. A psychiatrist. The fourth was a CIA doctor named Petersen. Also a psychiatrist. The rest don't matter so far as you're concerned, but they interested me.

'I then did another piece of checking on your stuff. I got a list from the Pentagon of dates and places where this Debbie Shaw performed. In a period of about eighteen months Symons was at the same camp as she was, on twelve occasions. I moved over to Immigration records and the print-out shows she came in and out at least four times after

203

she ceased to be a performer. And that's it, friend. That's how it is tonight, as Cronkite says.'

As Boyd sat there absorbing Schultz's information he remembered the words that Walker had said to Ansell – 'You don't like the Kennedys, do you?'

'What do we do, Otto? Where do we go from here?'

'If I had any sense I'd catch the next Pan Am flight out of here and go fishing for a month. How about your side? Has my information slotted into your piece at all?'

'There's a lot of indications that one or both of the psychiatrists are over here. The ex-soldier and the girl have been used under hypnosis in the last two years. The girl had been used in the last four months. I'm almost certain of that. And it can't be a coincidence that the guy you mentioned – Symons – was at the camps when she was. It was too often to be coincidence.'

'Go on.'

'You know what I'm driving at.'

'Maybe I do. But I want you to say it, not me.'

'This guy Symons is the direct connection. He can tell us what's been going on. He needn't talk about any US aspects. Just the UK scenario.'

'You don't think he'll actually talk do you?'

'Why not?'

'You realize what he's been involved in?'

'More or less.'

'You don't, James. But I guess that's understandable. I've already tried to trace Symons and Petersen. So far as CIA records are concerned they don't exist.'

'But you said you'd checked on the army camps where he and the girl had been.'

'I also said that those were Pentagon records. It was an accident that those existed. The CIA obviously don't realize they exist. They weren't operational records but nominal rolls so that rations and allowances can be drawn for officers and men accommodated at a camp. Routine administration. If he'd been a civilian on a camp his name would still have gone on the rolls. But he's not on CIA records any more. Not even the confidential ones. Because he's been stashed away somewhere. We've got dozens of official committees from the Senate downwards still investigating the Kennedy murders. And private investigation committees by the score. Journalists, broadcasters, private citizens. They're all in the Kennedy industry. It's my guess they daren't leave him around for anyone to question."

'Why not?'

'Oh for God's sake, Jimmy. His name's third on a switch list for a secret telephone number for the sole use of the mob and the CIA. Isn't that enough?'

'You mean he was part of an assassination plot?'

'I'm saying nothing, my friend. You read the books. Draw your own conclusions but don't ask me mine.'

'So why tell me all this if I can't use it?'

'I didn't say you can't *use* it. I just said you can't tell anybody else no matter who they are, what I've told you. How you use it is up to you.'

'Are you disturbed by all this, Otto?'

'I'm angry. I'm outraged by it. But I ain't gonna do a thing about it.'

'Why not?'

'Because I'm scared.'

And he pulled his passport out of his inside jacket pocket and opened it. It was made out in the name of Paul Jackson. When Boyd looked back at Schultz's face, he said, 'Thanks for putting me in the picture. Have you told anybody your end?'

'Not a soul. I wouldn't last two days.'

'You're sure it's as rough as that?'

'Quite sure. And if you're wise you'll take the same view. Have you told anyone I was coming over?'

'No.'

'Katie?'

'Nobody at all.'

'I'll go straight back tonight then. There's a flight in about an hour. I'll stay on my own. There'll be people around who might recognize me and I can lie that away, but not if they see me with you.'

'If you do get any more information will you pass it on to me?'

'Maybe. I don't promise I will. One last thing. I suggest that nothing about your investigation is passed to your liaison officer at Langley and nothing goes in the routine exchange of information summary. The item you saw could start them off if anybody reads the damned thing and it rings a bell. And remember if they go for you it won't just be the heavy boys, the top brass will have given their blessing. Don't imagine for a moment that you can debate the rights and wrongs with them. For them there will be only one right and that will be you – dead. There's too much at stake for them to do anything else even if it means knocking off a hundred people instead of just one.'

'But at least half a dozen people must know right now.'

'More than that, pal. Far more than that. But they've all got a heavy investment in forgetting what's happened. If you're wise you'll join 'em. Tell your boss that it's a dead end and you're wasting funds and time.'

Boyd half-smiled. 'Thanks a lot, Otto. See you.' And he stood up and walked away.

20

It was midnight when he got back to the flat and she'd waited up for him. There were three canvases propped up along the front of the settee. They were arranged so that he would see them as soon as he came in. He closed the door and leaned back against it looking at the paintings. They were of the creeks around Chichester. Bosham, Itchenor and Dell Quay. Thick but smooth *impasto* done with a palette knife, long tapering masts that took your eyes up to the solid blue skies and foregrounds that reeked of mud and mosses cradling the hulls of rotting dinghies and converted lifeboats.

He turned and saw her standing at the bedroom door, smiling. Smiling at his interest, and smiling with her own pleasure of knowing the paintings worked.

'They're beautiful, Katie.'

'D'you really like them?'

'They're beautiful as paintings, and wonderful in how you've made them seem to have movement. The boats just moving on the water. The breeze in the reeds and the sky, like you're lying on deck on your back.'

'Two are sold already.'

'Which two?'

'That's for you to decide. One's for you. Whichever one you prefer.'

'The one of Bosham.'

'I guessed you'd choose that one. Have you eaten?'

'Yes.'

'Let's have a drink to celebrate my sales.'

He poured them a generous whisky each and she sat on his lap on the armchair.

'Are you tired, James?'

'So, so.'

'You look tired. Or something.'

'It must be something.'

'You look a bit down. Is everything OK?'

He smiled gently. 'It's never really OK, my love. We only get what's not OK. And when we've made it OK we start on another new shambles.'

'Cartwright phoned. He said it was nothing important. He's a bit of a flirt your Cartwright, you know. Why hasn't he ever married?'

'He has. He married a Stradivarius when he was about sixteen.'

'How long are you staying this time?'

'I'm not sure. At least another two days.'

'Are you sure there's nothing wrong?'

'What's worrying you?'

'You. You've seemed far away these last two days. As if you weren't really here. I've seen you worried before, but not like this.'

'It won't be much longer, Katie.'

'So you are worried.'

'I guess so.'

'Can you tell me? Even vaguely.'

'No.' He sighed. 'I wish I could.'

'Let's go to bed.'

She lay in bed with her arms round him but they didn't make love, and for the first time since they were married she was scared. He had never before said that he wished he could tell her what concerned him. Usually when he was worried he was on edge, pacing around, unable to keep still, but she had never seen him like this before, uneasy, uncertain, barely listening or comprehending when she

208

spoke to him. His usual response was to snap out of his mood and take her out. But tonight he seemed lethargic. At the end of his tether, totally preoccupied by whatever his problem was. It was all out of character. He was always so self-confident, so self-assured. In control of himself and whatever problems he had. Maybe he had done something that might cause him to be dismissed the service. But they seldom did that. You got shunted to one side. To a desk job or a routine job. It was a long time before she slept, and when she woke the next morning he had already left. She turned to look at the alarm and it was only seven o'clock.

Boyd pressed the bell at the side of the door and waited. If Randall was there he would probably still be asleep. It was several minutes before the door opened and he recognized Randall from the routine description.

'Mr Randall?'

'Who are you?'

'I wondered if you could spare me a few minutes to talk?'

'No. I don't know you.'

And Boyd could see the almost empty whisky bottle and the glass on the table inside the room.

'My name's Boyd, Mr Randall. I think you could help me and maybe I could help you.'

'I don't need any help. What d'you want to talk about?'

'I wanted to talk to you about Debbie. Debbie Shaw.'

Randall was shaking his head as Boyd pulled out his ID card and held it up for Randall to see. Randall's mouth was open and he stank of whisky as he half closed his eyes to look at the card. He belched and looked back at Boyd's face, his eyes trying to focus.

'They send you from the hospital?'

'No. I'm nothing to do with the hospital.'

'The police?'

'No. It says on my card what I am. I'm an intelligence officer.'

'What's she . . . I don't understand.'

'Can I come in and explain?'

Randall shrugged helplessly and stood aside as Boyd walked inside and closed the door.

'You want a snifter?'

'No thanks. Just a chat.'

'You just chat away, pal. I'll be listening.'

'Would you like me to make you coffee?'

Randall half-grinned. 'You wanna sober me up. Is that it?'

'I've read the report you gave to Special Branch, Mr Randall. They seem to be keeping her in hospital a long time. I'm a bit worried about it.'

'Join the club, old man. I'm out of my bloody mind with worry, but there's nothing I can do. Not a relative, they say.'

'Has she got any relatives at all?'

'Nary a one. Nary a one.'

'Did you know that she's being held on a Section 72?'

'What's a Section 72?'

'It means that she can be held indefinitely in a mental institution and that she has ceased to be a voluntary patient. There's no appeal against such an order and only the Home Secretary can vary it.'

'Why are they doing this to her?'

'That's what I want to find out.'

'How can I help?'

'I don't know. I just want to talk to you. Talk about her. Every detail you can remember.'

'Why are you interested, Boyd?'

'I want to talk to Debbie myself. I think she could help me with something I'm investigating. You're the next best thing.'

'Let me take a bath and get sobered up and then I'll be able to talk.'

He talked with Randall for almost three hours. Not

gaining much information that would help his investigation, but he saw photographs of the girl and learned a lot about her. Irrelevant detail so far as his enquiry was concerned, but details that made him feel that he actually knew the girl.

As he sat in the taxi on the way back to Hampstead he thought about Randall. He was a strangely sad man, still with enough show-business panache to try and find some silver lining to his cloud, but so clearly failing. And so patently defenceless and unhappy. Randall seemed to have had a mutually satisfying but odd relationship with Debbie Shaw. He spoke about her as if the relationship was quite normal but it obviously wasn't. They had several roles for each other. The man was lover, brother and father, and the girl was mother, lover and friend. Neither of them seemed to have demanded much from the other and yet they seemed totally dependent on each other. Their lives had gone on day by day in a routine that suited them both. Both of them secure in their lives of business and pleasure. Not looking for anything more than that it would go on for ever. And then suddenly, shockingly, it had all ended. The girl's mental disturbance would have been blow enough, but Randall was now the victim as well. A victim of bureaucracy that gave him no status, no part even, in the girl's life. They were related by neither marriage nor blood and bureaucracy was impervious to claims of affection, love or dependence.

Boyd found it unusually depressing. He never allowed himself to be emotionally involved with anyone connected with his work no matter whether he was for them or against them, but there was something strangely familiar about Randall and his girl. He knew what it was, but he kept it lodged firmly at the back of his mind. Steve Randall and Debbie Shaw reminded him too much of Katie and Jimmy Boyd.

The phone at his bedside rang at three o'clock in the

morning, two days after Schultz had gone back. It was Schultz calling from an El Paso number.

'Is that you, Jimmy?'

'Yes.'

'I'm sorry if I seemed rough on you the other day. I guess I was being selfish. I thought about it on the plane coming back. Anyway it was wrong thinking on my part. I've done some fishing around for you down here in Texas. I gotta talk in parables, you understand?'

'Go ahead.'

'The doctor I recommended to you is right where you are now. You heard of a place called Northumberland?'

'Yes.'

'A town called Craster. The residence is Percy House. And the other doctor on our recommended list is there too. You might think they're Canadians if you didn't know any better. OK?'

'Yes. Message received and understood. And much appreciated. Are they here for long?'

'Indefinitely. But I'd guess they're being well looked after.'

'I owe you, Otto.'

'You sure do.'

And the line went dead. Boyd got out of bed quietly and padded bare-footed into the sitting-room. He sat on the couch, his head in his hands. Not in despair, but to exclude all distractions from his mind. He had arrived, he knew, at the point where he should not only report back to Cartwright, but get his opinion on what the next move should be. But if he did that Cartwright would have no choice but to refer upwards because of Carter's move against the girl. And then, almost certainly, the investigation would be called off. Carter's business nearly always took precedence over routine operations. And whatever games Carter was playing he'd put a stop to this investigation. In the past agents had argued their cases with skill or

212

anger according to temperament but Boyd could only remember two cases where Carter had failed to win the day.

If this investigation was called off George Walker was never going to live a normal life and he'd never even know why. And Debbie Shaw, a pretty girl, would never come out of that mental research unit. Even if she did she was always going to be vulnerable. Always under tensions that she didn't understand that would send her poor brain back to its nightmares. They had been ruthlessly abused, the two of them. And they were totally innocent. Picked almost at random, and methodically turned into zombies. No rewards, no praise, no pensions, no medals, they could be abandoned when they were no longer of use. Abandoned with a slow fuse burning to the bomb inside their brains.

So telling Cartwright was out. At this stage anyway. He didn't know enough about what the two had been used for and how to convince Cartwright to stand up against Carter. That meant that he had no real choice. He had to find out what had been done. Symons and Petersen were probably the only ones who knew.

He dressed and shaved slowly and worked out the first stage of what he had to do.

The armoury officer placed the two guns side by side on the table. One was a Walther and the other a Smith and Wesson snub-nosed Magnum.

'They've both been stripped and re-calibrated, sir.'

Boyd nodded, pursing his lips as he looked down at the two guns. They were both double-actioned and he was used to both models. He would have preferred the Smith and Wesson just because revolvers were more reliable than pistols. But there were too many protuberances that could snag on a pocket or a sleeve. He pointed and said, 'I'll take the PPK.'

'Right, sir. How many rounds do you want?'

'How do they pack them now?'

'Same as before, Mr Boyd. Packs of fifty and a hundred.'

'I'll take four fifties and a spare magazine.'

The armourer raised his eyebrows but said nothing as he turned away to the metal shelves. Two hundred rounds was a bit above the odds. Boyd sent him back for a pair of handcuffs.

From Facilities he drew a miniature transceiver with an electret speaker, and from Finance he drew an Amex card and a Barclaycard and £300 in cash. He walked in the drizzle from Century House to the bridge and hailed a taxi. He felt depressed and guilty leaving London and not seeing or phoning Katie. But there would be too much to explain and he needed to keep all the pieces of the jigsaw constantly in his mind or they would slip away again as they had done so often on this operation. Most operations went in sequence. A led to B, and B to C. But this operation was disjointed. Almost nothing that he uncovered seemed to connect to anything he already knew. It was almost as if two, or even three, different operations had got mixed up somewhere. Every ladder seemed to lead to a snake's head and back to square one.

He bought two drip-dry shirts, some underwear, and half a dozen pairs of socks and stuffed them in the canvas holdall with the gun and the other hardware. At St Pancras station he booked a sleeper and had a meal at the station hotel. Twice he got as far as putting a coin in the phone-box meter to phone Katie, and twice he reluctantly removed it and walked back to the lounge. An hour later the train rumbled out on its way to Newcastle.

It was six o'clock when the train pulled into the station at Newcastle Central and Boyd walked to the station hotel, bathed and shaved and breakfasted. At eight o'clock he walked to the roundabout and crossed the road to the police station. He showed his card, but the duty Special Branch man was not expected until mid-day.

214

The CID checked with several estate agents for the ownership of Percy House. The house was in the name of a family trust and was let on long lease to two Canadians. Their references said that they were both doctors from Kingston University, Ontario, on a two-year sabbatical. They were both writing books. One was Anthony Smith and the other was Peter Pardoe, and the lease was joint and several. There had been no complaints about damage from the quarterly inspection and the payments had been prompt and in advance.

The estate agency which had been responsible for the letting sent round the sales details of the house, a set of plans that had been done in 1920, and a couple of up-to-date photographs of the front of the house. When he saw the size of the house and grounds Boyd was sure that there would be servants. CID phoned the local constable who confirmed that a married couple lived in a converted outbuilding about fifty yards from the house. Their name was Chatton and they had worked at the house for ten years. He sent out to the bookshop for a six inch to the mile Ordnance Survey map covering Craster, and the three adjoining sheets.

He waited until noon but the Special Branch man hadn't shown up and Boyd walked down to Neville Street and hired a Rover 3500. At the supermarket at Gosforth he bought several packs of long-life milk, coffee, cheese, bread, butter, and half a dozen tins of pressed meat. A tin-opener and a knife, a razor, blades, shaving foam and a Camping Gaz heater completed his purchases.

An hour later he stopped to check the map, and a mile further on he was at the level-crossing at Littlemill and ten minutes later he slowed down as he approached the entrance to the driveway of Percy House. There was no name-sign, and he could see only the tiled roof and the chimneys. He turned right, on to a rough farm track and stopped the car. He could see the back of the house clearly, and the outbuildings, but there was no evidence of anyone in the house.

He reversed the car back down the road and headed south-west for Alnwick. He found what he wanted in the market square. A chemists and opticians that sold microscopes and binoculars. They hadn't got what he wanted but they could get it in two hours from their main shop in Newcastle.

Boyd had a leisurely coffee and then went to the main estate agents and asked about a cottage or a house on a short let. There were two. A large house at Wooler, and a cottage just a couple of miles south of Seahouses. They were honest enough to point out that it was isolated and the only access was a cinder track from the road. It had been the cowman's cottage when it was part of the farm. It was £10 a week for a minimum let of a month. He paid cash and they gave him the keys and instructions for finding the cottage. By the time he had finished at the estate agents the binoculars were waiting for him, and he paid by Barclaycard in the name of G. H. Merrick, one of SIS's favourite pseudonyms.

There were clumps of weeds, wild-parsley, thistles and couchgrass growing in the cinder track as the car crunched its way noisily towards the cottage. He sat in the car looking at the cottage before he got out. There was nothing picturesque or pretty about it. It was built of local stone with small windows and a grey slate roof. The windows were grey with dust and there was ivy growing over the blue-painted wooden front door.

He got out and walked round the cottage. There was a small orchard of very old apple trees, and a vegetable plot with Brussels sprouts that had gone to seed the season before and now stood three feet high in a dense jungle of rotting leaves. There were two milk bottles outside the back door and a pile of rotting windfalls by a wooden water butt

216

standing on four cinder blocks. But the big old-fashioned key turned smoothly in the door and it opened easily into the quarry-tiled kitchen and parlour. There was a Rayburn stove and a small electric double ring alongside the sink. The walls were at least eighteen inches thick.

21

Boyd switched off the lights, parked the car close to the hawthorn hedge and walked up the farm track, ducking under the wire strands into the field that led to the grounds of Percy House. He walked slowly, stumbling from time to time in the dark on the tussocky grass, until he came to the low stone wall that marked the edge of the farmland.

He could see the house now. There were lights in the downstairs rooms and he made his way across the well-kept lawns to a magnolia, and then on again to a group of three tall cupressus that marked the edge of the lawn. The gravel driveway was about ten feet wide and there was no cover until he got to the shadows of the house itself. He stood watching the house and he could hear faintly the sound of a piano.

It seemed an interminable walk across the gravel and despite his efforts the noise of his feet on the loose stones sounded outrageous in the stillness of the night. There were rose bushes in the border along the walls that snagged at his clothes, and it took ten minutes before he could look cautiously into the room. It was a big room lit by two large crystal chandeliers, sparsely but elegantly furnished. The polished oak floor gave it the appearance of an artist's studio.

He was looking across the top of a grand piano, its lid propped open. And a man was playing, easily and confidently, moving from one tune to another. From 'Smoke Gets in Your Eyes' to 'Try a Little Tenderness'. He was alone in the room, intent on his playing and as he changed key into 'Manhattan' Boyd saw that he was singing the words to himself. Smiling as he sang. For a brief moment the man looked towards the window, directly at where Boyd was standing.

Boyd guessed that the man was in his middle forties; his black hair smoothed back, the first signs of baldness at the temples. His face was so smooth and shiny that he could have been wearing make-up, and his dark eye-lashes were like a girl's, long and sweeping as he looked down at the keyboard. He played a few bars of 'Moon River' and then he stopped, stood up, closed the piano lid and walked across the room, switching out the lights as he left.

When Boyd moved on along the back wall he came to another lit window. A small window with drawn gingham curtains. Through the gap in the curtains he saw that it was a big old-fashioned kitchen. The pianist and another man were sitting at a table and an elderly woman was serving them food, smiling at something one of them had said. The other man was tall, wearing a sweater and jeans. The fair hair, blue eyes and square shoulders gave him a Scandinavian air. He was looking up, talking to the woman.

Boyd moved back to the narrow grass border that edged the drive and followed it round the house. At the far corner an open archway led into a cobbled yard and in the darkness he could see the silhouette of the outbuildings where the two servants lived. He was about to move on when he heard the back door open. As he pressed back into the shadow of the archway the woman went past, humming to herself, a shopping basket in her hand. When the light went on in the servants' quarters Boyd moved on. There were no windows on the ground floor on that side of the house and when he came to the front of the house he saw that he would be too exposed to check it carefully. He moved on quickly to the long window on the far side of the big main door and saw that there was a large hall, and in

219

the faint light from an open door he saw the broad stairs that led to the first floor. From the size of the house he guessed that there would be five or six bedrooms. Slowly and silently he made his way back to the car.

Back at the cottage he tried to work out a plan as he sipped his coffee. Despite the warm night it was unpleasantly cold inside the cottage and he walked outside, the mug of coffee in his hand. He could use the old ploy of checking meters or maybe pretend to be doing an inspection for the estate agency who managed the property. Both would give him a chance to look the place over. But it was wasting time and what did he expect to find? There was probably nothing there. They didn't need anything to hypnotize the girl and the soldier. There was obviously no guard on the place, not even a dog. And suddenly he felt quite calm. He was being stupid. He didn't know enough to decide how to tackle them. There was urgency, but even a week would make little difference. He put the empty mug on top of the water butt and listened to the night sounds. There were faint rustlings in the long grass under the apple trees and from somewhere near wood-pigeons cooed softly. And from far away he heard the long low roar of a train on the main-line to London.

It was still dark when he woke. He'd dreamed that Katie was running towards him on a sandy beach, her hair streaming, her arms outstretched and he hadn't been able to move, and as she ran towards him she seemed to get farther and farther away. It wasn't frightening, just strange, and he switched on the bedside lamp and looked at his watch. He had only slept for three hours and as he lay back on the pillows he knew that his thinking last night had been wrong. He couldn't wait around, he had to go straight in. Something could happen to Walker or the girl, or the two men could disappear. His eyes closed, and it was eight o'clock before he woke.

He spent the morning in Alnwick buying food and

220

various things he might need. He phoned the SB man at Newcastle to get him duplicate keys for the main door and the bedrooms of Percy House. He would collect them from the police station at Alnwick. He went to The White Swan at lunchtime and froze when he saw the pianist with a pretty girl at the bar. Despite realizing that the man would have no idea who he was, he left and went back to the market square and ate at the small café. He picked up the keys at the police station, signed for them, and went back to his car.

He laid out all the things he would need on the kitchen table, checking them carefully before he loaded them into the boot of the car and locked it. As he undressed he set the alarm on his watch for seven o'clock.

Just after midnight the last of the lights had gone out and Boyd started the car, drove down to the coast road and turned so that the car would be facing the right way for when he left. They didn't look as if they would be a problem but the quicker he could leave the easier it would be. He stopped the car just past the entrance to the driveway. The nylon ropes and the torch were on the passenger seat beside him. The Walther was in his right-hand jacket pocket. When he got out he opened all the car doors very slightly after he had switched off the parking lights.

He walked up the road until he guessed he was opposite the house and then climbed over the low dry-stone wall. The moon was full, and when he saw the house it looked almost as if it were floodlit. Treading slowly and deliberately he walked down the slope towards the house, across the drive and over to the porch. The porch was in deep shadow and he shone the torch on the lock as he gently pushed in the key. It turned easily and when he moved the handle he felt a soft gust of cold air as the door opened. He left the door slightly ajar and he shone the torch around the big square hall.

221

The stairs creaked alarmingly despite his keeping well against the wall, but nobody stirred. The bedroom facing the top of the stairs was locked, and he tried several keys in the lock. The third one turned the tumblers and he opened the door slowly. There was a smell of stale smoke, and he guessed it was not used as a bedroom. He shaded the torch with his hand and saw that the room was unoccupied. He found the switch, turned on the light and closed the door.

There were two trestle tables in the centre of the room. The kind that decorators use. They were piled with papers and books, with a space cleared for a portable typewriter. Against the far wall was a projection screen on a metal tripod. A slide projector and a 16mm sound projector were on a metal stand at the side of a metal filing cabinet. There were three worn armchairs and on an otherwise empty bookshelf was a small portable radio.

Boyd walked quietly over to the tables and looked at the titles of the books without touching them. *The Manufacture of Madness* by Thomas Szasz, *A Handbook of Contemporary Soviet Psychology*, and *Conditioned Reflexes* by I. P. Pavlov. He opened one of the file covers and turned over a few pages. They were typed, and the names in the text were in capitals which made them leap out from the page. He read the first line on the page twice.

'. . . the hypnosis programming of LEE HARVEY OSWALD was less complex. He carried out the instructions exactly, but the shooting of patrolman TIPPIT was an echo reflex. It was clear from the transcript of his interrogation at Dallas Police Station that there was no possibility of him recalling either the act or the hypnosis. Only fear on the part of the secondary collaborators outside CIA caused the killing of OSWALD by RUBY. This unnecessary action prevented us from continuing the . . .'

Boyd closed the file carefully and looked at the second

file. Every page was a graph or tables of figures. He took the first file and tucked it under his arm. That could be his equivalent of an insurance policy. He listened carefully at the next bedroom door but there was no sound from inside. He opened the door and put on his torch. It was a much smaller room, furnished as a bedroom with a single bed. There was nobody in it and he closed the door.

His hand was reaching for the old-fashioned brass handle on the next bedroom door when he heard a noise inside the room. The click of metal on glass and soft shuffling, and then the door opened. A man stood there, his eyes half open, a tumbler in his hand. He was wearing a red dressing gown draped over his shoulders. The man blinked and said thickly, 'Are you one of Carter's men?' Then he saw the gun in Boyd's hand. 'Say. What is this?'

'Go back in your room. Keep your voice down.' Boyd touched the muzzle of the Walther to the man's naked belly. He backed away slowly and raised his arms. There was a sweater and slacks on a chair by the bed.

'Put those on.' Boyd pointed at the clothes.

As he pulled on his shoes the man said, 'Just tell me who you are and what you want. There's no need for all this . . .' he shrugged '. . . whatever it is.'

'What's your name?'

'Smith. I'm just a doctor on leave.'

'Stand up.'

And as the man stood up Boyd knew that the handcuffs and the nylon rope wouldn't be necessary. He would come quietly enough.

Boyd looked at the man's pale face.

'You're Symons aren't you?' The man nodded, and Boyd took the file cover from under his arm turning it for the man to see.

'Did you write this report?'

Boyd saw real fear in the man's eyes. And the fear was not of him. He put the gun against the man's belly and said

223

softly, 'Did you write it, Symons?'

'Yes.' Symons's whisper was almost inaudible and in that moment Boyd did what his training and experience both abhorred. He changed his plan. This was the man who mattered. Instinct told him that.

'Walk quietly down the stairs to the front door.'

'What are you going to do with me?'

'If you cooperate and go quietly we're only going to talk. If you try and play games you'll get hurt. Badly hurt.'

Boyd waved the gun towards the bedroom door. 'Get moving.'

For a moment, at the front door, Symons hesitated and stopped, but he groaned and moved on as the muzzle of the gun ground against his spine.

At the car Boyd handcuffed Symons's hands behind his back and slid the cut foam sponge into his mouth before bundling him into the back seat.

Boyd drove slowly and carefully along the empty roads, through the small lanes and finally he turned into the rough drive up to the cottage.

The two men sat facing each other on opposite sides of the kitchen table. To a casual observer they would have looked merely like two men talking as they drank from the flower-decorated mugs. Only the fact that one man held his mug with both hands might have led one to notice that his hands were handcuffed. Boyd put down his mug and folded his arms, and Symons relaxed as he noted the traditional defensive gesture.

There had been no violence and Symons had had no sleep but he was slowly regaining his self-confidence. The Englishman was a slow talker and Symons assessed him as having a slow mind too. He could hold out without difficulty against this man's laboured thinking. And before long Petersen would be raising the alarm and the rescue would be in full swing.

224

'I can't believe you're an intelligence officer, Mr Boyd.'

'Why not?'

'If you were bona-fide you wouldn't be doing this. If the British authorities had any grounds for complaint they would take it up with the US Embassy.'

'You both have Canadian passports.'

'So what?'

'So you're an illegal entrant. You've committed at least half a dozen offences under the Immigration Regulations 1972. Any one of which allows a police officer to arrest you without a warrant.'

Symons smiled. 'But you're not a police officer. I'm quite willing to go with you to a police station right now.'

'Tell me about Walker.'

Symons smiled. 'I couldn't possibly discuss a patient with you, Mr Boyd.'

Symons was still smiling as Boyd's fist smashed into his face. His clenched hands came up to hold his nose and mouth as the bright red blood streamed through his fingers. Boyd made no move to help him. He just watched, still seething with anger at the man's hypocritical jibe. Slowly his anger subsided. When Symons moved his hands Boyd saw that the man's nose was broken and his soft lips were swollen and split.

'Tell me about Walker.'

Symons was trembling, shivering out of control, and as Boyd clenched his fist again Symons said, 'There's no need for that, you bastard.'

'Talk, Symons, and stop the bullshit. The next time it won't be just a punch on the nose.'

'You're going to regret this, Boyd. You really . . .'

And this time Symons screamed as the solid fist crunched into his battered face. He tried to stand up to get away from the pain, rocking his head, his eyes closed, his throat swallowing blood as he fought for breath.

When he eventually opened his eyes to look at Boyd they

225

were pleading for mercy, all trace of superciliousness gone. 'He's British. They wanted a suitable subject. All I did was programme him the way they wanted.'

'The way *who* wanted?'

'Your man Carter. And his stooges. Maclaren and Sturgiss.'

'Did Grabowski agree to this?'

'You know Grabowski?'

'Did he agree?'

'Yes. It was a deal.'

'What did you make Walker do?'

'He gave the *coup de grâce* to men who had sold or given away military secrets.'

'You mean he killed them?'

'Yes.'

'Why didn't they just do it themselves?'

'It's a standard precaution. If anything came to light. A body, say. Then there's no connection with anyone except the subject. And he could never be arrested and tried because as far as he's concerned he never did it. And was never in that place. That time or any other time.'

'You said it's standard precaution. You mean it's standard for CIA?'

'For Grabowski's people, yes.'

'How many murders did Walker commit?'

'Seven.'

'Where were they?'

'Two men and a girl in Germany. Two men in Holland. One in Israel and one in Athens.'

'Now tell me about the girl. Debbie Shaw.'

'We used her as a courier while she was travelling around the service camps in the States. Then we used her for carrying gold and drugs across combat lines for dissidents.'

'What about over here?'

'She killed two men in Dublin and one in Belfast. They

were IRA leaders. I gather your people were delighted with the results.'

'When did you stop using Walker?'

'He was due out of the army. And after he was released he went to see a psychiatrist, and we dropped him then.'

'How long did you use him?'

'About a year.'

'Is that why he can't remember anything about that year?'

'Yes. I put a memory block on him.'

'You programmed him to be a different person. What was the name of that person?'

'Dickens.'

'And who was Sergeant Madden SAS?'

'That was a second level. I needed that so that I could rationalize the violence for him.'

'And the girl?'

'She was Nancy Rawlins at the first level of hypnosis and Lara for the second level. The two levels weren't really necessary in her case. It was an early experiment to see if it would hold.'

'You realize she's a permanent patient now in a mental unit?'

'That was only because the hypnosis was filtering. When I found that she'd gone for treatment Carter had her detained for security reasons. I told him she was ninety-nine per cent locked-in but he wouldn't risk her being around.'

'Did you expect her to filter, as you call it?'

'No. It was always possible, but I'd controlled her perfectly for several years.'

'But it's always possible you were taking a risk?'

'Not really.'

'Why not?'

'I'd arranged a terminal programme.'

'What's that?'

'Self-immolation.'

'You mean suicide?'

'Yes.'

'How do you make that work?'

'She's programmed to do it when she hears a five figure number.'

'You mean you say the number and she just kills herself?'

'Yes.'

'How?'

'We had some research done. There's a high cliff on the south coast called Beachy Head where people frequently commit suicide. If she's in England that's where she'd do it.'

'And if she was somewhere else?'

'She walks into the nearest lake or ocean.'

'What's the number?'

'50556.'

'Why that number?'

'It doesn't come up in dates or clock times.'

'Can you undo it? Cancel it?'

'Possibly. It wouldn't be certain.'

'Why not?'

'I don't know. We haven't got that tested yet.'

Boyd looked for a long time at Symons in silence. Then he said softly, 'Does your conscience ever trouble you, Symons?'

'Why should it?'

'You know why it should, don't bullshit me.'

'You mean medical ethics and all that?'

'Yes.'

'I'm a CIA man first, a doctor second. The Soviet Union, the KGB do it. So we have to. We have to know how to use the method and how to combat it.'

'Forget being a doctor. Don't you have any scruples as a human being?'

228

'Are you married, Boyd?'

'Yes.'

'Ever thought about the animals that die in agony to test your wife's eye-shadow or lip-salve?'

'She doesn't use them.'

'Good for her. What about the drugs that save lives, or kidneys, or lungs or livers. Thousands of animals die to test them.'

'What's that got to do with it?'

'Millions of people will die in the next war. We're trying to prevent it happening. So maybe fifty or a hundred people die or get disabilities in testing. It's a very small sacrifice.'

'The ends justify the means?'

'Exactly.'

'That was the Nazis' excuse and Stalin's.'

'And now you're sitting there hoping I'll say that maybe they were right? So that you can label me as a Nazi or a sadist.'

'Not at all. I labelled you way back. You're a psychopath.'

Boyd saw the two red spots of anger suffuse Symons's white cheeks. 'You don't know what the word means, Boyd.'

'Now tell me about the Kennedys.'

'That's nothing to do with Walker and the girl.'

'I didn't say it was. But it is. That's where you started. Right at the top. And you've been working your way down ever since.'

'Boyd. You're having your bit of fun but you'd better remember one thing. I'm a senior CIA officer, privy to a lot of highly confidential information. They're not going to sit on their butts while some Brit does a bit of private enterprise kidnapping. You've got a few hours, maybe even a day, before Washington really starts leaning on your people. Then your people will be leaning on you. Meantime you can rough me up. There's nothing I can do to stop you. I didn't do the hoodlum training at Camp Peary so you're

229

in no danger from me. But when they come for you, you're finished.'

'Now tell me about the Kennedys. I've read your report but there's just one thing that puzzles me. How did they persuade you to do it?'

'Let me ask you a question. How did you trace us here? Was it one of Carter's men? There's only three, including Carter, who know about us.'

'You've forgotten about Washington, Symons. The CIA aren't all like you.'

Boyd saw the uneasiness change to fear in Symons's eyes. A different kind of fear. Disbelief fighting it out with fear that it could be true. That the sprawling machine that was used against others could be used against him. When that happens you can suddenly remember back to names and incidents, facts and rumours, when you were on the inside, when you never had to plead the Fifth or the First or the Fourth or even the Fourteenth Amendments. When it was normal to sit in a mahogany-panelled office round a table and discuss the feasibility study of the assassination of a dictator or a president; the advantages and disadvantages of a change of regime in some Middle East country; and the pros and cons of shovelling a million dollars down the pipeline to dissidents with unpronounceable names in countries that you couldn't find in an atlas because they were smaller than the State of Oregon. When altering the history, the destiny, of some foreign country was a matter of expediency not moral judgement.

Men who dealt daily in those terms spent little time discussing the termination of an individual life. They might spend a few minutes on a list of names, but one individual, theirs or the other side's, was not important enough to take up their valuable time. And when you had regularly sat-in on such meetings you were aware of how inexorably the machine worked. When the tick went beside your name it was just a question of time. And Symons was well aware, as

230

Grabowski himself was aware, that not only did many top CIA people deplore Grabowski's operations, but even those who approved accepted that an essential part of its function was its disposability. Officially, you and the others didn't exist, and when the need was pressing you didn't need to exist even unofficially. Grabowski would always survive. He was the exception. The rest were expendable. And he, Tony Symons, was one of the rest.

Symons looked at Boyd. 'D'you really mean that? The lead was from Langley.'

'Concerning your identity and whereabouts, yes.'

'Can we do a deal?'

'What kind of a deal?'

Symons shrugged. 'You give me cover and I'll give you what you want.'

'Maybe. You haven't answered my questions.'

'What were they?'

'About the Kennedys.'

'They just got in the way of too many powerful groups and people. They wanted to be the guys in the white hats. The knights in armour. They weren't, they were a couple of Irish Micks whose old man had made a pile of dough. They wanted votes; and by harassing the labour bosses, the Mafia, and investigating corruption in government, they thought they'd get the votes. And they were right. So in the end they had to deliver. Bobby was the number one target until John F got to the White House and then, as one of the mob once said . . . "Cut off the rooster's head and his tail will just drop off naturally." So JFK became number one target. They were actors those two. OK, they had good scriptwriters and producers, but they had no real talent. They should have gone to Hollywood. One of these days the country will do it in reverse. They'll go straight to Hollywood and pick a guy who plays the right kind of parts and make him president.'

'But he was put in the White House by the people's vote.'

Symons half-smiled. 'He was put in by a combination of every minority we have. The Irish, the Catholics, the blacks, the Hispanics, the poor, the manual workers. They were used and orchestrated just the same way any other political group makes a candidate into a president. There's nothing to choose between them, any of them. People expect too much. None of them matter. The Kennedys didn't matter. They were just figureheads. Prettier than most, but nothing more.'

'And the people who arranged their killings?'

'They were the people with real power. They proved that.'

'How did they persuade you to carry out these hypnotism programmes?'

'I need a crap.'

Boyd walked Symons to the toilet. Released his right hand and clipped the handcuffs and Symons's left hand to a pipe on the wall. Boyd stood outside the toilet door. When Symons called out Boyd released him, and Symons said, 'Can I wash my face?'

Boyd nodded and led Symons to the sink in the kitchen. He didn't fasten back the handcuffs when the washing was over. When they were back at the table Boyd returned to the question.

'What motivated you?'

'I guess at first it was the fact that I was picked out. Headhunted. When you're very young it's flattering. And then of course there's the sheer scope of what you can do. No more rats in experimental cages, but real people. Everything you do is new. Virgin territory. Maybe no more than three other psychiatrists in the world know the things that I know. There's no frontiers. Nothing's closed to you. And almost everything you discover has some use for the CIA or the Pentagon.

'You're not as vulnerable as even a four-star general.

232

There are thousands of three- and two-star generals with much the same qualifications, eager to take over and capable of doing the job just as well if not better. But there was nobody to replace me. Not one single soul could take over from me.' Symons paused. 'You won't be able to understand what it's like to be unique. It's almost like being God. I don't mean playing God . . . any totalitarian dictator can do that. *Being* God is different.'

'It didn't concern you that you were distorting people's minds. Maybe ruining their lives.'

'You mean people like Walker and the Shaw girl?'

'Yes.'

'I don't consider their lives are ruined. Walker is healthy. He's got a block of about a year in his life, but thousands of enlisted men have worse than that from their service. And his mind's not distorted. Just changed a bit.'

'And the girl?'

'Oh for Christ's sake. The reason she's detained is a security problem. If she's leaking she's got problems from time to time when it happens. Not much worse than having rather bad nightmares. She's still pretty. Nice tits and legs. She'll get by most of the time.'

'What about their parents, wives, husbands? They're affected too. Seeing somebody you love have nightmares while they're awake. Shivering, sobbing, vomiting. And none of them have any idea why it's happening or what caused it. They're seen as mentally sick people. And they are. You made them so.'

Symons shrugged and sighed. 'We don't see eye to eye. It's impossible to explain to a layman.'

'It isn't. You've explained. But explaining doesn't make it less outrageous.'

'Can we do a deal? I'll do my best to unlock the suicide programme.'

'Will you make a full confession and sign it?'

Symons's amazement was obviously genuine. 'A *confession*? There's nothing to confess, Boyd. I did my duty as required of me.'

Boyd nodded. 'I'm going out for about half an hour. I'm going to have to tie you up and gag you. Do you want to be sitting or lying?'

'I don't give a damn which way you do it.'

22

Cartwright took a plane to Newcastle and hired a car at the airport. The A1 was heavy with trucks and cars, and he hated driving at night. At Alnwick he missed the turn-off to the 1340 and it took him another hour to find the hotel at Beadnell. It was small and friendly and when he had booked in he asked for Boyd's room number.

He knocked on the door of Room 17 and tried the handle. The door wasn't locked and Boyd was asleep on the bed. Fully dressed except for his shoes and jacket. Cartwright closed the door quietly and looked around the room. Both the ceiling light and the bedside lamp were still on so Cartwright guessed that Boyd had only slept after it was dark. He could see no bag, no belongings of any kind, and Boyd's face looked as though he hadn't shaved for at least one day. And then the telephone rang. Boyd stirred and sighed, and opening his eyes he pulled himself up to lean against the pillows. As he reached for the phone he saw Cartwright.

'Answer it, James. There's no hurry.'

Boyd put the receiver to his ear. His speech was slow and hesitant.

'Yes . . . hi, kid. Thanks for ringing . . . I can't hear you . . . I'm OK . . . nothing special, I just wanted to hear your voice . . . that's probably because I was asleep . . . yes . . . yes . . . well get the rental company to fix it, that's what we pay 'em for . . . how's the painting going . . . good . . . sounds great . . . no, nothing special . . . not before the weekend at the earliest . . . just have a bath and a meal and then maybe I'll take a walk . . . it's small but nice. You'd like it . . . say I'd better go, someone's knocking on the door . . . I love you too . . . sometime tomorrow . . . bye, sweetie.'

Boyd swung his legs to the floor as he replaced the receiver. It was several seconds before he looked back at Cartwright.

'Why don't you sit down?'

Cartwright lifted the straight-backed chair and moved it so that he could sit facing Boyd.

'What is it, James, why did you want me so urgently?'

Boyd sighed. 'You won't believe it. I'm not sure I believe it myself.' He turned to look at Cartwright. 'Maybe it's better I don't tell you. Maybe I should just deal with it myself.'

Cartwright knew from experience that Boyd wasn't the kind who needed to dramatize his feelings or his operations. He said nothing as he looked at Boyd's face. It was pale and drawn, the nostrils pinched, and a small muscle was spasming under his left eye.

Boyd sighed again, a deep sigh. 'There are two CIA men. They've been living in a house a few miles from here. They've been in this country for nearly two years. They've got forged Canadian passports and they're not on the US Embassy list or any other list. They were sent over here to take the heat off the CIA from the Senate investigations into the Kennedy assassinations. John F and Bobby.' He paused as his eyes watched Cartwright's face. 'They're psychologists or psychiatrists. I don't know which. They hypnotize people for the CIA to use.' Boyd shook his head. 'They're out of some science-fiction scenario, Ken. It's incredible.'

Cartwright noticed the use of his Christian name. Boyd seldom called him anything but Cartwright, or maybe 'sir' if they were in front of other people.

'Don't worry, James. We can just ship them quietly back

236

to the States, or wherever Langley would like them to go. I can phone Washington tonight. We don't need to pressure them.'

Boyd shook his head. 'We do. They've been cooperating with Carter's group . . . doing the same sort of things over here.'

'What sort of things?'

'That soldier. The one who has nightmares. They hypnotized him, and Carter's people used him to kill people. At least seven, maybe more. And there's a girl.' He shook his head again, in disbelief at what he was going to say. 'She killed the two IRA men, O'Hara and Rafferty. They hypnotized her and told her to do it. She doesn't know she's done it. Neither does the soldier know what he's done.'

There was a long pause and then Cartwright said, 'I have to say it, James . . . are you sure about all this?'

'Quite sure.'

'Can you prove it?'

Boyd shrugged. 'Some of it.'

'Enough to convince a court?'

'I doubt it. Maybe if I had top-class medical help. I just don't know.'

'Are they still at the house?'

'No.'

'Where are they?'

Boyd looked away, towards the darkness of the window. 'I've got one of them stashed away. The other one is still at the house.'

'What do you mean – stashed away?'

'I collared him to make him talk. He's the one who matters.'

'Where is he now?'

'Can this be off the record?'

'No. Why should it be?'

'We can't just let those bastards creep back to the States

237

like nothing has ever happened. We should inform somebody over there.'

'Who?'

'Congress, the Senate, the President even. They should
know what the CIA are doing for God's sake. The one I've
got hypnotized Oswald, and the other one hypnotized
Sirhan Sirhan, these two goons programmed them to
assassinate the President of the United States and the US
Attorney-General, a presidential candidate.'

'And you're suggesting that the CIA arranged it?'

'Not the top brass maybe. But a group like Carter's
people. Killers. Thugs. Working with the Mafia.'

Cartwright didn't hurry to respond. If you've spent half
your life in MI6 you know things, and have heard things,
that often seem incredible, that may be the figment of
some over-heated operator's imagination. And almost
always they're true. But this was too much. It didn't hang
together, and it had a cast like *Birth of a Nation* with guest
stars. The President, his brother, the CIA and the Mafia.
And two men who could programme hypnotized people to
commit murder and not know what they had done. Even
half of it would have been too much. He should have kept
better contact with Boyd and then he would have seen those
first tell-tale signs of a man who was coming apart from
worry or exhaustion, or both.

'How long have you been at this hotel, James?'

'I got here about four o'clock.'

'How long have you slept?'

'A couple of hours.'

'You look worn out. Why don't you get a good night's
rest and then we'll sort this thing out together. One more
day won't make any difference.'

'I can't leave him there. He might get away.'

'Let me come with you. You can sleep in that place. You
need some sleep, James. You really do.'

Boyd shook his head. 'I need to know that we aren't

238

going to cover up for those bastards.'

'That'll be for other people to decide. Not you and me.'

'I can't go along with that, Ken. If our people let these two off the hook there's something terribly wrong with what we've all been doing.'

'This has got nothing to do with what you and I do.'

'It has for me.'

'Tell me.'

'I've done things . . . all sorts of things, that I didn't like doing. Pressuring people until they couldn't take any more . . . threatening to harm a man's wife . . . killing people . . . but to me it was in a just cause. The end really did justify the means. They were people who wanted to destroy us . . . our way of life . . . democracy. But I always thought there was a point . . . a line . . . beyond which we'd never go . . . not even as a last resort. They were always people in the business . . . agents, subversives . . . they knew what they were doing. Knew the risks they were taking if we caught them. But these are innocent people. A girl about the same age as my Katie. A pretty girl. These two bastards have turned her into a zombie. She's killed men in cold blood and she hasn't the vaguest idea that she's done it.' He paused and his voice shook as he went on. ' Do you know what the last thing was in her programming?'

'No.'

'Guess.'

'I've no idea, James. Tell me.'

'When somebody recites five numbers to her. Anywhere. Anytime. She kills herself. Wherever she is she goes to Beachy Head and jumps.' There were tears on Boyd's cheeks. 'That could be my Katie, Ken.'

'Where is the girl now?'

'In London. Held in a mental hospital on Carter's say-so. She runs a theatrical agency. She's successful. Every now and then she takes a few days' break and then she's back at her desk. And in those few days she's killed somebody and she doesn't know a damn thing about it.'

'We can give her protection.'

'How?'

'We can explain what's happened. Get her treatment. Keep her under surveillance.'

'And all that bastard has to do is phone her and say those five numbers and she's on her way to Eastbourne, and nothing and nobody can stop her. She won't just do it, she'll want to do it. Because she's been fed some rational reason for doing it. She's three different people and she might just as well be dead. Her brain is like a real can of worms.'

'Why did you ask me to come up to see you?'

Boyd sighed. 'Now you're here I'm not sure. I think I had some vague feeling that you could tell me that none of it was true. That you knew all about it and it was just a cover scenario.'

'And if it wasn't, what did you expect me to do?'

'I thought you might agree with me that it has to be exposed.'

'I can't believe you really expected that.'

'Maybe not expected . . . just hoped. I thought you'd be on my side.'

'I am on your side. You're one of my officers, and apart from that I like you. And I respect your judgement. But if half of what you've told me is provable, then deciding what action to take is not in my hands. You must know that. I've got an advantage over you. Several advantages. I've not been involved in all this, and I'm not tired out as you are. You're still in the woods and I'm outside. There isn't any choice for me, and that means there isn't any choice for you. It's for others to decide. From the sound of it the decision may have to be made by the Prime Minister. Meantime, you get some sleep. I'm in Room 21, let's have breakfast together about nine o'clock. OK?'

Boyd stood up slowly. 'What the hell are we going to do?'

240

Cartwright smiled. 'We're both going to get a good night's sleep.'

Cartwright drove the few miles up to Bamburgh and phoned a London number. He said very little beyond asking for an early meeting with the Deputy Under-Secretary. The problem he faced now was political not intelligence. All intelligence was political to some extent, but this looked as if it might be entirely political, and out of the area that SIS would consider as its own. It could end up as government to government with a dozen variations of a suitable deal. There were prizes in the situation for SIS if they cooperated with the CIA, but it would depend on the attitudes of the top echelons of both agencies as to how it should be handled. There would be men like Boyd in the CIA. Dedicated men. Where patriotism wasn't mere nationalism but was based on preserving a way of life. The sort of men who, long ago, had toiled and fretted over the writing of the American Constitution to protect the citizen from the state. There were times when those good men had to be over-ruled, their ideals set aside. And Cartwright was sure that this was going to be one of those times. He sympathized with the feelings of the Boyds of this world, but part of his own function was to decide when the man at the top had to be given an option on what should be done.

It was not that Cartwright was less scrupulous a man than Boyd and the others. Just that because of his longer experience he knew that there were times when expediency had to replace decency. The Boyds of SIS and CIA frequently went outside the law themselves, and when you were in that particular no-man's-land you shouldn't complain when others decided to go deeper into the slime. Protest if you like. Refuse to play a part in it. But don't, repeat don't, get in the way. And Boyd was shaping up to get in the way. For his own sake, and the service's sake, he had to be contained and stopped. He would give a couple of days to persuasion, but after that Boyd would have to be shifted sideways, away from the operation.

Standing outside the phone-box he looked up at the sky and then across to the impressive outline of Bamburgh Castle. He crossed the road and the grass verge, and took the narrow winding path down to the beach. The tide was ebbing and in the moonlight the sand looked white and clean. Out to sea there was a cluster of lights from the fishing cobles that were based at Seahouses, and on the horizon an Aldis light was winking from a Royal Navy frigate to the radio station at Boulmer down the coast. He turned to look up at the towering pile of the castle. It was more a fortress than a castle, but it had once been the home of the Kings of Northumbria, in the even bloodier days of the border wars with the Scots. Nothing much had changed except the means of waging war.

Cartwright was down in the small dining room by 8.45 and when the waiter appeared he asked for coffee and told him that he would wait for Mr Boyd. The waiter hesitated.

'Mr Boyd left. He checked out last night.'

'What time did he leave?'

'I don't know. I wasn't on duty last night. Do you want me to ask reception?'

Cartwright nodded. 'Yes, please.'

When the waiter came back the news was that Boyd had checked out just before midnight and had paid his bill in cash.

Cartwright ordered the full breakfast and a copy of *The Guardian*. It was going to be one of those days.

Cartwright phoned London and an hour later he stood incongruously on the wide golden beach as the RAF helicopter came clattering in from the sea. He stood there with his suitcase on the sands at his feet, watching the chopper settle down lightly a hundred feet away.

They flew him to Newcastle where a small white

242

Cherokee with RAF roundels was waiting to fly him to Northolt. Three hours later he was at the safe-house in Ebury Street waiting for the DUS. As he waited in the comfortable room he wondered how Parkinson would react to his news. Normally he would have had a pretty good idea of his senior's reaction but this time it was different. He wasn't even sure of his own reactions. But Parkinson was rated a 'sound man'. Well used to being the interface between SIS and the PM, he could absorb a good briefing competently and quickly, and could generally get the decision his service wanted provided he was convinced that they were right. Of medium height but stockily built he was known as "Flycatcher" by the irreverent, owing to his habit of listening intently with his mouth wide open. The humorists said it was to disguise his yawns, the more down-to-earth diagnosed sinus trouble, but the fact was that it was a purely personal idiosyncrasy that he had derived from his father.

Then Cartwright heard the slam of a taxi door, and moments later the muffled voice of the retired policeman who supervised the safe-house. Parkinson patted his chest as he arrived breathless at the top of the steep, narrow stairs.

'I told him we'd like some coffee, but later. Well . . . and what have you been up to?'

'It's quite a long story, sir.'

Parkinson smiled. 'They always are by the time they get to me. Let's make ourselves comfortable.'

Making himself comfortable for the civil servant meant no more than undoing the two bottom buttons on his waistcoat before he leaned back in the armchair.

It took less time to tell his tale than he had expected and Cartwright had said his piece inside fifteen minutes.

'Have you discussed this with anyone else as yet?'

'No sir. Obviously Carter knows part of the story, but he hasn't kept me informed. He won't know the latest developments.'

'You never know, Ken. You never know. I've not heard anything but I don't fraternize with Nick Carter unless I have to.' He paused and smiled. 'For his sake as well as mine. What the eye don't see the heart don't grieve about, eh?'

'I think the issues are clear, sir. Even if the decision is less so.'

'Do you now? Tell me the issues.'

'We either cooperate with Langley or we don't. We send them back discreetly and gift-wrapped, and leave Langley to decide their fate. Or we raise absolute hell at all levels. Their embassy here. Ours in Washington. CIA liaison. Even the White House direct. Eventually we agree to return them but only in return for something good we really want. Reluctant conspirators.'

'And which do you favour?'

'The discreet return.'

'Why that?'

'The sooner we wash our hands of all of it the better. We don't need to make a song and dance about it. It's not an occasion for pointing fingers. They don't like this kind of operation any more than we do.' He paused and shrugged. 'But we both cross the line when it suits us, and we need to. Mind you . . . without any attempt at being holier than thou I'm surprised that Carter has gone to these lengths. It's not our kind of game.'

Parkinson smiled faintly. 'Chaps like Carter can't resist a new toy you know. He gets his blackmail material on the CIA and instinctively he wonders how much it's worth. It never enters his mind that maybe you could get more out of it by doing nothing. So he borrows their new toy. Forgetting the ethics and all that, the way he's used it is merely adding another hazard to his operation. His old-fashioned thugs could have done it in half the time and with none of all this shambles for us to sweep up. And what about your chap Boyd? He's another complication.'

244

'I think in fact he's our only problem. Or *my* only problem. It always annoys me intensely when one of our own people gets on his high horse and pontificates. I sympathize with his views – most of us would. But if you're in the service it's self-indulgent. We're in a game that officially doesn't even exist. Almost everything we do is open to criticism from some source. If we tap the phone of some Irish thug preparing bombs in a semi in Willesden we are infringing the liberty of the individual. But when he kills seven innocent people we get kicked for not knowing what's going on.

'But I got over being indignant about that sort of thing in my first year of service. We have to make our own rules and standards. When somebody goes too far they get the chop or demotion. Carter's gone too far in my opinion. But who decides how far too far is? Not me, thank God. And certainly not Boyd.'

Parkinson nodded and his smooth fingers touched his grey silk tie. 'Carter's been extremely naïve in this matter. We give him a lot of rope but the understanding has always been that the outcome has to be worth the moral black-out. This little circus isn't worth any risk at all. Do you think you can talk Boyd out of his indignation?'

'I'm not at all sure that I can. I think in some queer way he's identifying this girl with his wife. They're much of an age. Both very pretty. He sees it as happening to her.'

'Sounds a good solid citizen.' Parkinson turned his head very slightly so that he could watch Cartwright's response from the corner of his eye.

'The only solid citizens we can afford in SIS are those we stick behind desks. Shuffling papers and scribbling notes for their monograph on *Mediaeval Guilds in East Anglia*. Field officers should be committed.'

Parkinson smiled. 'Now steady on. I can remember you complaining about the kind of chap we were recruiting

245

some years ago. And you said we shouldn't be taking on chaps who were eager to do the job. We should be looking for the reluctant virgins who had doubts. Your own words, Ken. You quoted Philby as the example of the committed man. You've said to me a number of times that you valued your music because it kept you at arm's length from being the dedicated SIS man always wearing blinkers. Yes?'

'I'm afraid so. I suppose that's why I was so hot under the collar about Boyd. He reflects my own views too closely for comfort. The only difference is that I've been in the racket enough years to make me tend towards the long view.'

'Would you like me to put someone else on to dealing with Boyd?'

Cartwright looked surprised as he turned towards Parkinson. 'What made you suggest that, sir?'

'Because the obvious solution is one you won't like,' Parkinson said very quietly.

Cartwright didn't reply and Parkinson stood up. 'I'll have to miss out on the coffee. Got a meeting before lunch. Keep me in touch.'

Parkinson's meeting was in his own office, and his secretary pointed towards his room and nodded as he walked through to where the black Gothic script said 'M. F. Parkinson MBE Deputy Under Sec.'.

Carter was already waiting for him, and Parkinson nodded to him as he walked round to sit at his desk. As he sat down he looked across to Carter.

'I got your message. How long will it take to move her?'

'I'll need a Home Office transfer authorization and some pressure on the two doctors. And I'll need to make arrangements for her at another hospital. That will take some time. Medical people can't stomach being told what to do by their inferiors.'

'See Penny about the transfer authorization and you

should have it back from the Home Secretary's office within the hour. Hire an ambulance and take her to one of the safe-houses. The one at Petersfield's available. Get Facilities to lay on one of our own nurses. Don't stand any nonsense from the two doctors and make them sign the Official Secrets Act form. Point your finger at Section Two.'

Carter stood up to leave but Parkinson waved him back to the chair.

'I gave you the benefit of the doubt when I agreed to let you go ahead with these two Americans. You'll recall, I hope, that I pointed out to you that the prize wasn't enough for the risk. You remember?'

'Yes, sir.'

'Was I right?'

'Yes, sir, but we've had practical experience of a new weapon, a new method.'

'Rubbish. The two Americans may have, but you haven't. You couldn't repeat it without them. You've no more learnt how to do it than watching Menuhin play the fiddle on TV teaches you how to play the violin.'

'I'm sorry, sir.'

'We've got a complication now.'

'What's that, sir?'

'Cartwright's chap Boyd broke into the house and took off with Symons. Boyd wants to expose the whole thing. The naughty CIA and their collaborators in SIS. Abuse of the minds of innocent victims. It would make Watergate look like the vicar's tea party.'

'What's Cartwright going to do?'

'That's what worries me. I think he'll make the right decision in the end. But if he's backed into a corner Boyd's only got to get to a telephone and call Reuters and the balloon goes up.' Parkinson pushed a trayful of files to one side. A symbolic clearing of the decks before he looked across again at Carter. 'You'd better provide some insurance,

Carter. Or we'll all be writing our memoirs in the Tower.'

'Do we know where Boyd has taken Symons, sir?'

'No. You'd better get your people up there doing their bloodhound act. You get my meaning I hope.'

'Yes, sir. I'll deal with it.'

Parkinson nodded brusquely as he reached for the internal telephone.

23

Maclaren drove the XJS with Sturgiss in the passenger seat and Carter stretched out asleep at the back.

Cartwright had flown up on a scheduled flight to Newcastle where there was a message for him at the airport to phone London. Signals Security had monitored several coded calls addressed to him from Boyd, on one of the SIS operational channels. Cartwright phoned the Special Branch senior at Newcastle and asked for a transceiver to be sent across to him.

He hired a car at the airport and as soon as the radio had been delivered he headed up the A1 for Beadnell. He booked into the hotel and then walked to the empty beach. In a hollow in the dunes he extended the aerial and turned the switch to Channel Five, the frequency Boyd had been using, and pressed the transmit button. Slowly and carefully he said, 'Everest calling Snowdon . . . Everest calling Snowdon . . . are you receiving?' He turned over to receive and waited, but there was no reply. He called twice again and then looked at his watch. It was only three o'clock but he seemed to have been on the move for weeks.

The tide was ebbing and the white sand glistened in the afternoon sun, and far across the bay he could see the shape of Bamburgh Castle, its grey stones purple in the reflected light from the sea. On a rock beside him a sandhopper explored the skeleton of a small shore crab that was embedded in a thatch of orange lichen, and in the smooth stones at the high-water line a sea anemone swayed in a rock-pool, betrayed by the tide. It was like being a boy again, and his father giving him a magnifying glass, pointing out some rare wild flower or insect, telling him always to notice everything he saw. To find out what it was, its life-cycle and its habitat. But the magic had all ended when his father died. And now it wasn't wild flowers and insects that he observed so minutely, but people. Their life-cycles and their habitats. Trying to assess their strengths and weaknesses in case it might some day be of use.

And that thought brought him back to Boyd. He had never really fathomed Boyd. He was loyal and experienced and had been consistently successful in all his operations. But there was part of him that seemed to be hidden away. Not deliberately perhaps, but it was there. A cut-off point. And his loyalty. Was it to the service or that pretty young wife of his? Which would get the casting vote if the chips were ever really on the table? He hadn't worked out what he would say to Boyd to make him conform. He had sufficient confidence in his own powers of persuasion to be able to convince Boyd that the rules were the rules. And the particular rule in this case was that you did what you were told to do by the appropriate authority. When he knew that it was straight from the Deputy Under Secretary Boyd would surely conform. Some protest of course, but that was reasonable enough. There was a lot in what Boyd had said, but there were times when moral judgements had to be put aside and expediency ruled. That, of course, was what Goering and the others had said in their own defence at Nuremberg. But that wasn't a just cause.

He looked at his watch again and went through the radio drill. Boyd came back on the second call.

'Snowdon calling Everest. I hear you.'

'Everest acknowledging. Hotel in one hour. Confirm.'

'Confirm. Over and out.'

Cartwright pushed down the telescopic aerial and slid the set into his jacket pocket. A breeze had come up and he shivered momentarily as he brushed the sand from his trousers.

Cartwright had ordered tea and toast in his bedroom and as he poured tea for them both he said, 'Have some toast. You look half starved.'

'What's going on, Cartwright? What's the word from Mount Olympus?'

'The DUS asked me to pass on his congratulations for the good work you've done. He feels that you've placed us in an extremely strong position *vis-à-vis* Langley. For once we've got all the aces, and he's very grateful.'

'What's all that add up to on the ground?'

'He wants us to get the two Americans back as quietly as possible. And then we'll decide what we want from Langley.'

'And Walker and the girl?'

'Walker? Who's Walker?'

'The ex-soldier who has nightmares.'

'Of course. The name escaped me for a moment. Every effort will be made to help him sort himself out. Every effort.'

'And they'll release the girl?'

'If it's medically feasible, James. Her mental health has to be the first consideration. But everything will be done.'

'Did you go along with this?'

'Of course. I had no choice. It's a direct order.'

'Not for me it isn't.'

'James. Be reasonable. They'll want to please you. There's talk of an MBE, even an OBE, for your good work. Don't make it more difficult for us all than it already is. Be reasonable.'

'And if my idea of reasonable isn't the same as yours, what then?'

'That's a hypothetical question, James.' Carwright leaned

251

forward to touch Boyd's knee. 'Help me, James. You won't regret it.'

'That's a word you shouldn't have used, Cartwright. Regret. It's been in my mind for days. One thing I know is that if these bastards get away with what they've done, and it's me who lets them off the hook, I'll regret it for the rest of my life.'

'For God's sake, Jimmy. You've done far worse than this many times.'

'Sure I have. But not to innocent people. The ones I killed were in the business. They knew the risks the same as I did. It was them or me. It could have been me. But not Walker and the girl. They were just bystanders. These bastards just decided they could be useful, and took them. They don't even know what's been done to them. They didn't volunteer. There were no risks for these bastards. If it worked – great. If it didn't – too bad. This isn't what the SIS is all about. It isn't what this country's about. Nor the United States. It isn't what I'm all about either. You have to draw the line somewhere, Cartwright. I wanted to hear what you'd have to say. I hoped you might have found some scruples while you were down in London.' Boyd stood up and Cartwright looked up at him.

'Your scruples are at other people's expense, Boyd.'

'How do you make that out?'

'If it was just that you wanted to draw the line for yourself you could take some leave and be out of it. Or you could resign.'

Boyd shook his head slowly, 'You really don't understand do you?'

As the door closed behind Boyd, Cartwright wondered what to do. And as he was thinking the phone rang.

'Yes.'

'Is that you, Cartwright?'

'Who's that?'

'Carter.'

'Where are you?'

252

'In a dump called Seahouses.'

'What the hell are you doing up here?'

'Playing sheepdog, pal. What's the position with our friend?'

'Why are you up here?'

'Flycatcher's orders. Didn't he tell you?'

'No.'

'Well, what's the situation?'

'He won't cooperate.'

'So what's he going to do?'

'God knows.'

'OK. Now listen, you stay right where you are. I'm taking over as of now. We've found where he's holed up. But don't interfere. I'll come back to you when we've dealt with it.'

'What are you going to do?'

'What do you think, sweetheart?'

Cartwright could hear the derisive laugh long after he had hung up.

Carter posted Maclaren and Sturgiss at the back of the cottage, and the marksman with his rifle in a piece of dead ground where the lawn met the wire fence of the adjoining field. Their small van in Post Office livery was parked a hundred yards down the lane alongside a telegraph pole. Grabowski and Carter were crouched below the window of the wooden shack at the far end of the cottage. There was only one way for Boyd to get to the cottage and there was still light enough to see him clearly.

As Boyd turned the car into the bend in the lane he glanced at the Post Office van as he passed. He wondered why it was there, and then he jammed on the brakes. Switching off the engine he got out of the car and walked back to the van. He stood on the grass verge and looked up. As he had thought, it wasn't a telephone pole, it was a pole carrying the electricity supply to the farm across the fields and to the cottage. So why a Post Office van instead of a van from the North East Electricity Board?

The doors at the front of the van were both locked, and when he tried the double doors at the rear they were locked too. He looked around but there was nobody in sight. Everywhere was quiet except for the distant lowing of cows and a blackbird singing in the hedge.

He walked slowly back to his car and unlocked the boot. He looked through the tool-kit and took out the tyre-lever and the heaviest spanner. Despite all his efforts the tyre-lever was too thick to go between the door and the body of the van. Taking off his jacket he draped it over the driver's side window and smashed it with the spanner. Sliding his hand through the jagged hole he released the lock and opened the door. Sitting in the driver's seat he went over the interior, checking it carefully. There was nothing. And the rear of the van was completely empty.

Back in the road he stood away from the van. A working van was never that empty. There would be job tickets, cigarette ends and packets, driver's manuals, toffee papers. Some sign of human beings. There was something wrong but he didn't know what it was. And then he saw it. The tiny tell-tale shadow.

Standing alongside the van he ran his nail along the edge of the 'P' in Post Office and it lifted, the whole legend coming away as he peeled it off. It was hand-lettering on a self-adhesive strip. He threw the strip into the ditch and walked back to his car. Sliding into the driver's seat he reached across and unlocked the glove recess and took out the gun. Watching the road ahead he smacked his hand against the base of the magazine and heard it snap into place.

Boyd sat there trying to remember what the area looked like on the map. All he could remember was the orchard at the back. Further back still was a pond or a lake, and marking the boundaries were rough wooden posts carrying three or four strands of barbed wire.

He walked back down the lane, past the van to the five-barred gate. It rattled and shook as he climbed over. Five or six black and white Friesians stood flicking their ears in the shade of an oak tree, chewing the cud, saliva dripping from their soft mouths as they stared at him. He looked at his watch and then at the sun: it was just touching the top of the oak tree. Boyd headed across on his rough bearing towards a hawthorn bush on the far side of the field. Beyond the hawthorn hedge was a small coppice of silver birches, and bending low he hurried towards it.

The copse had been allowed to run wild and thin saplings grew everywhere, with runners slanting up from the roots of established trees to impede his movements. At the edge of the copse he stood just behind the outer clump of trees.

Forty or fifty yards ahead of him he could see the marksman. He was dressed in a loose brown suede jacket and lightweight slacks. His rifle was on the grass beside and in front of him, turned on its side, its thin leather strap already looped to take his hand. The butt was custom-made, so was the cheek rest. As Boyd watched, the man lifted the rifle, pulled it to his shoulder, and raising his head he looked through the telescopic sights. He held the rifle there for a minute or so and then placed it back on the grass. The rifle had been aimed at the concrete slabs where he would have parked the car.

Slowly and quietly Boyd went back through the copse and skirted around it away from the sun. It was beginning to set, casting long shadows from the trees, and Boyd sat waiting for the light to go.

Almost an hour later he moved off in the darkness, heading towards the orchard at the back of the cottage. A tangle of wild blackberry bushes snagged at his clothes as he reached the first of the ancient apple trees. Their branches were so low that he had to crawl. The thick overgrown grass was wet with dew and his trousers clung heavily to his legs when he eventually stood up. He could

255

see the back of the cottage, barely distinguishable in the special darkness of dusk before the moon comes up. There would almost certainly be a man at the back of the cottage. And then as his eyes became accustomed to the darkness he saw what could be the shadowy shape of a man at the near corner of the cottage. He waited, breathing shallowly and then the shadow moved. There were no lights on anywhere in the cottage but there could be someone inside. He would have to take this first man with his hands, or the marksman would be around to help him.

Boyd turned up the collar of his jacket to hide the light colour of his shirt. He moved forward slowly on all fours, and then a hand grabbed at his ankle and a heavy body flung itself on top of him. He twisted to one side as a hand grasped at his throat. As he bent his legs to fend off the man a boot landed deep in his belly, and above him a man called out. Boyd reached out for where the face must be and the man grunted as Boyd's fingers scraped his face and then grabbed for his throat. The man twisted violently but Boyd's strong fingers were squeezing his wind-pipe. Slowly his fingers pressed on the man's throat until he felt him sagging heavily on top of him. Then a boot crashed against Boyd's head, stunning him temporarily, a torch shone on his face and a voice said, 'That's him. Go on.' As the muzzle of the gun jabbed at his eye the pain was almost like an anaesthetic and when the bullet crashed into his skull he didn't even feel it. He died instantly with no need for a second shot, and as Carter looked down to the pool of light from his torch he saw Boyd's right hand shaking violently as the last messages from his nervous system did their work. The fingers closed, gripping tightly, and then they relaxed, spreading out again in the wet grass.

Grabowski gripped his gun tighter and smashed his foot against the cottage door. It swung open easily and he realized that it hadn't been locked. He glanced around the living room and walked through to the old-fashioned scullery. There were used plates and mugs and dirty cutlery in a red plastic bowl filled with water, and all the signs that this was where they had been, but there was no sign of Symons.

Walking back into the living room he saw the narrow flight of stairs. Slowly and cautiously, peering upwards, the gun pushed forward, he made his way up the stairs. The first bedroom was empty, the second bedroom was locked. Bracing his back against the wall he put his foot up beside the lock and pushed. For a second the door held before it sprang open. Symons was lying on the bed, his hands behind his back, his ankles roped together, and a roughly cut piece of foam rubber sticking out of his mouth. His face was bruised and bloody, his nose swollen to twice its normal size.

There was a gush of blood from Symons's mouth as Grabowski pulled out the gag and he moaned softly as Grabowski turned him over to release his hands. When he saw the handcuffs Grabowski turned him onto his back again and putting the gun on the bed he untied the ropes binding Symons's ankles.

'How're you feeling?'

'Terrible. I think he's broken my nose. Why did it take so long?'

'It's only been a few days.'

'Can you get a key for these handcuffs, they've cut into my wrists.'

'I'll have to get a key from the local police.'

'Where's Boyd?'

'He's dead.'

'For Christ's sake. What happened?'

'He was shot.'

'Who shot him? You?'

'No. Not me. I gotta talk seriously to you, Tony.'

'What about?'

'Remember when we were talking, way back just before Dallas? You said that if anything happened to you the bomb would go off.'

'Yes. I remember it very well.'

'And you said if you died from natural causes the same would happen. Remember?'

'Yes.'

'Well that's always worried me. That's what I want to talk about.'

'No harm in you talking, Ziggy.'

'I don't need to talk much. I just want to know what you've done. I assume you've done some sort of disclosure of the MKULTRA experiments and you've stashed them away someplace.'

'That's more or less right, Ziggy. But I'm not saying any more, old friend. Those things are my insurance policies.'

'I'm aware of that. Nevertheless I want to know where they are.'

'No way, Ziggy.' Symons smiled a battered smile. 'You know better than that.'

'OK. We'd better get down to the essentials. I've known you for a long time now, Symons. You're a clever fellow. You've done a good job, so I don't want you to come to any harm. You've been drawing an active service special allotment for years now. The same extras that top field agents draw. But you're not a field agent and you'd never have survived as a field agent. They're maybe not so bright in some ways as you are. But they've got several things that you ain't got and won't ever have. Like guts for instance. When I start putting you through the wringer you're gonna scream like a stuck pig. I don't much like the sound of men screaming so I thought we might find a way to avoid it.'

'You mean you'll turn the heat on *me*? I don't believe it.'

'Start believing, lover boy. I'll put you through the mincer without a second thought. I might even enjoy it. You've been a cocky bastard when you had the chance.'

Symons was trembling as he shook his head. 'You wouldn't. You couldn't. Not after all I've done. I'm one of your team.'

Grabowski said softly, 'See this gun?' He reversed it in his hand, the barrel gripped tightly and he slammed the butt hard, like a hammer into the palm of his left hand. 'I'll give you ten seconds to start talking, Symons. After that I'll finish off what Boyd started on your face.'

Symons turned his head away as if to avoid a blow and he said harshly, 'What d'you want to know?'

'Where's your stuff? The cosy little time-bomb that reveals all?'

'Can we do a deal, Ziggy? We could share it. You need some insurance just as much as . . .'

The butt of the revolver crashed against Symons's mouth and teeth. For a moment he was silent, wrapped in a shroud of pain. And then he screamed. Again and again. Falling back on the bed he buried his face in the softness of the pillows. And slowly a red stain spread from the pillows to the sheets.

Grabowski turned him onto his back and leaned over him. 'Where's the stuff, Symons? Or do you want some more?'

'It's in the house . . . Percy House . . . on Kodachrome slides . . . in a pack . . . seventy-one slides.'

'Where is it? The pack?'

'It's with . . . all the other packs of . . . slides . . . it's marked on the label . . . ARTLUKM . . . our code reversed.'

'And what releases it to the waiting world?'

'A letter . . . my lawyer . . . he's got a set too . . . unopened . . . sealed with superglue.'

'Who's your lawyer?'

'Miles Roper . . . Roper and Callagan . . . Boston . . . at Harvard together.'

'No other copies?'

'No . . . I swear it . . . please Ziggy . . . I'm haemorrhaging

259

'. . . get me . . .' Symons's eyes closed.

Grabowski knew that it would be safer to check on the slides first, but it would complicate things too much. He pointed the gun at the bloody mess that was Symons's face and fired twice. Symons's body jerked from the first shot but there was no visible response to the second.

Back at Percy House Grabowski found the pack of 35mm slides and prised it open with a knife. In the darkened room he projected the first ten slides and that was enough. He dropped all the slides and the pack into the Aga cooker in the kitchen and stood watching as the yellow pack twisted and bubbled, and then suddenly the gases ignited and the pack and the slides flared and melted, grey smoke pouring from the glowing liquid residue. He put back the hotplate ring, lowered the bolster and then walked back to Carter and Sturgiss in the sitting room. He passed Cartwright sitting on an antique chest in the hall, talking on the telephone. Boyd's body was being flown to London. Symons's body had been sewn up in a canvas sack.

All night Carter's men removed all evidence of the two Americans from Percy House and from Boyd's occupation of the cottage.

The convoy of two cars and a light van made its way to the local authority rubbish incinerator at Alnwick in the early hours of the morning. Carter and Grabowski stood watching as the sack containing Symons's body and everything from the house and cottage were swallowed up in the glowing maw of the furnace, until there was nothing left but a layer of fine grey ash in the pit below the steel grating. Cartwright was already on his way back to London.

Grabowski went back to the hotel, booked himself into a room and put in a call to a Boston number. It was only eleven in the morning over there and that gave them ample time to carry out his instructions.

260

The law firm of Roper and Callagan reported the break-in to the local police the following day but neither the slides nor the sealed letter were reported missing. Just two IBM Selectrics and a Sirius micro-computer. It was Grabowski's guess that they hadn't even noticed the other missing items. And there was no reason why they should: He had a whisky with the night porter and then headed back to the cottage.

24

George Walker sees Dr Ansell from time to time, just for a check-up. Once or twice a year he has one of his nightmares. They leave him screaming and sweating, but he has almost got used to them and he takes them in his stride. Ansell has tried in vain to establish what triggers them, and in his case-notes he attributes them to responses to the accumulated tensions that affect most people one way or another.

Walker now works as a computer programmer for a national insurance company that omitted by oversight to ask him to fill in an application form. He has not married and still lives with his parents. He has no friends and he devotes all his spare time to a model railway layout that he has built up in a small shed in the garden.

Debbie Shaw is in an asylum for the incurably insane. She owes her survival to being the thirty-first item on an SIS policy-making agenda on the hottest autumn day since records were kept. The item was to discuss whether she represented a security risk if left alive. The meeting had only got to item twenty-five by eleven o'clock in the evening. The DUS had been called away to the House at ten to see the Prime Minister, the man from the Joint Intelligence Committee had never heard of Debbie Shaw, and the new man from Berlin had suggested that item thirty-one should be dealt with at Cartwright's discretion. Cartwright would be the last person to admit that he had been moved by Boyd's words or thoughts, but he came down in favour of Miss Shaw being moved to a place of permanent care and treatment.

Debbie Shaw wears a threadbare towelling bath-robe, several sizes too big for her because it was once the property of Steve Randall. She doesn't remember him and she has no visitors.

She gives little trouble to the staff, sitting most days in the same wicker chair. She knits a scarf that the nurses have to unravel from time to time when its length exceeds twelve feet. She sometimes sings to herself quietly as she knits, and one of the young doctors once said amiably that she ought to be a singer.

About once a year she is a problem. A passive problem, refusing to eat or drink. Sitting silently, not knitting, in her own small cubicle. Refusing to talk. It never lasts more than a week and force feeding every other day keeps her alive. She is still pretty, apart from her pale face and the purple shadows under her eyes. Male patients proposition her from time to time but she just smiles.

Steve Randall gave up his act and lives now in one room in Pimlico. He has been arrested several times on drunkenness and vagrancy charges. He goes to see *Dr Zhivago* whenever it's on and sheds tears when it comes to the bit where the man and the woman sit on the bench under the trees and the leaves blow along the street.

He appeared once on a TV show called *Where are they now?* and was congratulated by the producer on a gallant performance. He goes irregularly to meetings of Alcoholics Anonymous and despite being an obvious backslider he is well liked by everyone in the group. He survives on Social Security payments and small hand-outs from a show-biz charity.

Grabowski retired a year after his visit to Northumberland

263

and lives on the outskirts of Kansas City. He receives a good pension and is popular in the neighbourhood. He tells tall stories of foreign parts to the young kids, and tends his garden with love but no skill. He spends his spare cash on a fine collection of foreign stamps, and is visited from time to time by men in Lincolns and foreign sports cars. Rumour has it that he had been a sports writer before he retired. He neither denies nor confirms it, but it is held as significant that on the only occasion when he was co-opted as anchor-man on the tug-of-war team for High School fathers they achieved the only win in the history of the event. Only he and a doctor in Washington know that he is dying slowly of cancer. Petersen, who now teaches Psychiatry at a well-respected college in North Dakota, visited Grabowski once, but the meeting wasn't a success. As Petersen afterwards reflected, there was not what he would call a meeting of minds.

At a meeting in a private room at The Travellers four men considered at some length what they should do about Carter, Maclaren and Sturgiss. One of them, in the early stages of the meeting, had said a few words on the lines of 'only doing their duty and should not be disadvantaged for so doing'. Nobody picked up the ball because they all knew only too well that they were not there to consider the pros and cons of the three men but how to dispose of a potential embarrassment. They had a replacement for Carter already in mind and Maclaren and Sturgiss were neither here nor there. All the meeting wanted was to make sure that whatever arrangements were made they satisfied the three men so that there was no possibility of any come-back in the future.

One of SIS's legal advisers drew up suitable documents for the three men to sign. Carter was paid £57,000 and a tax free pension of £2,500 a year. Maclaren and Sturgiss were each paid £17,000 cash, tax free. Sums arrived at as being capable of withstanding future criticism on the grounds that there were redundant steel-workers and miners receiving similar redundancy payments.

Carter lives in Bradford, his home town, and has shares in a north-east fun-fair, a Scarborough holiday camp and a small chain of betting shops. His wife of twenty-five years, a stout, jolly woman, speaks proudly of his long service in the Merchant Navy. A cover story she always believed.

Maclaren owns fifty per cent of a drinking club not far from Debbie Shaw's old offices in Wardour Street. He married a quiet girl who likes violent love-making and they live happily enough in a small detached house in Ilford. He sees Sturgiss from time to time who pimps for five girls in Portsmouth. Sturgiss too is happy in his work and has been financially successful, his money invested in Krugerrands. Maclaren had once asked Sturgiss what the Kraut girl had been like when he had her before she'd been shot and Sturgiss genuinely couldn't remember either the girl or the occasion until Maclaren had retold the story. Sturgiss had thought Maclaren an odd sort of fellow to remember it all.

The Deputy Under Secretary read the lesson, standing at the brass lectern with its eagle wings spread to support the huge Bible, lifting his eyes from the page every few lines as if to show that he wasn't just reading, but passing on the prophet's words as they originally came to him.

As they walked down the aisle the organist was playing *The Day Thou Gavest Lord is Ended* and as they went slowly down the path of the churchyard to the open grave Katie realized that of all the people there the only ones she knew were her mother and Cartwright.

At the graveside she barely heard the vicar's words, and when they lowered the coffin into the grave she didn't look down but up to the soft blue autumn sky. The big white cumulus clouds were quite still. It was the kind of day they would have enjoyed on the Seamaster, messing about in Chichester creek.

Nothing about the ceremony moved her. She despised the whole rigmarole as she knew Boyd would have done. The decisions about the type of handles on the coffin, the choosing of hymns, arguing with her mother who wanted to invite people back to the flat after the funeral. All of it was meaningless. She shed no tears, and was oblivious to the hands that took hers and the lips that pecked her cheek. All she wished at that moment was that he was waiting for her at the flat and could share her disgust with this whole circus of death. If only he could come back, just for five minutes, so that she could say how much she had loved him.

The Deputy Under Secretary hurried to her as she reached her car. 'Just a brief word, Mrs Boyd. Perhaps a word of down to earth practicality might help. I put a very strong case to the Minister, and I was grateful that he agreed that a full pension would be paid. Full salary, and index-linked of course. The whole of your life-time. And of course the Fund will look after all today's expenses.'

When Katie didn't reply beyond a nod the DUS turned to her mother laying a plump hand on her arm. 'She's been so brave, this dear girl. It hasn't gone unnoticed. And now . . .' he shrugged '. . . we must leave her in your safe hands.' She didn't believe a word of the rigmarole they had told her. Jimmy Boyd was dead and that was all that mattered to her.

In the shared official car back to London the DUS sighed without looking at Cartwright.

'Thank God that's over. D'you think she rumbled anything?'

'I'm sure she didn't.'

'Very attractive . . . soon find someone . . . amazing how

266

our chaps always get pretty girls.' He chuckled. 'Except you and me of course. What are you doing tonight?'

'I've got a ticket for the Festival Hall.'

'Who is it?'

'Itzhak Perlman.'

'What does he do?'

'Plays the violin.'

'Does he now. Is he any good?'

'He's one of the three best in the world.'

'Really? I must remember that. One should know these things.'